GARDENS OF

PLENTY

RON ARIAS

PEACE CORPS WRITERS

Dedication

To my grandsons, Nene, Ren and Kino

Acknowledgment

I must first thank my son, Michael, for his editing help and encouragement in the completion of the novel. Several supportive friends and my partner, Karen de la Peña, also provided key suggestions for ways to bolster the story of Joseph Fields.

And I deeply appreciate the efforts of the following persons who helped me in the early stages of my research: UC Merced professor Manuel Martín Rodríguez for hosting me in his native Seville; John Emelin and Jane Hazen for driving me through the backlands of the Mexican state of Pachuca; John Wagner for giving me lodging in Jalapa, Mexico; Nick Viner, former director of the Jewish Museum of London, for a key suggestion; Todd Zonderman for driving me from Edinburgh, Scotland, to the Isle of Mull and the site of a Spanish Armada shipwreck; Alfred W. Crosby, Jr., author of *The Columbian Exchange: Biological and Cultural Consequences of 1492*, for his encouragement; and University of Arkansas epidemiologist David W. Stahle, a coauthor of "Megadrought and Megadeath in 16th Century Mexico" in *Emerging Infectious Diseases*, for his research into the devastating effects of the pandemic scourge known as *huey cocoliztli*.

I also want to acknowledge my original inspiration in the creation of my main character and his tale: the account of Miles Phillips in Richard Hakluyt's *The Principal Navigations, Voyages, Traffiques and Discoveries of the English Nation.* Beyond this book, I've of course relied on many other published sources. One was particularly helpful, *The Queen's Slave Trader: John Hawkyns, Elizabeth I, and the Trafficking in Human Souls* by Nick Hazlewood.

Finally, I thank my meticulous copy editor, Eileen G. Chetti.

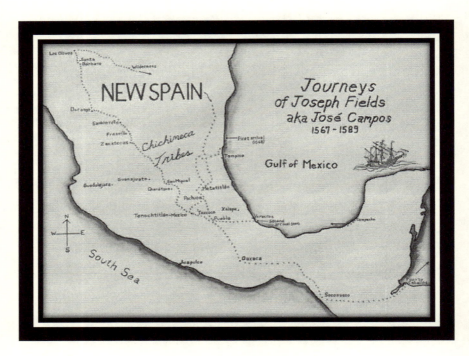

Drawn by Ron Arias

Contents

To withdraw is not to run away, and to stay is no wise action, when there's more reason to fear than to hope.

-Miguel de Cervantes

Chapter 1 – Scrivener

Found yourself a home, eh, Ratso? All comfort and quiet, no one yelling in your ear, "Scrub the deck, boy, scrub it hard, scrub in the wee cracks, scrub, scrub, scrub!"

I hold the lantern steady. You're watching me. Your eyes shine, and your whiskers are still. You've got it better than I do, my little friend. You can run and hide. I cannot, not really. Wherever I am, they'll find me. Go on, disappear. No? Let's see if I move my hand—ah, that's it! Run, hide!

The *Mynion* rises and drops down with a thump. Up, up, up, then down, down, down with a thump. Over and over. Creaking, grinding sounds all around, moans and mutterings. I'm alone in the bow, leaning against the coils of tar-stinking rope, away from the crew, until it's morning and I'm called to duty.

We've been in the storm for some ten days—since soon after leaving Plymouth on the second day of October 1567. We lost two sailors and a longboat, and the leaks in the hull planks won't stop. They get plugged, and more appear. Ah, but now the skies are opening up, the seas are calming.

Most of the crew stay below, still curled up in whatever space they can find, useless to climb into the rigging, pull lines, or work the bilge pump. They groan and whine, retching or relieving

1

themselves belowdecks in tubs or tethered buckets. If they don't reach them in time, the mess runs between barrels, sailcloth, and other stores. In the forespace of the deck below me, even the pigs, goats, and chickens are sickened by all the pitching and rocking.

Nicky and I never lose what we eat. He's the other ship's boy, younger than I am, nine or ten, I think. I'm thirteen or thereabouts. And there's an older boy, the captain's page, we call Hawk because of his hard stare.

We empty buckets over the side, keep the gun deck clean, especially around the powder kegs, swab the decks and fetch things like ropes, water, or hardtack for the sailors on the rigging and spars. I like climbing the lattice of lines, feeling the ship rise and drop with each swell, swaying through the air like a seagull swooping from side to side, up and out and then down, again and again.

It's how I imagined my time on a ship going to the Spanish Indies. Free as a bird in the air, free to sing, to dream, and, in Deacon Brown's words, to seek a good and fortunate life. My mates and I were busy doing our sums when the town crier shouted from over the Greyfriars wall about the return of mariners from across the ocean. They suffered storms and scurvy but came back laden with silver, gold, and pearls, telling tales of marvelous new lands filled with strange beasts and a bounty of new foods.

"Who would like to go to sea?" Deacon Brown asked us.

We all shouted, "Me!"

As Deacon Brown waved his hands for us to settle down, I imagined climbing up to the crow's nest, searching the horizon for this wondrous new land. The mariners had survived the journey to paradise and back—why shouldn't I sail across the sea to such a place?

Our teacher blasted us for dreaming that we might easily cross the ocean, saying it was not for the fainthearted. "But someday one of you lads might sail with the likes of Captain General John Hawkyns."

I vowed to myself that I would be that lad. I would leave England just as I promised Father. He said I should flee my homeland. I thought he meant that I run from the plague, the same pestilence that took him, Mother, and Sister Mary.

On my thirteenth birthday, almost two years after the Queen's men snatched me off the street in Southwark and put me in Greyfriars, I decided to escape because I feared a flogging. On that day, I was to be made an apprentice to a stonemason who liked to whip his new boys as a grisly kind of welcome. The thought of a whip cutting stripes into my back scared me more than catching the plague.

So I left London, going to Gravesend, courtesy of a kindly boatman. Then I walked on the Roman road going to Rochester, stopping only to muck out a pigsty for a widow named Millie in exchange for a bowl of cabbage, carrots, and a chicken leg, which I ate under the sad, watchful eyes of her long-eared hound, Scout.

On the way to Rochester, an old charlatan robbed me of my sole possessions—Mother's wooden spoon and nit comb and the penknife given to me by my dying father, a scrivener. But with the help of a minstrel in a Chatham tavern, I found the thief and recovered my things. Then by good fortune I was taken aboard the *Mynion*, a man-of-war with four masts in the Hawkyns fleet bound for Plymouth. There, with the Queen's blessing and more vessels, the ships gathered to set sail for Africa to capture Negroes to sell in the Spanish Indies. My plan was to stay in the New World. But an old mariner, a veteran of two runs with Hawkyns, scoffed at my scheme. When I asked him if I could stay in the Indies, he laughed. "Only slaves stay behind. We sell them for hides, silver, and pearls, and that's it. They stay; we go."

"None of us gets to stay?"

He shook his head and laughed again. "We're English, boy. In the Indies they call us heathen Lutherans. To the Spaniard, we're all devils. So you tell me if you want to jump ship and throw the dice. The Spaniard's more than happy to make you a slave or put your bum in prison. Better yet, put the torch to you. Big public thing is the stake. Cheers and jeers, that's what you'll hear!"

I hear the sailors and soldiers who are too sick to rouse themselves cry out. Nicky is among the sickest. He's weak and feverish. I try to revive him with soggy hardtack and broth, but he refuses to eat. I pray that he can be treated on land and given proper meals.

I move away from my sleeping spot and curl up next to a cannon carriage to listen to crewmen go on about the need for repairs and fresh water. "Joey," a voice whispers. I feel a tap on my hand. In the dim light, I see a familiar figure reaching for my arm. "Joey, write me a will."

I say nothing, thinking of Father. Would I remember the words he taught me? And I have no quill, no ink nor paper for the task.

"Joey, please."

"I can't."

"For the love of God, please."

"I've nothing to write with."

"You say you write."

"Yes, but I need a quill, a bit of ink, paper."

I know him as Budgie, a shepherd from Devonshire. He told me he lost his flock of sheep in a card-game wager, then left his wife and two children for work at sea, hoping she would survive by mending clothes and washing other people's laundry.

Now I hear Budgie catch his breath before repeating his plea. Three other men move closer. "I've a gull's feather," one of them says. The quill is soon produced, and I move to the morning light coming from the open hatch. From the cloth around my waist, I pull out Father's penknife. I sharpen the blade on a clay jug, then I move

5

to sit before a small wooden chest with a flat top. I strip most of the feathers on the quill's shaft, leaving a brushlike fan of bristles on one side near the tapered end. Finally, I fashion a split point.

When I finish the quill, I call for lampblack and water. "Now the ink," I say to the onlookers. The circle of sailors and soldiers that has formed around me grows quiet.

"How much do you need?" a seaman asks.

"Depends on how much paper I have. Got paper?"

"I'll ask the bos'n."

A while later, Hawk comes down from the main deck with his usual superior air and drops two sheets of paper onto the sea chest. "Captain wants you to know this is good use of idle time," says the page with a snort and walks away. Soon enough I have what I need: paper, quill, and a cup of soot.

From what I understand, most of the crew and soldiers have left behind their last wills and testaments in England so that if they die at sea they will leave something to their family, friends, and debtors. But many of the newer, first-time voyagers do not have such documents and regret not leaving written word on how to dispose of their things.

"Budgie," I say, "just so you know—I'm not a notary, nothing official. I only write."

"I don't care, just put it down. Got to have something."

6

His reason for leaving home, it seems to me, is no less desperate and urgent than mine. He lost his sheep and ran away. I lost my family and ran away. And I kept my promise to Father. Near death, he gave me his penknife and whispered, "You must flee England. Promise me."

I asked him why and all he said was to ask Jacob, the London apothecary who sold him ink.

"Joey," Budgie says, "the will."

"Aye."

I tell the nearest sailor to hold the pewter cup with the ink steady, and I begin to write on the sheet of paper before me. It's the first time I've done scrivener work since I wrote for the women of the stews in Southwark.

I ask Budgie to say his full Christian name. Before the silent stares, I begin to pronounce the words as I write them.

In the name of God Amen.

After these words, the rest flows from the nib as if the quill were guiding itself.

I Roger Parker being in parfytt mynde & memorye make here my laste will and testament. First I bequeathe my soule unto the hands of the lyving God and my bodye where yt shall please my company. I will that my wif Sara dwelling in Topsham in the countie of Devonshyre shalbe myne executrix to recyve all sayd parcels and duties as belongit vnto me. I give to her a cut Jerkin and lynnon clothe, a cut dublet, a shirte & a newe paire of shewes.

I stop writing and blow on the page. I've done most of the talking, often pausing to dip the quill into the cup. I wait for Budgie to correct himself, and when he doesn't, I say, "New shoes? Really?"

"As God's me witness. Won 'em fair 'n' square."

The seamen, many without shoes, laugh, and someone says, "Swears you and the devil!"

Aboard the *Mynion* any sort of footwear is for officers, soldiers, or those standing watch. Wet leather shoes and boots aren't of much use on a wooden deck awash with seawater and would certainly hinder men in the rigging. Suddenly, what I'm doing at this moment feels as if I'm performing a sacred ceremony for Budgie and for all the men gathered under the light coming from the open hatch. Even Nicky, still sick and doubled up next to a cannon carriage, watches with glistening eyes. I pronounce each word aloud, as Father did with his clients, so that what I call the testator hears what I'm writing.

"Please," Budgie says, touching my writing arm.

"Yes, new shoes," I say. "What else?"

"Me home, every stick of it."

"All to your wife?"

"That's me wish."

I finish and feel pleased. I've kept the attention of my audience with words and tiny marks, curves, dots and lines. All that's left is a signature. I ask Budgie to make his mark at the bottom of the page, and he slowly draws the letters R and P. Several sailors also sign as witnesses, one man with an eye patch who makes various odd marks that he says are his given names.

"How did you learn to write?" the man with the eye patch asks.

I tell him my father was a scrivener and taught me in Greenwich. I used to sit on a stool by his side on the street, listening to him recite letters and petitions that people asked him to write. When he wasn't writing, he would watch me mark my board as I learned to write sounds and read words. Later, after the Black Death took my family, I went to London and wrote for food and bed on the streets of Bankside.

"And how's it you speak so proper?" a voice asks.

"For the same reason, my father. He sought to speak correctly. English was a gift from the Queen, he would say, something to respect."

Returning to my little ceremony of words, I write my own name, Joseph Fields, at the bottom of the two sheets of paper I used for Budgie's will. When I'm done, I hand over the sheets to the gambling shepherd from Devon. He thanks me, and I stand to leave the men gathered around the chest. The ship doesn't pitch and shudder as much as it did during the storm, but I still must spread my legs and be careful of my balance.

"Hold on there, boy," says another voice. I turn to see the scowling gunner with the red beard and Irish accent. For some reason, I ignite the nasty in him.

"My turn," he says and orders me to write his will and testament, a short one because he possesses almost nothing. But I have no more paper and say so, which earns me a hard slap on the side of my head. Before I can suggest we ask the ship's officers for more paper, an excited voice from above deck calls out, "Land ho! Land ho!" Everyone cheers. Even little Nicky stirs. He lifts his head and utters a faint "Land, land ho."

Chapter 2 – Bucket Duty

We're anchored in a bay. The calm waters seem to have revived Nicky's spirits, so much so that he goes over the rail for a swim with Carlos to check the state of the hull planks. The ship's carpenter and caulker tells us he came from Essex and his birth name is Charles. But he spent some years mending hulls in Spain and likes being called Carlos and boasts that he speaks the language he calls *cristiano*.

After Nicky's swim, we lie on the main deck warming ourselves, but Nicky keeps scratching and picking at his scalp. So I tell him to sit up, and I'll get rid of his lice with my mother's nit comb.

Earlier in the morning, the captain and most of the crew and all the soldiers rowed to the port of San Sebastian in longboat runs. The few men left behind sit on the fore- and aftdecks, mend sailcloth, sing ditties, or throw dice, while the red-bearded gunner fishes off the aftdeck, cursing the tangles of kelp he hooks again and again.

I pull out Mother's comb from my waist cloth. As soon as I begin running it through Nicky's shaggy blond hair, I sense his agitation drain away. After I finish catching lice and nits in the comb's tiny, narrowly spaced teeth, we stand by the rail and watch the screeching seagulls whirl overhead, some of them touching down on a spar or on the tallest of the three crow's nests. Nicky says that the birds look small and are nothing special, not when compared to the graceful white-bellied pelicans that glide over the water near his home in Cornwall.

As he's telling me this, I feel drawn to him as a friend I can count on to be my mate in anything we do, someone I can trust with my life. Years ago, Father told me that people are collectable, like interesting stones—some good, some bad, some a bit of both. He said I should try to collect only the good stones, saving them in a make-believe bag tied around my waist.

I tell Nicky about my bag of imaginary stones and that he's now in a bag with Father, Mother, Sister Mary, a few steady mates at Greyfriars, a wherryman who took me down the Thames, and a farm woman who fed me. Nicky thanks me for the gesture. It's an honor, he says with a laugh, as long as I don't lose the bag in the sea.

We watch a pelican dive into the water and moments later surface with the pouch beneath its bill bulging with its catch.

"Teach me to write," Nicky says.

My eyes are stuck on the pelican, and Nicky repeats himself.

"I'll teach you," I answer, "but you have to show me this." I stretch out my arms, moving them forward one after the other, then pulling them back one at a time.

"What's that?" he asks.

"Guess."

"Pulling lines?"

"Swimming."

"Not like that," Nicky says, giggling.

"Then show me."

We stand, and he asks me if I've ever been in deep water.

"Never."

He climbs onto the rail and invites me to join him. "Time to get wet," he says.

"Careful, lads!" Red Beard yells from the stern. "Sharks about."

I look at Nicky, who shakes his head and waves away the comment. Then he springs forward and dives into the water.

Nicky told me he comes from a poor family that lives near the shore. As long as he can remember, he loved being in water. His mother called him "Fish Boy," and he was the only swimmer of her five children. His father had sailed the English and Dutch coasts most of his life, and after he died Nicky followed his example. With his mother's blessing, he looked for maritime work in Plymouth and, like me, found it as a ship's boy on the *Mynion*.

I've only touched open water in the river Thames. Now I'm faced with a jump into the ocean. I hitch up my pants, make sure my penknife and comb are secure in their pouch, and then I climb up on the rail and step into the air. I hit the water feet first, feeling cold and afraid I'll never stop going down. Then I stop and slowly begin to rise. I can see Nicky's legs next to the ship's hull. Suddenly, my head's above water, and I can breathe again. Nicky grabs my hand and pulls me to the webbing that hangs on the side of the hull.

"Do this," he says, cupping his hands and beating the surface. "Do like a dog, move your front paws up and down."

"And my legs?"

"Move 'em like . . . like sheep shears, up and down, open and close."

I let go of the webbing and start to go under. I'm frantically kicking and moving my arms, swallowing water and spitting it out, gasping but staying afloat. My dog imitation isn't working, as I go under again, swallowing and choking.

"Here!" Carlos shouts from above. He tosses down a small wooden block with a line attached to the ship.

I dog-paddle to the float.

"Good," Nicky says, leisurely swimming on his back. "Now let go of the wood and do it again."

14

I practice my kicks and strokes until I get tired and have to cling to the wood. Nicky waits for me to catch my breath. "Let go of it, Joe," he says, urging me on with a wave of his arm. "Kick-kick stroke! Kick-kick stroke!"

I launch myself again, this time without clinging to the float but splashing about on my own until the coaxing begins to take effect. I swallow a lot of water. I'm determined not only to stay afloat and breathe but also to move forward.

After a while, Nicky says, "Watch this," and he slips completely under the water's surface. Minutes pass, and I finally call to Carlos, "He's gone!"

"Aye, but you needn't worry about him," Carlos says, leaning over the rail and peering down. "He likes to swim con los peces," he says.

"What?"

"With the fish."

Carlos likes to pepper his speech with Spanish words.

"Where's Nicky?"

"Shark got him," Red Beard says and spits over the rail. "Look for blood."

"He's teasing," Carlos says.

"Did he drown?" I ask.

"No."

Just then Nicky appears. He swims toward me from the bow of the ship. He waves a hand, then resumes his strokes, moving with ease alongside the hull.

"I thought you had drowned," I say.

"Never! Not Fish Boy."

"All right, *muchachos*!" Carlos yells down. "Boats are coming back."

We scramble up the ropes, climb over the rail and collapse on the deck, both of us grinning and dripping wet.

"Thank you," I say. "I owe you some writing lessons."

"Let's go, *vámonos*!" Carlos shouts from the poop deck. "Mop up the puddles!"

Then he tells the crewmen to gather the canvas and store the sails below.

While Nicky goes down the hatch ladder to fetch rags, I tug off my clothes and wring them out over the side, then pull them on again. I figure the sun will dry them soon enough.

Nicky climbs out of the hatchway and tosses me a rag, and we begin drying the wet spots. While we are doing this, we talk about my make-believe collection of stones. I tell him the first stone in the bag is my mother because my father used to say she was the heart of goodness. And she was.

"Was your father your second stone?" Nicky asks.

"Yes."

"Do you have many stones?"

"Not many. There's my sister, Mary, a few mates from the streets, a boatman named Wayne, Millie the farm lady who fed me, and a minstrel who never gave me his name."

I told Nicky I was fooled by an old man with a limp, a fellow I met after leaving Millie's place. I was on the Roman road to Rochester, and while I was washing myself at the edge of a stream, he took the knife, spoon, and comb from my bag, leaving stones in their place. Later, on the Rochester bridge, when I opened my bag, I discovered the theft. The minstrel saw me crying and carrying on over the loss, and he asked what was the matter. I told him, and he said I was lucky the man didn't take my life as well.

When I got to Chatham, I saw the old thief enter a tavern without a limp. I followed him in and accused him, shouting that he'd taken my father's penknife and my mother's comb and spoon that I carried in a cloth bag with the bread and cheese Millie gave me.

I looked like a beggar, and no one in the tavern believed me. They shouted for me to be tossed out. But the minstrel, who had followed me to the tavern, heard my description of the knife and the mark on its handle. He banged on his tambourine to get everyone's attention, then asked if the accused could describe what was carved into the handle. When the man could not, he was rousted out, and my knife, comb, and spoon were returned to me. Then the innkeeper asked to see the knife. After looking at the mark on the handle, he said it was the Hebrew symbol for life, something he learned from a Jew in Amsterdam.

"Can I see the knife?" Nicky asks. Before I can take it out of my waist pouch, Carlos surprises us from behind, clapping us on our backs. "Good work, lads! ¡Estupendo! And you, Joey—you'll be a swimmer soon enough."

"I want to dive," I say.

"Not what it seems."

"But you like it."

"Never."

"Never?"

"Aye, never have."

"Then why do you do it?"

"Fear, fear it is."

"Of what?"

"Leaks. This old tub is so rotten you might as well call it a coffin."

Carlos holds up his right hand, hiding his thumb and little finger. "This much wood is between us and eternity. So I strip the weeds, scrape the barnacles, feel for worm rot, finally plug and patch the holes. Otherwise"—and here he slaps me on the back again—"down we go, down to the briny bloody bottom!"

I wince, but Nicky laughs.

"Don't go diving, lad," Carlos tells me. "You read and write. Why waste all that with diving and scraping?"

"I guess I want to swim."

Carlos proposes an exchange. He will let me dive with him after I learn to swim. He will show me how to fix leaks, and I will teach him how to read and write. I agree, but I say I'd also like to learn what he calls *cristiano*, or Spanish.

"Fine," he says. "You teach me letters; I teach you *cristiano*. You too, Nicky."

We shake hands with Carlos, or *manos*, as he calls them, and our first lesson begins. *Barco* is "ship," *vela* is "sail," *mar* is "sea," *cielo* is "sky." After a while Nicky and I are answering Carlos with a snappy "*¡Sí, señor!*" From the beginning we both like the sounds of the new words—*agua, viento, pescado*. I feel as if I'm hearing a new kind of music, some of it sounding like the Latin I learned from Father and Deacon Brown.

With each lurching pull of the oars, the ship's longboat is coming closer to the *Mynion*, with other boats going to other ships. I recognize Captain Hampton, who sits in the bow dressed in his greatcoat and top hat. When the boat draws alongside, the rowers raise oars, and the captain points to a man crouched in the middle with his head down and face hidden. His tunic sleeves are torn, and his arms are bound at the wrists. The captain orders that they be untied, and when this is done, he shouts, "Up you go!" The man stands and raises his head. With a start, I see Budgie's puffy, bruised face. The old shepherd appears even more pitiful and sunken-eyed than when he was begging to have his last wishes written. He reaches out from the longboat and grabs a line. As he steps onto the webbing, one of the rowers yells, "Papist dog!"

I think his immediate fate will be painful. In London, I saw what they did to Catholic heretics—at the pillory stocks, at burnings and hangings, and at the whipping post. What's it going to be at sea?

Since the start of the voyage, the captain has ordered every man to attend Protestant morning and evening prayers. If the weather and seas allow, he leads the services from above on the poop deck. The seamen, even the sick, kneel and recite the Creed and the Paternoster, asking God to keep them safe and protect the Queen— all of this in English with not a word of Latin.

It's not much different from daily prayers at Greyfriars. When any of my mates wavered, they got the switch or the paddle, depending on which one Deacon Brown grabbed first. I'd been spared punishment because of what Father told me—that he'd been a Catholic but converted to the English church. And he warned me and Mary never to speak ill of the Queen nor blaspheme the faith, telling us, "Just profess to be a good Christian and say your prayers." I did what he told us, and I never got the switch or the paddle.

After they pull Budgie aboard, two sailors push him toward the mainmast. I think he'll be flogged. But first, the captain addresses the crew: "Whilst some of you were having great amusement in the tavern," he says, "this man was in a papist chapel praying to idols of saints. He will now suffer the punishment for heresy."

Budgie hesitates when he's ordered to hug the mainmast. A sailor with a length of rope slaps him on the head. "You deaf?" the sailor shouts. "Do it!" Budgie extends his arms on each side of the mast, and another crewman binds his wrists. When the captain announces that thirty-five lashes will be counted out, Budgie utters a guttural sound and begs for mercy.

"Begin!" the captain orders. For an instant, the several unwound strands of the scourge, which are knotted at the ends, dangle above the pinkish white skin. Then the flogger raises his arm behind his own back and brings the rope down with a snap. With each thwack, one of the crew calls out a number, and Budgie cries out and squirms. As the flogging gains a regular rhythm, he groans, hardly moving, welts, cuts, and rivulets of bright-red blood spreading over his back.

I'm sickened by the sight and look away, first at the water, then at the crew. Though all hands are present as witnesses, several sailors behind the standing crew are leaning against the bulwark, casually muttering. I know some of them are secret Catholics, like Red Beard. I've seen his string of rosary knots. He just hasn't been caught.

Budgie's slumped over, quivering through his ordeal. I turn away again, flinching at the sound of the whip striking flesh. "Steady there, lad," Carlos says as he walks by. "You must watch with thick skin, like your little mate does." Of all punishments, whipping strikes me as the most degrading, reducing a man to his most naked, raw self in front of everyone.

Most of the crew are younger than Budgie, baptized in England's new church. They watch stone-faced, but one voice curses Budgie for doing the devil's work. "The old bugger was talking to saints. Deserves every bloody stripe!"

Nicky and I watch from the quarterdeck. Suddenly, Hawk squeezes in between us at the rail. "They caught him kneeling before statues," says the captain's page. Then he praises the sailors for exposing Budgie as a heretic.

I feel sorry for him and say so.

Hawk shakes his head. "Is that right?"

"Yes," I say. "The man does no one harm."

The captain's page smiles, then his face breaks into a devilish grin. Budgie is now so bloody and motionless that he looks dead. "At least he had a last will and testament," I say.

Hawk glares at me. "And you wrote it."

"I did."

"Helping a papist."

"What?"

"You helped the papist. You're probably one of them too."

"I am not!"

"You wrote his will."

"I only wrote his last wishes."

"So you say."

Nicky then blurts, "Joey's teaching me to write!"

Hawk spits on the deck between us, almost putting his spittle on my toes. He warns me not to be too clever. "Keep to your station, worm. Fancy words ain't gonna help when the captain finds you out." Before I can think of a proper answer, Hawk steps away and climbs down to the ship's waist, where the whipping has just ended.

Sailors untie and drag Budgie to the hatch. Others lift and lower him into the hold. Some crewmen turn away, and several stay looking at the trail of blood.

"All right, boys!" the big boatswain shouts to me and Nicky. "Clean up the mess!"

I fetch a bucket with a line attached and drop it over the side. It fills with water, and then I haul it up. I splash the seawater over the bloodied part of the deck, then Nicky begins to scrub with a brush while I pull up more water to throw on the deck.

When we're done, we go below to see how Budgie is doing. He's belly down on a patch of torn canvas near the stern of the gun deck. A bloody cloth covers his back, and he's whimpering. Nicky asks one of the crew if Budgie will live, and the sailor answers, "Wouldn't wager on it."

Later that night, Budgie dies. In the morning, with no prayer or ceremony, he's carried to the rail and dropped into the sea. I can only hope the captain or first mate has kept Budgie's last testament and they get it to the man's wife. I think he deserves at least that much.

***

By the time all the ships gather to hoist sails and leave for the African coast, I've learned to swim, and Nicky and Carlos are able to read simple phrases written on scraps of sailcloth. It's the end of October, and by then my mind is filled with so many Christian words that I go about my daily chores repeating them, often to the annoyance of others. "For bloody sake," one sailor tells me, "speak your own tongue, boy! Make sense!"

24

GARDENS OF PLENTY

The grand enterprise of collecting slaves is about to begin, and the boatswain tells Nicky and me that whenever the ship is anchored, we are to stay aboard and tend to our usual tasks. "Amuse yourselves, lads, but stay with the ship."

At every stop on the voyage south, from the desert coast to the warm Cape Verde Islands, we climb aloft into the rigging to look around and watch for other ships. Once, we see what turns out to be a Portuguese caravel, which some of our ships attack and take. It's loaded with enough mullet to feed the crews of all the ships. Another time, we go after six French ships. Soon, they lower sails and heave to—all except one caravel. The *Mynion* gives chase, firing a cannon shot over its bow as a warning. It turns out to be a Portuguese vessel, which Hawkyns claims, along with its crew, some soldiers, and jars of biscuits. As for the French ships, our captain general buys from them quantities of figs, almonds, and cider.

The greener the coast becomes, the more the fleet drops anchor near the mouths of rivers. Our sailors and soldiers then leave in longboats to pursue their mission to capture Africans. They return sometimes days later with fresh food, monkeys, parrots, and water, as well as tales of battles with natives who attack them with poisoned arrows. As the weeks pass, we hear that many Negroes are captured and put on other ships in the fleet. So far, none have been put aboard the *Mynion*.

On really warm days when the ships are anchored and duties are few, Nicky and I sit on the highest spar to feel the breeze. No one can hear us talking, so we practice our Spanish words. We call them our secret tongue. I feel as if Nicky is a brother, or at least my new good stone. And I make a confession. I tell him I escaped from Greyfriars and not to tell a soul.

In English, Nicky answers, "On me mum's honor," then he jabs an elbow in my side. "Mates forever?"

"*Siempre.*"

Suddenly, Nicky cocks his head and points. "Bos'n! Negroes!"

In the distance, I see a longboat emerge from the mouth of a river, heading toward the *Mynion*.

The boatswain motions to the sailors sitting on deck, men who had been singing and swapping stories while stitching sailcloth tears. "Alright, lads, stow everything!" The seamen rise and begin gathering the sails to take below. We climb down the ratlines to the main deck. When the men finish stowing things, they stand ready. The rowers ship oars, and a crewman throws up a line. The naked black figures are crowded in the center of the boat, hands bound in front of their bodies.

The first mate orders the Africans to come aboard. After much prodding and pushing, they begin to climb up the crosshatch of ropes to the rail at the ship's waist. One of the rowers from below shouts for them to climb faster, poking their behinds with an oar. After they all climb onto the main deck, Captain Hampton, with Hawk behind him, comes aboard and orders the longboat rowed back to shore for more captives.

Nicky and I are on the poop deck, watching the Africans, three women and thirteen men. They're huddled by the mainmast. Some are shaking, and a few are crying. Besides having their hands bound, the captives are hobbled by two sailors with a basket of chains.

When all are shackled, they're made to stand in a line so William Cornelius, the *Mynion*'s barber and surgeon, can check each one as another man makes entries in a ledger. There are no names, only a word or two about appearance. "Tall male, short male, girl of bearing age, scar on forehead." This goes on for some time, is shouted, repeated, and written down. After the inspection, the captain orders two men, both armed with clubs and switches, to force the Negroes down the hatch ladder. "Hit if you must," he says, "but mind where you strike. We want to sell the merchandise, not damage it."

The Africans are pushed to the hatch amid much shouting by some of the crew. This herding of people seems a lot like moving cattle belowdecks, except the animals are lowered by rope into the hold. And these poor souls are treated the same as beasts.

"Why?" I hear myself say.

Nicky pokes me. "Why what?"

"Why treat them this way?"

"Joey, they're slaves."

"I know, but I don't like seeing them pushed around like cows or sheep."

Nicky nods and is about to say something when Captain Hampton, with Hawk by his side, shouts for another boatload of Negroes to come aboard. They're treated the same as the first group and also shoved to the main hatch. When the last and largest man in the line reaches the open hatchway, he whirls about and cries out in Spanish,

"¡No soy esclavo!"

"What did he say?" the captain asks.

"It's Spanish, sir," Carlos says. "Means 'I am not a slave.'"

"How so? Ask him."

Carlos steps down to the main deck and speaks with the big fellow, then calls up to the captain. "Claims to be a freed man who worked in Spain. He went back to his people and then we captured him."

The captain raises his eyebrows. "Freed? I think not. Take him below."

A sailor hits the big Negro with a switch and the man cries out again, "¡No soy esclavo! ¡Allah ayúdame! ¡Allah akbar!"

The captain looks at Carlos. "Carpenter?"

"He asks for Allah's help. It's what the Mohamids call God."

"Indeed."

"Aye, Captain, Allah the greatest."

"Greatest?

"It's what they say, sir."

"Get him below!"

As the African is being shoved down the ladder, I notice Hawk staring at me. Then he speaks to the captain and points to me. The captain nods and says something to the boatswain. He steps down the stairs to the main deck and, oh my, comes my way. He pushes Nicky aside and shouts in my face that I am to serve as the Negroes' cleanup boy for the remainder of the voyage.

"Aye," I say.

"Louder!"

"Aye, sir!"

"Doing what?"

"Bucket duty among the slaves, sir."

"More to it than writing words, eh?"

"Yes, sir, more than writing words."

"What's that?"

"Words don't—"

"Speak up!"

"Words don't stink."

I scream. He's pinching my left ear.

"My dear maggot," he yells in the same ear, "I've a mind to toss you over myself, scrub you from the manifest. Yes, I think I will! You won't exist!"

He lets go of my ear and shoves me toward the hatch. "Now, go meet your new mates."

Chapter 3 – Darkness Below

I'm a rat, crouching behind coils of tarred rope, creeping about in the shadows, doing my duty among the slaves, a cloth covering my nose and mouth. I feel like a slave myself, though the biggest difference between me and the Negro rats is that they're in chains, and I'm not. I no longer tend to the duties of a ship's boy. No more fetching, scrubbing, wiping, and coiling. And never again writing.

Like the rats, I stay fearful and cautious, keeping to the darkest places. I walk on bare feet, seldom speaking, eating whatever broth, hardtack, or scrap the cook gives me from the galley pot. Asleep, I feel my gut ache for anything to fill it. Millie feeds me dream fare of cabbage, chicken, and carrot stew, one delicious spoonful after another. Whatever goes into my mouth, it's her stew, her bread. That's how I eat, how I swallow—with Scout licking my feet for salt. No matter how foul the air or what I'm given to eat, I pretend it's from Millie. I never gag, never bring up what I eat. I reckon that if my rat mates can live in a seagoing pigpen, so can I. If I'm to see the Indies, I have to live as Ratso lives.

What have I done? What sin? I wrote Budgie's last will and testament, but I didn't know the man was a heretic. I never committed heresy. I can recite the Paternoster and many psalms better than most of the pious among the crew. Yet I was ordered below and banned from daily worship on the main deck, all because

Hawk invented a story, a lie. Deacon Brown invented stories for us all the time. One day we could be knights charging a giant or a dragon. The next day we might be mariners sailing to the New World. Harmless stories but never lies.

I sing the hymn, what I remember from services in Greenwich, "O deliver me from the deceitful and unjust man," I sing. It's what I remember from services in Greenwich. It was one of Father's favorite hymns. And now I pray the Lord delivers me from the unjust men aboard this very ship.

I hear shouts to unfurl sails, then I hear the cheers. We have our slaves, and the vessel is finally heading westward, leaving the Guinea coast and starting the voyage across the ocean. I try to stand, but the sudden pitching of the ship keeps me off balance. I spread my legs and move across the deck toward the hanging lantern. I take it off its peg, reach down for my big bucket, and turn to get started with my chore.

The Africans yowl and moan. How many are there? I've forgotten. Fifty-six? Sixty-six? Something with six. Each ship has its share of human cargo. I'm guessing five hundred in the fleet, but my rat's mind can't say for sure. In the flickering light, I see them ahead, spread over the deck, sitting hunched over or stretched out. I duck under a crossbeam and hang the lantern. A woman's shriek slices through the wailing and moaning. I start emptying the small vessels into my bucket.

"*Mozo*," I hear. It's a low voice calling me "lad" in Spanish—what Carlos, the ship's carpenter, sometimes calls me. The cristiano tongue he taught me.

"*Mozo.*"

I don't answer.

A rat doesn't answer. Again, I hear the voice, but louder. It must be the big African who speaks Spanish. He's chained. He can't harm me. Ahead of me in the shadows is his large figure sitting upright. I must stay busy, be the odd rodent without a tail. Don't answer, keeping to my chore.

The deck is wet, and I'm afraid of slipping. If only I had four feet. I've never seen a rat slip on a floor, although once I watched three of them crossing a mooring line, then drop into the water when a gust of wind shook the line.

I step between bodies on each side of the deck, trying to keep my balance. I take tiny steps and have to ignore the big man calling out.

I turn around and move toward the ladder, haul the bucket up to the gun deck, get to the stairs to the main hatch, and clamber to the top. "Nicky!" I call out. He appears and lifts the bucket.

"I have it," he says and goes to drop the contents over the side. While he's gone, I gulp the windy, salty air. Nicky hands me the bucket, and he says in Spanish, "How's it with the Negroes?"

I don't answer.

"What's wrong?" he asks, now in English, and hands me the bucket. "You don't look right."

As I take the handle, he stoops down and says, "Here," placing a biscuit in the palm of my right hand. I retreat down the ladder of narrow stairs. I reach the deck and tuck the hardtack under the cloth around my waist.

On my second round among the slaves, the same low voice cries out. I want to see the face and lift the lantern to see more of the man. I see him.

"*Agua, por favor*," he says, pleading for water I don't have. I want to ignore him but I can't help answering, "*Sí.*"

He looks surprised, then asks me who I am. "Another rat like you," I say in Spanish. "Yes," he says, "but who are you? What's your name?" "José." "I'm Hassan." Again, he pleads for water, but I go on collecting. In the glow of the lantern's light, I try to ignore all the outstretched hands and pleas of other slaves spoken in words I don't understand. Why would this man Hassan say he was free? Weren't all black slaves captured or bought in trade? Weren't they all meant to serve others? The Romans kept slaves, some of them from Britannia. And Carlos said he had known white men who'd been galley slaves and pulled oars for years. But maybe this man, Hassan, truly was given his freedom by his Spanish master.

GARDENS OF PLENTY

I return to the gun deck, then move on to the next ladder up to the main hatch. After the handoff to Nicky, I go down again and approach the gunnery seaman with the red beard, the man who wanted me to write his last will and testament. He's with a group of men gathered by a cannon carriage. I ask if there's water for the Negroes. "Papist dung!" he yells and reaches for a mallet. As I back away, he grabs the mallet and flings it at me. I duck, and it flies overhead. "They get no water and no victuals until the bosun says so. Now, shove me my mallet." "Losing your touch, Red," I hear one sailor say, chuckling. "Shut your hole!" the big gunny answers. I hate the man and must stay away from him. Next time the mallet might catch me square on the head.

I move among the slaves, holding the lantern high, and cross over to the glistening face and body of Hassan. I tell him there will be no water for now. He sighs, his bound hands suddenly beating his chest as if in prayer. "And food?" he asks. I tell him there will be none for now. We speak in Spanish, and I remember the biscuit Nicky gave me. "Bizcocho," I say and pull the square hardtack out from the fold around my waist. I offer it to Hassan, who takes it but only seems to study the object. Then he raises his eyes to the others, shouts something, and is answered by many voices. He places my gift in the open hand of the man behind him. It's then passed into the shadows from hand to hand to a person Hassan calls la cabecilla. I fumble the sense of the word and have to ask him for its meaning.

35

I'm thinking "little head," which doesn't make sense. "Like a ship's captain," Hassan says, "like the chief, the head of everybody." I nod that I understand, and Hassan asks why I can speak Spanish if the ship is English. I tell him the ship's carpenter taught me what I know. "He's the one who translated what you said about being free and not a slave." "Is he Spanish?"

I'm about to answer when several of the crew appear at the hatch from the deck below, shouting that they have gruel. When the sailor with the lantern reaches me, he pushes me aside to make way for two men carrying a large, steamy pail. Two more sailors with clubs and whips make room down the middle of the deck. Another crewman scoops portions of the watery mixture into the few wooden bowls he hands out to the Africans, who are begging with extended arms. With one hand he points and gestures for them to share the bowls.

After this feeding comes the water. Hassan shouts something to the others, and this time they hold their bowls steady as sailors fill them with water from leather bags. "Like scared children they are," Hassan says to me. "They have no idea how to save themselves."

Intent as I am on keeping to my rat ways, I can't help being drawn to this man, at least to listen to him, to hear the softer sounds of a new tongue, repeating words, asking for meaning, testing his answers. Spanish now seems to give me the freedom to think and speak what I can't say in English to my captors.

GARDENS OF PLENTY

With the end of the first days of rough seas, I talk to Hassan as often as I can. He corrects my Spanish, repeating words so I can practice pronouncing the sounds. I tell him of my escape from London to follow my dream of crossing the ocean to the Indies. Afterward, he does what Father used to do—speak in sayings. *"Nadie es profeta en su tierra,"* Hassan says, and I ask what that means.

"You can't be a prophet in your own country—not until you leave and see other lands." For such a large and muscular man, he now speaks softly, calmly, as if he were sitting in a chapel pew, not here, naked and in chains. We talk a lot, and he tells me that when he was a boy, not quite a man, he'd been captured by another tribe and sold to Spanish slave merchants. They tied his hands and made him walk until they reached the sea coast and a ship that would take him to Spain.

In Seville, Hassan saw great houses, streets of stone, and crowds of people speaking and shouting unknown words. A potter bought him to dig clay, which he did for years, digging and hauling, chanting songs with other slaves. Then he was taught to make pottery on a wooden wheel. He worked with Spaniards and was allowed to sell his bowls and jars in the markets, living the life of a merchant. But everything changed after a mule kicked and killed his patron. Before the man died, he told his wife and children to free the slave Hassan and give him money for his years of service.

A free man, he used the ducats to pay for passage back to Africa on a Portuguese caravel bound for the Guinea coast. He

37

found his village in ruins with only a few old people to tell him his parents had died and his two brothers had been captured by warriors from another tribe.

With nothing to keep him home, he started walking toward the sea, hoping he might find a ship to return to Seville or Lisbon. He hadn't gone more than a day's distance when white soldiers discovered him hiding in a tree. They stripped him of his Spanish clothes, then bound him to a long line of other captured Africans.

"Alive or dead, I'll be free again," he says. We're squatting in near darkness because the candle in the lantern is almost burned out. Hassan's hands must be trembling because the manacles on his wrists start clinking as he repeats the words, "Alive or dead."

It's the first time I wish that a black African were free, that all the Negroes were free to return to their homes. "You're treated no better than a beast," I say, "yet you keep your dignity. How is this possible?"

For a long while, he's silent, then he speaks. "Dignity deceives, honor does not."

It sounds like a riddle or something Father might say. After a while, the words make sense. I can squat with slaves in a floating hell and maybe pretend to be dignified. That would be deception. But keeping my honor isn't about how I appear.

The truth is inside me. I'm either honorable or I'm not—and only I know this.

Chapter 4 – Cast Away

Mornings and late in the day, if the weather holds and the seas permit, the crew gathers up top to pray and sing hymns. The captain usually leads the service. Every white hand on board, well or sick, is present, all except me.

I'm below, half asleep, listening to the hymns when I hear Father's voice. It rises above the others. Then I feel a pat on the top of my head. "Bear and forebear," the voice says. I wait for another touch but feel nothing. "Father, is that you?" I say and wait. I sit up and look aft across the deck. I see nothing but the shapes of the Africans.

"Eh?" someone mutters. "Father?" "It's me, Hassan. We need to sing too." "Yes," I answer, thinking I should also start another round with the bucket. I rise and step forward, lift the lantern off the peg, pick up the bucket, and head to the crowd of bodies. I've grown used to the moans, cries, and coughing, sometimes hearing faint singing. I also hear the wailings after death, the same as I heard in Greenwich and London. "O deliver me from the deceitful and unjust, deliver me, deliver me," I mutter, repeating the words over and over.

When we left the Guinea coast, I began marking the days on an overhead timber. Today, I scratch the wood for the twenty-second day of the voyage. I hang the lantern and go to retrieve the vessel that's between a boy about my age and a girl who usually greets me with a smile. I like her smile; I like her. I wish we could speak to each other.

I want to know who she is. Sometimes when I'm sleeping, she comes to me and speaks English, speaks words of play. And she laughs. I give her a name. I call her Princess, and she calls me José. And we hold hands. Yes, a dream I can't forget.

I'm walking like a crab, moving sideways with my lantern in one hand and the slop bucket in the other. Clumsy me, I trip on her outstretched arm and fall on my thin little Princess. The boy nearby and others holler at me, words I don't understand. I try to push up with my arms and hands. I slip on the wet floor planks, then roll to one side, across her legs, thinking she will cry out. But her body is still. I tap her bony shoulder, hoping she'll stir. I wait for her eyes to open, for some movement, for the smile I want to see. Around me, the voices have gone silent, and then I hear a woman from across the deck. She wails and others join in. I cry too. My chest heaves, and I can't stop; I can't stop this feeling of hurt that strangles my breath. I set the lantern and bucket down and wait for the sobbing to stop.

I've already seen six or seven lifeless bodies. Until now, Hassan has told me when someone dies. He usually nods in the direction of a corpse, and I inform the crew. But my Princess is the first departed soul I discover on my own.

The wails continue long after I tell a sailor on the gun deck, after two other crewmen come down to roll the body onto a strip of canvas, after they drag it away, after their burden disappears up the ladder and through the hatch. "Peace eternal," I whisper. It's what Father and Mother would say whenever a death cart passed our lodging. But the plague didn't strike the girl. She died only because she's a slave, taken from her home and deprived of nearly everything. And she got no word of farewell before they dropped her into the sea. Nicky tells me that dead slaves are dumped over the rail as easily as slop. "Not even a pause for a prayer," he says. "Angry the crew is, Joey, for they see money lost."

Nicky tells me that whenever a mariner is given to the ocean, the men kneel on deck all pious and prayerful. "Awful's the dying, Joey. Some die from Guinea worm, some from wounds they got when fighting the blacks. It's the bad fever now—and a good deal of bloody flux. Who goes next is all they're thinking."

I saw the plague take my parents and my sister. I watched the men of the death cart carry them out in a dirty cloth after each one died. I prayed for their salvation, crying and shouting for God to help me. How could I live without them? I prayed for help, I prayed to live, somehow to go on, day after day. And I did. Now I pray for myself and the Africans, pray that we live to walk on land again.

I'm a rat that prays. More than that, I'm a rat that's afraid. I'm living in fear for my life. Will they dump me overboard? I say nothing of my woes and fears to Hassan because he is shackled in place, a black man with a misery of his own, a misery much worse than mine. And I'll never let on to Nicky that I fear I may die here in the dark.

Father, what can I do? I think of you and me, of Mother and Mary. That time we went to the meadow beyond the forest. We took food to eat, tossed our raggedy ball, laughing when we joined hands, running round and dancing till we all fell down. I hear myself laugh. Is it me, a rat no more? Yes, yes, I have to be me again.

When Hassan again mentions singing, I don't expect anything more than prayers for the dead and dying. But in the faint light that passes through the sides of my lantern's sheets of horn, I see him burst with words of his own or another language not Spanish. He has lost a lot of his muscle so that the power of such a sound is as startling as hearing the other voices answer in a chant.

Hassan and his chorus fill the gloom with regular sounds. I begin to hum along, then I join the voices and do the same as I did at Greyfriars whenever my mates and I sang hymns. I close my eyes and move into a kind of trance, singing for the soul of my little Princess.

"Shut them up, Joey!" I hear Nicky yell from above.

"You tell them," I shout.

"Stop them!"

I sing on, slapping the deck in rhythm.

"Make them stop or you'll get the whip."

"You made that up."

"Bosun's words, as God's me witness."

I pick up the lantern and cross over to where Hassan sits with his legs drawn up, his chained hands around his knees. I ask him to stop the singing. "If you don't, they're going to whip me."

Hassan stops chanting, then shouts to the others. Their voices trail off until all that I hear is the creaking of the ship's timbers and the voices singing above us.

"You shouldn't sing with them," Nicky says.

"I want to."

"The captain knows you speak Spanish with the heathen slave."

"He's not a heathen. He prays to Allah."

"But you sing with him."

"So?"

"They already call you a heretic. You want to be tossed over too?"

"If they wanted me dead, they'd have done it already."

"Just be quiet when the crew sings."

"Yes, fine."

"Amen."

***

RON ARIAS

I've marked forty-eight days on the timber. The slave chants have died down, and Hassan's voice has dropped to a whisper. During the day's feeding, he surprises me by predicting everything will soon change and that he and the others will be given beer instead of dirty water, meat instead of sour soup, and everyone will be brought up for clean air and a dousing with seawater. "They'll bring us back to life," he says. "They want us to look strong for the auction."

I am pleased for my friend and the others but believe I won't be part of the plan to fatten the slaves for the market. And when they're all sold and gone, my duty will be gone. Before that happens, somehow I have to slip away.

I tell Hassan about the first African I ever saw. I was by the river with my mother, and we watched a naked man with a rope around his neck being led off a ship and into the street. He looked sick and not well-fed, and my mother said he was probably on his way to an auction.

Hassan shakes his head. "Sometimes a slave is already sold or promised to someone before leaving the ship or is given away to pay a debt. The ship that took me to Seville had two slaves promised to a family as a gift."

Odd, I think, that a person would be given as a gift, like a doll or a ribbon for a girl's hair.

On the fifty-second day of the voyage, Hassan's prediction comes true. I'm ordered up to the main deck with the Africans able to

44

walk. It's my first time breathing open air in almost two months. I'm as filthy as the Africans are, my body dark with grime. When my eyes adjust to the sunlight, I see Hawk standing by the mainmast. The captain's page pinches his nose, calling me stinking scum. "A washing ain't going to clean you," he says. "You can't scrub away heresy."

Just then, Carlos steps close to me and says to ignore the page. "Steady on, Joey. *¡Ánimo!*"

The buckets of cold ocean water revive my spirits enough so that when I return belowdecks with the slaves, I begin to think they and I might soon leave our floating prison. Hassan thinks we're nearing land because he saw a bird flying in the distance. Another good sign is that the Africans are given meat in the daily stew. "To cover our bones," my friend says. "It's what you do for cattle before taking them to market."

None of this fare is doled out to me. But the Africans give me bits of meat, salted fish, hardtack, and beer from newly opened casks. Their kindness soon makes me feel less like a rat and more like me, like Joseph Fields.

Hassan remembers that in his village rats are hunted to be roasted and eaten, but in Spain almost no one but Africans takes advantage of this delicacy. "Believe me," he says, "a hungry slave, black or white, will not hesitate to eat a rat if there's nothing else to eat."

When he lived in Seville, Hassan met a lot of slaves brought back from the Indies. They and others coming from Africa filled the streets of the city—many of them freed men and women mingling with everyone else. He heard so many stories of slave life in the Old and New Worlds that it seemed he knew all about the voyages, the slave markets, the owners, the escapes, the captures and, for the luckiest, the freedoms given. He says he prays to Allah every day for his freedom and for my freedom too.

I ask if he can put in good words for Nicky, who is now sick with scurvy. He's grown so weak over the past few days that he can hardly lift a bucket. I figure that my prayers to a Christian god as well as Hassan's prayers to Allah have to be more powerful than praying to only one god.

I know in my heart that answers to prayers can be fickle. When the Black Death struck our home, I beseeched God to save my family. But they all died within days of falling sick. What good were my pleas? Either my prayers reached deaf ears or my family was being punished. But for what? They were good people.

"Land ho!" someone up top shouts. "An island!" I hear whoops and oaths to the Almighty. I'm crying, slowly at first, then in sobs. I feel released from what I thought would be a slow, rocking death aboard the *Mynion*.

Hassan waits until I stop crying, then asks, "What are they shouting about?"

"An island. They see an island."

As the ships draw close, I hear the island's name, Dominica, and I learn it will be our first anchorage in the Indies. Nicky speaks to me from the hatch opening in a slow, weary voice. He says the fleet will stay long enough to collect fresh water and gather what fruit or game they can find or trade among the natives. And before his illness gets any worse, he will be left on the island. Maybe rest and native food will cure him. "Joey, they're leaving me with the Caribs."

"Who tells you this?"

"Cornelius."

"The barber?"

"Yes—and Red Beard. He says I would not be eaten because I'm too skinny and sickly."

"They're trying to scare you."

"I don't want to leave."

"You'll die if you don't."

"Might die anyway."

"Well, at least you'll have a chance."

"Wish you could come with me."

"I'd like that, but how? I'm going to miss you."

My best mate is leaving. He's been my eyes and ears for everything outside my rat's world—and my only helper with the waste bucket. Through the crosshatch of slats, I say goodbye and good luck. I catch a smile, and then Nicky moves away and is gone.

After we pull anchor and leave Dominica, the *Mynion* sails for other islands and mainland ports with names like Margarita, Borburata and Cartagena. I wish I could see some of the splendors of these places, but from where I am in the hold, I never catch sight of the Spanish Main.

Many slaves leave the ship, pulled up through the hatch. Sometimes I hear musket shots or feel the ship rock from the booming cannon blasts. Other times I see Carlos when he comes down to look for leaks in the hull. He speaks to me and Hassan in Spanish, telling us that merchants and landowners want slaves but that the Spanish Crown is against the traffic in Africans. "Some Spaniards love us for what we bring; others would rather see us rot in hell."

At most of the stops, two or three crewmen come down to where the Africans are. "Five up!" one shouts to his mates. "Let's go! Not that one! Take five from that lot over there." The sailors call the Negroes "goods" and goad them up to the main deck to be washed in seawater and then swabbed with palm oil to look their gleaming, healthy best, as Carlos says.

Soon, only a small group of slaves is huddled together below. I think it's strange that my friend, who is easily the strongest slave on board and the only one who speaks Spanish, has yet to be taken away

48

for sale or barter. Carlos says a healthy African slave who speaks *cristiano* is worth much more than one who doesn't. Hassan himself doesn't know why he hasn't been taken ashore, though Carlos thinks it's because Hassan is a "prize specimen," probably to be used in a trade for costly goods. That never happens because once most of the fleet's cargo has been sold or traded, we sail north, away from the mainland. After a few days and nights, we are struck by an awful tempest that forces the fleet westward. After many days, the *Mynion* is so battered that a lot of her timbers leak, and her bilges are flooded. Carlos says we have also lost much of our sailcloth and rigging. The rickety hand pumps can't keep up, nor can he plug all the new leaks. Around us, I hear voices shouting about doom and drowning if we go down. Truly, Nicky is lucky to be on an island and not with us to meet such an end.

Gradually the storm eases and the violent rocking stops. Someone shouts to lower a boat because the fleet's flagship, the *Jesus of Lübeck*, is approaching. Soon I hear that the captain general himself will be boarding. And then from the sound of things up top, I think he does board us. Not long afterward, two mariners come down to unshackle Hassan. "Why?" I ask. A sailor pushes me aside. "How would I know?" he mutters. "Hawkyns' order, not mine."

Hassan's transfer is so quick that I have almost no time to dart between the sailors and give my friend a quick hug. He says I'm a good *mozo* and then they pull him away, but not before he tells me, "Maybe we meet again, José, in this life or the next."

"*¡Ojalá!*" I shout above the din of voices from the newly

boarded mariners. Hassan taught me that ojalá means "God willing" or "Allah willing," and I cling to the word as I would a prayer. I so want to meet my friend again in this life and not wait for the next. I will miss our talks, miss his strength, his composure. In many ways, he reminds me of Father.

By the time the fleet reaches an anchorage, only five slaves are left on the *Mynion*. Sailors speak of New Spain and being near the port of Veracruz, but I can't see land through the cannon ports because the smoky gun deck is crowded with activity, as if a battle were about to start. And it does, beginning with great cannon blasts, followed by explosions all around. I can only huddle below with the slaves, quivering and shaking with each thud amid the constant shouting of orders and yelling.

The smoke and heat from fires are so awful that I long to scramble up the ladder to the gun deck. At least that way, I might get to where there would be some breeze coming from the cannon ports and hatchways. About then, I hear the frantic call to set sail. I feel the *Mynion* move with the waves. The noise and screams of fighting gradually soften as the heat and smoke are left behind.

About noon, I hear more shouts coming closer, becoming louder. Then there's a great commotion above on the main deck. After a while, I hear that English sailors and soldiers from another ship are boarding our vessel. Many of these men scramble down the ladders, pushing me and the Africans aside, crowding in wherever they can.

From the light of lanterns, I can see that some are wounded and smeared with blood. I hear that all but two of the fleet's ships—ours and the *Judith*—were burned and sunk by the Spaniards and that hundreds of men have perished. Only the general master himself, John Hawkyns, escaped with survivors in longboats, and now they are with us on the *Mynion*.

The Spaniards don't pursue us that day, but another storm hits us. When daylight comes, everyone speaks of losing sight of the much smaller *Judith*. They loudly curse its captain, Francis Drake, a kinsman of Hawkyns, for abandoning them.

Most of us aboard the *Mynion* are a sorrowful lot. As the days pass without water and food, some men resort to drinking seawater or they chew leather and lick any wet surface. Most of us are starving, and the weakest and sickest begin to die.

After about two weeks of high seas bashing the ship, some men are delirious and talk of eating the dead. Others speak of mutiny. I revert to my rat self, not speaking, hiding, trying not to be noticed, waiting for what will happen. I am weak and hungry, and I don't know how much longer I can stay alive.

For the good of everyone aboard, Hawkyns asks for volunteers to be left on land to lighten the Mynion's burden. In the end, I think he chooses men he values to stay on the ship, including several Africans, since they would be worth something in trade. I join a hundred or more crewmen ordered to go ashore. Although I hear a lot of whining about death at the hands of natives or the Spaniards, I can't wait to get going.

***

I emerge from the lower decks for the last time on the eighth of October 1568, as announced by Captain Hampton. This is more than a year after our departure from Plymouth. For a while, I'm blinded by the sunlight, but then I welcome the brightness of color all around, especially the blue-green sea. I'm doused with a bucket of seawater and cursed as a vermin-ridden heretic. I've been living for so long in the darkness that I feel more like a starving rat than a starving human. I never speak, never see my make-believe bag of stones. What good is such a game now? Seems foolish. I can no more speak to them than I can pray to God. I even doubt the wisdom of Father's sayings. They do me no good. Most of the voyage has been a purgatory of want. None of that. I must make my own good fortune.

Red Beard grabs me and cuts a few handfuls of my hair. "That should keep your bugs from jumping onto other heads," he says, laughing and shoving me away. Next to me is another boy, Myles, who boarded the *Mynion* with Hawkyns. "Have faith," he says to me. "Struck down but not destroyed." Ah, another silly, useless saying. I recognize the biblical words and nod.

Myles must not have heard the accusations of heresy against me because he gives me a friendly elbow poke in my ribs. "Don't lose hope, mate," he says. "Our general promised to return for us in a year's time." I say nothing because in my heart, I hope Hawkyns does not return, at least not for me.

Myles and I are among those squeezing into the second, overloaded longboat, along with the barber and surgeon, Cornelius, and Red Beard. I move toward the stern just as lines are tossed, and the rowers start pulling away from the *Mynion*. I never want to see the ship again. I have such dark thoughts about my floating hell that I only want to watch for the strip of white beach I can glimpse every time we rise to the peak of a swell pushing the boat from behind.

While we are seesawing up and down in this way, the *Mynion's* first mate orders the rowers to put some muscle into the task. What muscle? Most of us are all bones. Every day I must tighten the waistcloth that holds the pouch with my penknife, spoon, and comb. They are my sole possessions, and I'm afraid of losing them.

As we near the shore, the swells grow higher; twice the boat almost capsizes. When the first mate orders everyone out, I hear a few men say they can't swim. "In the water, lads!" he shouts, ignoring the pleas. "Swim for your life!"

I watch the first men drop over the side. Moments later, two of them disappear under a wave and never come up. "Over you go, my little heretic," Red Beard shouts. "Swim for your life!"

I rise to jump over the side, but then he grips me around my chest and heaves me forward. I hit the water and go under. I feel cold and there's a sudden silence. I begin kicking, pulling myself upward with my hands. I break the surface and gasp for air, then start to swim for the line of sand ahead. My arms and legs move as I was taught.

Kick-kick-stroke, kick-kick-stroke. Fish Boy would be proud.

Chapter 5 – Dancing Plant

I can't get up. All night I lie in the wet sand; all night it rains. And now I can't move, can't rise. With the sun starting to light the sky, I watch tiny black flies crawl about on my arms. I listen to faint voices and look across the sand to a single tree with thick branches. I see figures. Some are standing or squatting; others are in the tree, and it looks as if they are eating something. They're also drinking from a bag and passing it around. If I could reach them, I could eat and drink, and I'd be saved.

Or would I? Why would they want to save a papist? The men of the *Mynion* probably passed word to others who were with Hawkyns about the boy who was punished for heresy, put with the slaves. The figures I see would no sooner help me than they would welcome the devil himself. I can't make out the big gunny, but the thought of his hands on me, of him ordering me around, gives me shivers.

I crawl up the slope away from the water, keeping my distance from the men. I creep across the sand inch by inch so they won't notice me moving toward the reeds and grasses. I move into the green wall and sink into a muddy marsh. I taste the salty water and spit it out.

On my hands and knees, I move in the direction of where the men are but stay hidden in the reeds, feeling my way forward over the mushy bottom. I raise one hand from the mud, and just as I part the tall stems, I feel a sharp pinch on my other hand. I scoop up whatever it might be and see that I caught a crab big enough to eat. I've eaten crabs before, like those I found along the banks of the Thames, but I always roasted or boiled them before eating. I don't hesitate to eat now. I lift the creature by one of its legs, hold it belly up with both hands, and bite down to pull away the hard bottom, exposing the soft stuff inside. Then I feast, hardly tasting, chewing, and swallowing.

As I go on catching and eating crabs, I'm bedeviled by tiny flying insects that keep me slapping at my face, neck, and arms. My only relief comes when I cover my skin with mud.

I'm getting closer to the big tree, but I no longer hear voices, only the clicking and popping of insects and the calls of gulls and other birds. When I can see the tree's highest branches, I move the reeds for a peek at the men.

They're gone.

I leave the marsh and step across the ground. It's littered with the stones of the fruit they've been eating. I swallow what bits I can find, then struggle up into the branches to eat dark fruits that look like berries. Near the top of the tree, I can see that the marsh stretches into the distance to a forest. And below me not far from the tree, I see the hole the men must have dug in the sand to get their water.

I climb down, step to the edge of the pit, then slide down to drink from the puddle at the bottom. Afterward, with the sea on my left, I follow the many footprints leading in the direction that I reckon is south. I ignore the three sets of tracks going off to the north, guessing I'll have better luck following the larger group.

I come to where the marsh blends into dry brush that stretches ahead to hills. I continue south, following the swath of footprints among the flattened weeds. The tracks narrow into a path through high grasses, like a weedy tunnel with streaks of sunlight filtering through.

I'm tired, stretch out on the matted grass and fall asleep. In my dream, Millie's black dog, Scout, licks the salt from my ankles and feet. Suddenly, the dog stops licking and disappears into the thick grasses. I follow him and come out into a clearing where I see him trot toward Millie's cottage. She's outside, tossing scraps of something to the two hogs in the sty.

As I move closer, I see that the sty has become an enormous pool filled with food of every kind—mutton for the dog, vegetables for the pigs and chickens, and mounds of bread, cheese, and fruits for my friends Carlos, Hassan, Nicky, my Greyfriars mates in their usual blue smocks, Deacon Brown, and the Africans aboard the *Mynion*. Everyone sits at the edge of a moving, floating feast, grabbing, eating, and singing with the minstrel from the Chatham tavern. He's dancing on top of the revolving mound, singing King Henry's lyric about loving the good life in good company.

I run past Millie and dive onto a slab of cooked mutton. Others appear in the pool, rolling about, snatching, and munching whatever floats by—cabbage, turnips, carrots, baked apples, fish. "Dad! Mum! I'm alive! I'm here! In the New World!" My own shouting wakes me, brings me back to the weedy tunnel. I stretch my arms and rub my eyes. If only the dream were true. Crouching down, I move ahead. How long have I slept? Have to hurry. By now, the men are probably two leagues ahead of me.

At the first open space, I come to a stop. Can't move forward. I stare ahead, as still as I can be, unbelieving. What I see—is it real? What happened? The only movement comes from the swirl of black birds, vultures, I think. When it seems safe to move, I step forward toward the bodies. I pause at each one and see that flies are already busy over the dead flesh.

I can see the place is perfect for an ambush. As kids playing at war in Greenwich, my mates and I would wait for the enemy to walk into open spaces. Attackers would be like fish swimming into a net. Then we would pounce on the surprised invaders.

So many unarmed, weak men must have been easy targets for a barrage of arrows. I count eight bloody punctures in eight different bodies, thinking the arrows must have been withdrawn to use again somewhere else. There are no other bodies.

I recognize a young *Mynion* soldier who caught an arrow in the chest and fell backward. Most of his scalp was torn away, leaving a bloody patch without hair. The man's eyes are still open, and his yellow and red blouse is torn, as if it were ripped away because the collar and part of a sleeve remain around his neck. Poor fellow, he was a soldier who once gave me extra hardtack and told me he thought sailors ate better than soldiers.

The mess of death is awful, and I must get away. All but a few of the footprints appear to trail off to the south. I decide to go westward into the forest. I figure the attackers are natives, not Spaniards, because all the wounds are more like cuts or slits made by arrowheads and not holes made by musket balls. I know the size of the hole because in Greenwich, I saw the wound of a bloody, dying thief, shot by a guard in front of the Queen's palace.

I think I'll be better off meeting natives rather than catching up to my shipmates or running into Spaniards. The English will see me as an enemy Catholic, and the Spaniards will accuse me of being a Lutheran heretic. Both would rather see me dead. Also, by moving into the forest, maybe I won't be easily seen.

As I go toward the west, the brush and trees grow thicker and higher. Before nightfall, I come to a grassy spot by a stream, lie down, and soon fall asleep. Once or twice I think I hear leaves rustling, but whatever it is—maybe a deer or a rabbit—I'm never completely roused.

When the first light begins filtering through the trees, I rise and begin crossing streams and crawling among the tangles of vines and giant leaves. In front of me, about ten paces ahead, is a large lizard with a head that looks like a dragon's—at least like those I've seen on family crests in Greenwich and London. It frightens me at first, but I realize the animal is food, probably good meat. If only I can bash it with a rock. And rocks are everywhere on the ground. I pick up one that I can hold in one hand, one that appears to have been shaped into a rectangular block.

I creep forward, my weapon raised, but the green creature crawls upward with jerky moves. It disappears across vines that are growing from the cracks of what looks like a stone wall. I continue and reach the end, or corner, then turn to follow another stone surface covered in thick roots and vines. There, in front of me, I see what I think is a root that moves. Ah, a small snake. I bash it with the stone, then open its underside with my teeth.

After my little feast, I climb a jumble of stone steps high up to the flat top of the structure. Trees are all around, and at my feet are many shells, colored beads, and the blackened signs of burned-out fires. I look across the forest and not far away through a break in the wall of green. I see what looks like a giant stone head with a wide, flat face. The nose spreads, and the lips are fat like pillows. I want to get closer to the head and start down the broken steps, but the vines and forest cover block my way down. Finally, I find what appears to be a narrow, brush-beaten path down into the forest, away from the round stone sentinel.

I follow the opening for a while, but then it begins to rain so hard that I can't see where I'm stepping. I squat and wait. When the storm passes, I continue into the thick brush even though I've lost the path.

Over the next several days, I have more luck finding food. Relying on my rat instincts, I find frogs, snails, slugs, snakes, some flowers, and wormlike creatures as long and as thick as my middle finger. I don't want to use my penknife for anything but making quills, but hunger forces me to use the knife to sharpen the point of a stick so I can spear fish in streams I cross.

To protect myself from the sun and heavy rains, I wear wide, flat leaves that I tie over my head and shoulders as if I were wearing a large bonnet. I must look like a walking plant, a strange green creature that might startle grown men like Carlos and Hassan.

I hike westward in the direction of the sunset, at one point struggling up and over a steep mountain, going from warm to cool to warm again. I see families of deer, three black bears, birds of many colors, a very large cat, monkeys, and a waddling piglike creature with a long snout.

I fancy myself fit for this wondrous new world. I feel as if I'm a thinking citizen of nature, not a fierce and barbarous savage. Maybe I'm like the natives on Dominica, where Nicky was left. I want to believe they are people of some reason, not the savages the *Mynion* sailors called them. Surely, I'm thinking, the captain wouldn't have left my best friend to be killed by cannibal natives.

Covered as I am in large, slick leaves, I'm starting to feel comfortable in my giant garden. I think of myself as just another forest creature, though one without a tail, claws, or wings. Of course, I know I'm quite different. I have wit enough to think backward and forward. I believe the animals around me can't think as I do. I can remember my past life and wonder about tomorrow, but can a snake or bird do that?

As I plod along, collecting or catching my food, I begin to think I've found my patch of paradise. No more stinking seaborne jail. I'm free to roam this or that way, be a laughing fool if I choose, a dancing plant with legs and eyes, able to move from place to place, able to think and dream.

What would have happened if I had stayed in London, gone off with the stonemason to pound rocks? I never would have seen this land. On a hillside, resting on a ledge, I gaze across the forest top in the direction of the sea. This is my realm and maybe I'm its ruler. But rule what? With no subjects in sight, I'll have to content myself with my fellow forest creatures, from the tiniest ant to the greatest of birds that I've seen swoop down for a kill.

What would it be like to rule such a land? But then what would be the point of ruling? Here, every creature goes its own way, following its own rules for living.

I wonder how rulers think. My only memory of knowing something true about a ruler was when Queen Elizabeth and her attendants stopped in front of Father's table on the street in Greenwich near the palace. I was sitting on my box next to Father, who was writing a letter for a woman addressing her merchant husband. When the Queen approached us, we stood and bowed, and the client curtsied. "Go on," said the Queen. "I want to listen awhile."

Father continued writing what the young woman said, sometimes suggesting a change in wording. After he finished the letter, the Queen said, "Splendid," then asked him for his name.

"David Fields, Your Majesty."

"And this is your son?" she said, looking at me.

"He is, ma'am."

The Queen smiled at me, then turned to Father. "Excellent, Mr. Fields. You command our language well."

"My father's dream, ma'am, that I should speak and write the English tongue to perfection."

"You do indeed, as will your son, I would imagine."

"Oh yes," Father said, and both he and the Queen looked at me again.

"And your name, son?"

"Joseph Fields, mum."

"A good name. Will you write as your father does?"

I was nervous and looked at him. "Yes, mum," I said.

"And be a loyal subject?"

"Always."

She removed the lacy glove on her right hand, leaned forward, and patted me on my left cheek. "Carry on," she said, turning away and walking on with her retinue.

I remember that after the client left, Father told me the Queen nodded and seemed to like his suggestion to change the word "touch" for "caress." I asked him what the difference was and he said a caress is sweeter, more gentle than a touch. And then he told me even a queen can show a gentle side.

As I sit on the ledge, I want to exult in the vastness before me. I know the word "exult" because in one of my Latin lessons, Deacon Brown reminded the class that "exult" is *exsultare* in Latin. On that day, he lifted his cassock, stepped up on his chair and raised his arms before hopping off, shouting, "*Exsultare!* Leap for joy, lads. Exult!"

And we followed his example, jumping off our benches, yelling, "*Exsultare! Exsultare!*"

Days later, I come to a sunlit waterfall that empties into a clear pool. I step close and see a fish bigger than my hand. I raise my stick and stab it through its middle. I eat all the meat I can find on the bones, from the middle to the tail. Then I suck the head clean inside and out.

I hop around the edge of the pool. Through the slanted sunbeams, purple and yellow butterflies flit before the splashing waterfall. I'm cavorting and shouting Spanish forms of the verb "to leap." "*¡Salto! ¡Saltas!*"

I get no further than "You leap," because at that instant I'm hit hard on the right side of my head and I fall.

Chapter 6 – Captive

"Here, eat this," the soft voice says in Spanish. I feel something being pushed into my mouth. With one hand, I feel my aching head. It's wrapped in cloth that covers my eyes down to the tip of my nose and upper lip. I breathe through my nose. I'm curled up on my side, hands bound together, and a rope tied around my neck. My covering of leaves and grasses is gone, and I hear the waterfall splashing into the pool, along with men's voices speaking words I can't understand.

The same woman's voice speaks again. "Can you hear me? Do you speak *cristiano*?"

I nod, my mouth and throat so dry I don't think I can speak at all. Then I whisper the Spanish word for water. She asks me for my name.

"José," I say.

"My name is Izel."

I repeat the name, which rhymes with "wee bell."

"Stand up, José."

I try to push up from the ground with my left hand. "I can't," I say, groaning and trying to rise again. I feel the neck tether pulling me. I roll to one side, get to my knees, and slowly stand. I see only black.

"Come," Izel says and pulls me to the right, almost a yank. I stumble. Then I step forward, my feet apart. Izel tells me to kneel and drink water, which I do by scooping it up with my hands. When I finish, she says we have to walk.

I get up and go wherever I'm pulled. When I lag, the rough rope jerks my head one way or another. It hurts. Izel sometimes apologizes as she yanks me about. I ask her to remove the smelly cloth around my head and she says she can't; she isn't allowed. I want to tell her that even a horse in harness is allowed to see the ground, but I don't know the Spanish word for harness.

I ask why I need my eyes covered. She answers that her savages don't want me to know where they are because if I'm a spirit or a devil, I might tell other evil spirits where the tribe is.

"Who are you?" I ask.

"I told you, Izel."

"No, who are the men, who are all of you?"

"Savages. They fight the Spaniards and others."

"You're not a savage?"

"No, I'm a slave."

"A slave."

"Yes."

"Are you black?"

She giggles. "Yes and no."

"What? I don't understand."

GARDENS OF PLENTY

Izel answers that she wears black and rubs her skin with charcoal and ash because her mother told her the savages fear black and they like colors. Izel says she's a Nahua who was captured by Chichimecas from the north. She tells me there are different kinds of Chichimecas. Not all are barbarians. The men who took her were Guachichiles, which in her language, Náhuatl, means people with heads painted red. And they are the fiercest savages of all the Chichimeca tribes. She calls them Guachis or "devil savages."

I repeat the new sounds and she corrects me on words I mispronounce, just as Hassan did.

"But what color you call them doesn't matter," she says. "Red, green, yellow—they're all savages."

"And you're their slave?"

"Like you."

"What?"

"Yes."

"No!"

"Shh."

"I'm no slave!"

"Quiet! They'll beat you, maybe kill you."

From then on, Izel and I talk in low voices as we walk or trot along after the men.

It's an exhausting pace at first, but I get used to it. Maybe I'm getting stronger.

I trip, stumble, and fall down. Izel helps me up but then scolds me for being clumsy, for not lifting my feet when I walk.

She either yanks me forward with shouts or treats me kindly. She doesn't know exactly why the warriors have not killed me, guessing it's because I don't have long hair or because I looked like a tree spirit when they found me.

"They knocked you down," she says, "and told me to find out if you were really a spirit."

"I'm not."

"I know. You were bleeding. Spirits don't bleed."

"If you tell them I'm not a spirit, will they kill me?"

"I don't know."

"So don't tell them."

"When the time is right."

"Why didn't they kill you?"

"Because I can speak your tongue."

"My tongue?"

"What the Spaniards speak."

"I'm English."

"But you speak cristiano."

I rant in English, invoking the Queen, the river Thames, and my family's past in Greenwich. I stretch the truth, since I know nothing of my forebears. "And my name is really Joseph."

"Yo—sef?"

"Jo, Joseph."

"Josef."

"Yes. But now I'm José."

I finger the spoon and penknife in my pouch. I think the men might kill me if they no longer think of me as a spirit. But before that can happen, I'll cut myself free and run for it.

Izel seems pleased that I'm not a Spaniard, that I'm from another tribe or nation called England. I can hear the change in her voice, a softer tone. But whenever she speaks of her devil savages her voice turns hard. She says she calls them that to their face and they just laugh.

She tells me only one man among the Guachis speaks Náhuatl and none speak Spanish. So when a group attacks the Spaniards, she goes along with that man to translate what the Spanish survivors can tell them about where wagons, mules, and soldiers are. Her devil savages then attack and kill the Spaniards and other natives, laughing and doing the same as they do when killing cattle, sometimes cutting up the people.

I mistake the Spanish word cortar for horcar. "Hang them?" I ask.

"No, cut," Izel corrects me. "I've seen them cut everything, every part of men and women. They will do the same to me if I look away and don't laugh. For them, killing people is a party. I have to laugh."

"How can you laugh at that?"

After a moment's silence, my tether is yanked and Izel says, "I want to live."

The Guachis must have stopped because she tells me we can sit and rest. I lower myself to the ground and listen to her go on about how the men color their heads and bodies red and yellow before they go out to attack. They look ferocious in feathers and different animal skins. She describes them attacking and I imagine the Guachis looking like giant cats, serpents, eagles and bears, wearing skins and feathers, taunting their victims, dancing and screaming at them, ordering them to dance before they kill them.

She says that not long ago near the sea coast, her devil savages attacked a group of men they thought were Spanish. But the white men were terrified and appeared already near death. They couldn't fight and were helpless, so the attackers stopped before they killed more of them. The living were allowed to walk away, pointed in the direction of a Spanish town. Before that happened, they stripped the men who'd been dressed in clothes with color, then they put these clothes on themselves.

I tell her I was with the same skinny white men but got separated and was left behind.

"Wait here," Izel says.

I hear the rope drop and the sound of her footsteps moving away. After a while she returns. "I told them you're not a spirit and not Spanish. You're from a different tribe of white men."

"What will they do to me?"

"I don't know."

"Kill me?"

"I don't think so. When they kill, they do it right away. The same as when they hunt. They love to kill and eat, and it's fast. They don't wait. Now, get up." She pulls me to my feet. "We're going into the mountains."

If they don't kill me, then what? What would Father say? Bear and forbear, most likely. Or something is better than nothing, my something being my life. But it's no longer mine. I've nothing else but my breath, my walk, and my thought of the moment. In a blind world,

I have nothing else. Even thoughts of bearing up and holding on to life give me no consolation. I'm no more than a blind dog on a leash.

I suppose my lot could be worse—like the fellow whose head I saw on a pike in front of Newgate. I saw him the morning I fled Greyfriars. I was watching the men and women with their baskets of flowers and vegetables, chickens, bundles of wood and thatch, and a parade of sheep, horses, hogs, and carts with barrels of ale, all headed to the markets of Cheapside. I wondered how many prisoners were inside Newgate, found guilty of everything from murder and treason to witchcraft and robbery. I pushed my way through the crowd to get a better look at the man's head. The birds had taken out the eyes, leaving only dark pits. From where I stood, I could not imagine the man had been alive. Black were the sockets, only a darkened husk of a face, a mask.

I touch my own mask, the cloth over my eyes. I don't have eyes either, no face, really. Ah, but at least I'm alive.

Izel says she can't talk much because she was told to treat me like a bad dog. To make a show of this, she often whacks me with the rope, all the time shouting angry-sounding words I can't understand. But between breaths, she apologizes, using her sweet-sounding voice, saying she has to appear angry and mean.

Along the way, she gives me water with a kind touch, pouring from a gourd, or she slips bits of food into my mouth as if I were a baby. During the colder nights, we share a deerskin and talk in whispers until sleep takes us. She names things, like nuts, berries, and slivers of rabbit, deer, or birds that the Guachis shoot out of the air. "They're very good with arrows," she says. "One time I saw five of them hit a bird in the air so many times that only feathers fell to the ground."

That's the only time I hear her admire anything about her devil savages.

I have no idea how old she is or anything about her, and my head wrap is on so tight that I can't even peek at her. But I can breathe in her scent when she comes close. It's an earthy, sweaty, sweet scent. I try to imagine what she looks like, but the figure and face are vague, a blur. Who is she, really?

I slip in questions whenever we stop to eat, to sleep or to relieve ourselves. I don't want her to watch me when I squat. I ask her to close her eyes and tell me how she was captured. "Try to see what happened," I tell her, remembering Deacon Brown's words whenever he asked me and my mates to remember something that happened to us, something we should remember with our eyes closed.

Izel says she lived in a Spanish town with her parents, who belonged to a Spaniard she called an encomendero. She helped her mother in the patrón's house, playing with the family's children and learning to speak cristiano. Then about a year ago, when the Guachis attacked her town, they were in the patrón's house and her mother rubbed charcoal all over her body to protect her from the attackers. Izel hid in an empty wine cask. Her mother had told her that they fear black and if they found her, they'd think she was a devil.

"How old were you?" I ask, standing up.

"Twelve, I think."

"And now?"

"I don't know, fourteen years, maybe fifteen."

"Open your eyes."

"Yes, fifteen."

We start walking, this time at a good pace to catch up to her savages. Izel asks me my age.

I want to say fifteen but I feel a sharp yank pulling me to my left. She warns me of the rocks on that side, yelling her usual abuse, along with a few slaps of the rope.

I ask her if she belongs to any one savage.

"Never! My mother always said that if they ever caught me, I should say I belong to the Spaniard, that I'm his special woman."

"You were hiding?"

"I was. I waited in the barrel until I thought they were gone. Then I ran to the church. But two Guachis were outside cutting meat from a cow, and when they saw me running, they came into the church. I think they were scared of me because they never touched me. But they put a rope around me and pulled me out of the church."

"Did you tell them what your mother said?"

"I spoke in Náhuatl and one of them understood me. I told him I belonged to the Spaniard, that I was his woman."

I wonder if this is true, that she belonged to the Spaniard and shared his bed. I knew it was possible, since I'd seen girls her age and younger working in the stews of Southwark.

"Were you his special girl?"

"Yes and no. Special because in Náhuatl that's what my name means, one of a kind, special. I didn't lie."

"You weren't really his woman?"

"No, I committed no sin."

"Are you Catholic?"

"Yes."

"I'm not."

"Not Catholic?"

"We say Christian, something like Catholic but without the pope."

I ask Izel what the savages believe.

"Nothing," she says. "They believe in nothing. I don't know, but that's what I think. They have no churches, no temples. At night they shout to the stars."

I try to imagine such people. I think of some of the mariners I'd known on the *Mynion*, cruel men who professed Christian faith but never showed it in their treatment of others, especially the Africans.

"If you're a slave," I ask Izel, "who is your owner?"

"No one. No man will take me because I'm black."

I'm pulled to the left and I stumble. Izel warns me that the trail is steeper and that if I go to the right, I'll fall off the edge and die. "Little steps, English. Take little steps."

She's calling me "English" now and only sometimes "José." I assume she likes my being English, an enemy of the Spanish. She hates them for killing so many of her people, taking their lands, making them slaves. In the time of her grandparents, they destroyed the great city of Tenochtitlán, built by the people who spoke Náhuatl and who are called Mexica, which Izel pronounces "Mehsheeka."

But she despises her devil savages even more for killing her parents and brothers, something she never saw but can easily imagine—now that she's seen how swift and cruel they can be in their attacks. "In my dreams," she says, "I go back to that day so I can save my family. I want to warn them, to turn them into birds that fly away. I want them to be safe and return when the devils are gone." I want to see them again and live as before, live with streets and houses, where you can grow plants, where you can sell and buy things in the *tianguis*."

"Tankees?"

"No," she says, giggling, and slowly pronounces *tianguis*. "The place where you buy and sell everything. A market."

I think of London's market streets with their piles of cabbages, beets and carrots, hanging rabbits, ducks and spreads of fish.

"My savages," Izel says, "live in caves or under sticks or under nothing. They have no houses, no markets. They live naked, killing and taking what they want. What do they give the world but death?"

I haven't spoken to anyone in this way since I traded stories and ideas with Hassan. And never with a girl my own age.

"And the Spaniards?" I ask. "What did they give your people and the Mexica?"

"I'm not Mexica but like them we speak Náhuatl. So I'm Nahua. Mexicas are the people of Tenochtitlán."

"What did the Spaniards give your people?"

"Hmm. The Virgin? The little Virgin?"

"That's it?"

"The church, the priests, nuns."

"What else?"

After a long pause, Izel says, "Chickens!" and we both laugh.

I trip and fall. This time I'm on my feet before she can help me up.

"One foot is bleeding," she says. "I can bind it with a piece of my huipil. But I have to hurry. Don't sit, just stand—so they don't think we're resting."

She quickly wraps my foot with a strip of cloth and we move on.

By the time we arrive at our destination, Izel has wrapped both of my feet twice. I sit on the ground, pull my knees up to my chest, and hope the head cloth will finally come off. I hear babies crying and the shouts and voices of children and other women. I still have no idea who will own me or what I'll be doing. Why would they march me for days if they were going to kill me? Izel says I might belong to everyone or just serve one person. She thinks she belongs to everyone, even the children.

The air has grown cooler in the afternoon, and when my cloth finally comes off, I feel a breeze on my face. I blink a lot and shield my eyes, thinking it might be daylight. But after a while I can see that the sky is dark and the sun probably has set. All I can make out at first is a woman's silhouette against the flames of a fire she is tending with a stick. Then the figure is gone and I'm surrounded by mostly naked children and women, some pinching my face, others rubbing my arms and belly with their hands. I look up and around, searching for someone who might be Izel. I call her name.

"Yes, I'm here!" says her voice from behind the shiny faces lit by the fire. "They say you belong to the old lady. She can hardly walk, so you have to carry her."

"Old lady?"

"The chief's oldest sister. She's a kind of witch and knows how to cure."

My first clear view of Izel startles me. I can only stare and smile. I already liked her voice and at first I thought she might be beautiful. But after she told me how dirty she looked covered in charcoal, I thought of her as ugly. Now I see and hear her, matching the voice with a kind of beauty I've never seen before.

"I wanted to wash the black from my face so you can see me as I am."

Besides the sweetness of her face, what strikes me most is her head covering, so different from the long tangles of the other women. Izel's hair is buried under coils of twisted black yarn piled on top of her head, making her almost as tall as I am. And her body, unlike those of the other women, who only wear a patch of leather hanging from their waists, is covered by her huipil, a black tunic that reaches to her knees.

At first, the women and children back away. In the fire's light, Izel's clear skin appears bronze. One woman mimics her

Spanish when she speaks. All around there is giggling. The women point, their grimy faces peeking out from wild mops of hair.

Izel ignores them as she unbinds my hands and removes the rope from around my neck. I stand and clap my hands together. I'm now the main attraction, an odd, white-faced prisoner, and my audience stares at me as much as I gawk at Izel's lovely face. I think I should celebrate the moment, so I jump in the air and recite a few forms of the Latin verb *exsultare*.

Everybody but Izel moves back. "What was that?" she asks.

"A prayer," I say and again jump up, this time clapping my hands and shouting her name.

When she smiles, I notice a sparkle in her eyes. It's the same look Mother would give me whenever she praised something I did. And then she would kiss me on the forehead.

"Come, English. The chief wants to see you."

Izel leads me across a clearing that is lit by several fires. I'm surrounded by women, children and a few skinny dogs. Behind the flames sits a man with a stern, unpainted face. He stands. He's tall and stares at me with a puzzled expression. His hair reaches below his waist, a flap of leather covers his loins, and around his neck hangs a string of what looks like pieces of dried meat or fruit dangling from black braids.

The Guachis' leader speaks to another man and he speaks to Izel. She asks me if I want anything."

"Water," I say.

Izel tilts her head back and gestures with a thumb to her mouth. The chief raises a hand and moments later a woman brings me a glass goblet filled with water. I lift the vessel to my lips and swallow in gulps. The chief then takes the glass and begins to laugh. Soon everyone is laughing and hollering. Then the chief waves me away.

Izel tells me that her savages took the goblet from a church far away near the town of Xalapa. They brought back meat and many scalps but the big prize was the cup.

"Why did they laugh?" I ask.

"I don't know."

"Something I did?"

"I don't think so. Maybe it was the cup. Yes, the cup made them laugh."

"What?"

"The cup's like a memory, like a memory of that day."

"And that's funny?"

"No, I think they remember the feeling of what it was like."

"When they attack."

"Yes. It's what they feel when they kill their enemy. I've seen it. They yell a lot and laugh."

Chapter 7 – Escape

I carry the old woman on my back, her rear end slung in a deerskin, legs dangling, arms around my neck and shoulders. I don't know her name. I think of her as "Hump." Neither Izel nor I know the word in Spanish, so my burden becomes Hump, which is also Izel's first spoken word of English.

I care for the chief's sister as if she were a wounded bird, for the tiny woman is cursed with a shortened, lame leg and can hardly walk even with a stick. Wherever the band settles for a day and night or more, I set her down, spread out a deerskin for her to lie on, and then go with the women and children to collect sticks and brush to make a crude shelter. I also help put cactus spines around the camp to protect us from enemies.

I feel I have a place and a purpose. Izel says everyone does something. She points to the young man who carried Hump before I did. He smiles and laughs a lot or makes others laugh. He never paints himself as a warrior and never goes on attacks, always staying to make arrows and bows or amuse the children. He twists cactus or sinews of animals for bowstrings or chips away at obsidian to make arrowheads. Izel says he does this as well as or better than any warrior can.

I start calling the maker of bows and arrows "Chuckles" in English because he amuses the band by doing things like twirling baskets on a stick, juggling stones, or imitating dogs, deer, vultures, jaguars, and rabbits, chasing and catching the smaller children. When I come back from gathering wood or collecting cactus fruit with some of the women, Izel tells me in Spanish what "Chuckles" did while I was gone. To her, he's the only Guachi who isn't a savage.

This playful young man also teaches me to make my own arrows and a strong bow, showing me by example and not by words. This allows me to go with some of the young boys to hunt for small animals. It's with them that I learn to stalk my prey and shoot. They laugh at my many misses but then shout their pleasure whenever I hit something we can eat.

***

Caves shelter us best, but sometimes we make do with stick shelters or simply sleep in the open. I go out in the morning's first light to collect cactus fruits and insects to eat. Unless the band has just feasted on a deer or one of the wild dogs Izel calls *coyotl*, I'm usually hungry, having to feed Hump and myself. If my collection of fruits and tiny creatures is small and doesn't please her, she yells at me and hits me with a stick.

When we're in the dry lands, I get water from certain plants and roots. Watching Chuckles and the women, I also learn where to find water in the hidden pockets and hollows of dry creeks and riverbeds, filling gourds and skin pouches with water. When we eat,

Hump fancies my mother's wooden spoon and likes to use it to slurp cactus juice into her mouth.

Beyond basic words like "come," "fire," and "water," I can't speak Hump's language well enough to have a conversation. But the two of us most days get on fine, especially after I made her a rigid basket seat that faces backward. It's easier for her to sit in and for me to carry. Hump now rests on her woven perch and can see those trailing behind us. With all the walking I do under her weight and the few pelts, baskets, and gourds we carry, my legs grow stronger, my arms and shoulders bigger.

As Hump's helper in treating the sick or patching wounds, I sometimes carry patients to her. Today I bring her a moaning warrior with part of an arrow shaft sticking out of his thigh. He just returned from a fight with another Chichimeca band. She massages the area, pours an herbal juice on the wound, and manipulates the shaft while the man is drunk on a liquid Izel calls *pulque*. Slowly, the shaft and arrowhead emerge. Hump binds the wound with leaves wet with *pulque*, and the dazed warrior stumbles away.

I'm convinced that the chief is so satisfied by how I take care of his sister that he stops watching me, no longer afraid that I might turn into a spirit and disappear with the old healer.

I tell Izel that Hump probably sees me as something like a son, more than just the obedient white beast carrying her from one place to another. Izel laughs, shaking her head. "If you break your leg and can't carry her anymore, Hump will have you cut up for everyone to eat. She won't even cook you!"

"What are you saying?"

"Listen to me, English. If you no longer have a use, they kill you and eat you. Hump won't care."

Izel reminds me of Deacon Brown, exaggerating things to scare his pupils into paying attention. I tell her I can't believe what she says, and she shakes her head again. "When they attack a town or a line of mules loaded with silver, they see us as the enemy— Spaniards, Indians, blacks. They want all of us out of their land."

More and more I want to escape this world of a slave. Izel, who is ordered about by the women, also wants to escape. But how can we? When? We are their slaves, forever being scolded or hit with sticks, or sometimes stuck with cactus spines.

Today, I notice Hump sitting by our shelter scratching her head, clawing at her long tangles of hair. I take my comb out from the pouch, walk over, and squat down beside her. I show her how I comb my hair, producing lice for her to inspect. Then I crack the critters between my fingernails. I gesture that I can do the same for her, and she laughs, tilting her head back and opening wide her nearly toothless mouth.

I move behind her and begin to comb. I use the side with the wide-spaced teeth first. Then I flip the comb to use the side with the small row of tightly spaced teeth. The strands of her gray mess are long and thin, and I pull slowly from her scalp out to the ends, gathering mostly lice and nits. When I show her my harvest, she snatches the comb from my hand, removes her tiny tormentors, and eats them. After swallowing, she smiles and returns the comb. Then she leans back into me, tilting her head close to my nose.

I think Hump and all the tribe could use a good scrubbing. The Guachis almost never wash themselves, living with filth until they die. Izel says that's why their bodies are washed and cleaned before being burned. Hump gives off a rancid smell that I've grown used to. I'm not as put off by the different smells as Izel, who says that her savages wouldn't know what to do with soap.

Hump seems pleased with my combing, and now other women who've been watching, one by one, offer their heads for me to comb. They sit on the ground and wait for a turn. Children come close to watch, and by the time darkness comes, I've combed another six heads of dirt-encrusted hair.

The next day I undo more tangles of hair, ridding the women of lice, nits, fleas, dirt, bits of food, crusty red dye, and tiny black balls of dried blood. The men ignore my grooming show until Hump throws rocks and yells at the women waiting to be combed. I think she's bothered by all the attention the combing has drawn. To the men, such a display by the chief's sister amuses them because they laugh at what I'm doing.

The mother of perhaps the fiercest warrior appears to be a leader among the women. She insists on being first whenever I wave the comb to signal that I'm ready to start. She's proud, loud, and stern with the others, but she quiets down under my steady strokes, making little squeals and curling her toes. When I tell Izel about Squealer, as I call her, she warns me not to be too good at combing.

"What?"

"English, you don't know about those sounds?"

"She likes it."

"Well, I hope the man she belongs to doesn't hear about it. If he does, no one can help you."

"But they all like it."

"Too much."

"Listen to me. In Náhuatl we say it's too late when a person is already trapped in sticks and rope."

I shrug. I can hear Father.

The women are all different, and I give a name to each one. Happy approaches with a giggle, Sad always seems about to cry, and

Crosseyed is so shy she comes with her head down and never makes a sound, hiding her face as much as possible. All but one woman appears to like the combings. I can never comb Whiner in the right spots of her scalp. When I pull back on her hair, she elbows me in the stomach, slaps my hand, yells at me and points to parts of her head, as if she's scolding me for missing something.

I finally get what Izel means about the sounds women make. Before Squealer's man comes for my scalp, I decide to stop combing all the women except Hump. I shake my head, make faces, and wave my hands to shoo them away, all of which greatly pleases Hump.

At night, after the fires die, Izel unwinds the black yarn on her head and grooms herself with my comb. Other than that, the comb now touches only Hump's head and that of a boy I name Skunk because of a natural strip of white hair that begins at the middle of his forehead and runs back down to his waist.

When the whole band of Guachis is on the go, Izel is treated as every woman's slave. Dressed as usual in her black huipil, she gathers food, collects wood, fetches water, and grinds seeds. There's always some task to do. But when the band stops so a woman can give birth, they keep her away from the mother and baby.

I know Izel will never get over her hatred of her devil savages. They killed her family, and she's now their slave. But I can never feel such anger at the tribe. I've grown to admire, even envy, certain things about the Guachis. Shooting a bird out of the sky with one arrow shot or outrunning a deer are feats amazing enough, but nothing can compare to the way they feed themselves.

Sometimes we come to a stretch of rocky wasteland where I think there's little or nothing to be found that we can eat. But then I leave Hump and join almost everyone else to harvest a day's food for the entire band of about sixty people. Berries, seeds, flowers, cactus fruit, mesquite pods, mice, rabbits, snakes, beetles, spiders, and scorpions—all are found, collected or killed and then eaten on the spot.

I've gotten to where in one morning I can gather and catch more than enough bounty for me and Hump. Izel finds her own food, but we often share with each other.

Our hunger makes spiders, lizards, and snakes a fine meal.

I've also learned how to protect my feet, especially for the ball game. I started by playing with the children. And Chuckles has taught me to make my own buckskin sandals. They help me run over broken ground while pursuing the ball. In Greenwich, I often outran all children my age or older, but here with the Guachis, I think of myself as a tortoise. I can't always keep up and can only marvel at their speed and endurance. When I'm not tending to Hump, I like to run with the boys and young men. I'm learning the ball game well enough so they no longer jeer at my efforts. We chase the wooden ball, two teams of five players on each side. The hardest part for me is wedging my kicking foot under the ball and flinging it forward.

After a game, everyone celebrates by drinking a lot of the nopal brew. Some players also eat tiny fruit that Izel says makes them go mad. So far, they haven't offered us any of their brew or mad fruit. I can only believe it's because they see us as slaves who are not to be indulged.

The first time I saw this kind of madness was when everyone was celebrating a raid on a Spanish caravan loaded with goods for the north. The men had returned with sacks of meat, mirrors, knives, and rolls of colorful cloth. An older man, after eating the little fruits and drinking *pulque*, tied a deer's head on top of his own and ended up vomiting and falling to the ground. He got up, as so many others did, and danced for two days and nights, rattling shells, growling, and calling to the sky. Chuckles, ever the jester, was the only one dancing and singing without, as far as I could tell, taking the brew or fruits.

***

For the most part, the cactus and mesquite hills and plains we live on are rocky and rutted. But today we leave this dry land and climb up to a mountain pass to the east. Then we descend into a forest of pine trees. For days, our trek leads us into a valley of leafy trees and thick bushes until we reach a clearing where we stop to make camp. As usual, I kneel down to let Hump's feet touch the ground so I can drop my bow and quiver, then I slip out of my harness. But as I loosen the ropes holding her basket seat, I suddenly feel the old woman's weight gone, and I hear a thump. I turn around and see her body face down on the ground. She's not moving.

90

Two women cry out. Others begin shrieking, and soon Hump is no longer my charge. Chuckles and an older man lift and carry her across the clearing. They place her before the chief. He stares at the small figure and begins to cry. Before long, everyone is sobbing and wailing. Dogs are howling. Izel says Hump nursed most of the band through illnesses, treated their wounds, pulled many of them out of their mothers.

I watch everyone circle around. I can't help crying. Suddenly, I miss the old woman. I miss her weight, her touch, her gaze, her frowns, her grin, her laughter. She was fragile, and all the jostling and bumping had to have worn her down. I remember when I first carried her. She was my burden. But gradually she became a part of me, the me on my back, the me that gave me a place among these people, the me that let me live. Now she's gone to the afterworld. My angel is gone.

What will happen to me? Maybe I can do something else for the tribe. I can shoot arrows well enough to hit rabbits and birds on the move. I can find things to eat. Surely I can be of use.

"Izel, will the chief blame me for his sister's death?"

"I don't think so."

"What will I do?"

"English," she says, squeezing my hand, "just watch."

A cluster of wailing women begin to touch and stroke Hump's body. I see the men and children move back.

"Come," Izel says, pulling me away. "Let's find wood for the fire."

Suddenly, everyone but the women around Hump moves out of the clearing and into the brush. We follow them, find and break branches and bring them back to toss onto a growing pile. The women pour water from gourds onto the naked body. Then they wipe Hump dry with strips of the clothes taken in raids, lift her up, and place her on a deerskin that covers the pile of brush, sticks, and branches. The chief, who is moaning and crying, pushes the women aside and places a rattle, necklace beads, and a handful of red cactus fruit on his sister's wrinkled belly.

When he leaves, I step close to the body, expecting maybe to be stopped or clubbed in the back. But nothing happens. I place my comb on Hump's hair just above her forehead, followed by my spoon next to her hand. I whisper in English, "May your gods and good spirits be with you." Then I back away.

Starting with a tiny smoking ember taken from another fire, the first flames under the healer's body rise through the kindling. Their mournful wailing becomes louder, and the men and women gather in a circle around the pyre and start to dance in a kind of shuffle. As the fire goes down, the pulque is passed around, with men and women leaving the dance to drink from a gourd, then rejoining the dancers. From what I can see, everyone but me, Izel, the children, and Chuckles eats the madness fruit.

Izel and I keep outside the circle, watching at a distance. The children wander off to lie down, then the women and men, led by the deer-headed chief, slowly move away from the dying fire and settle down. Some shout to the stars and half-moon.

Chuckles, who's curled up near the embers, appears to have fallen asleep.

"Let's go," Izel says.

"What?"

"Now!"

"Wait, my bow and arrows."

"No, you can't. Someone will see you."

"But—"

"Let's go! Just stand up and walk away."

We leave the mourners and Hump's charred body, stepping around sleeping shapes, moving toward the darkened edge of the clearing. I stumble and almost fall on one of the children. It's Skunk, the boy with a streak of white hair. I see his look of surprise. Then he smiles and closes his eyes.

Chapter 8 – Running

We stumble on in the dim moonlight, pushed by our fear, holding hands, often tripping, falling, having no path or fixed direction. We're running for our lives, running to get as far away from the Guachis as we can. Just knowing how good they are at tracking prey keeps us from stopping to rest.

As the sky begins to brighten, Izel pulls me sideways, and we collapse on a patch of weeds. I lie still, listening to our heavy breathing until the sounds are soft, and I relax into sleep.

When I open my eyes, it's daylight. Above the trees, I see blue sky. I turn my head to see Izel next to me. She's sitting up and stretching her arms. I watch her rewind the deerskin strap around her ankle. I wonder how long her sandals will last. Mine will soon be useless, and I'll have to run on bare feet.

"Let's go," she says and stands up. She grabs my hand and pulls.

"Go where?" I ask, looking around at the trees and thick brush with no path that I can see.

"It doesn't matter," she says. "They find us, they kill us."

"I think we came from there," I say, pointing to some broken branches between thick trunks of what appear to be oaks.

"Good," she says and steps off in the opposite direction.

I follow her, and right away we're darting between and around bushes and trees, jumping over vines. We cross streams, descend into gullies, climb over boulders, and up hillsides through tangles of bushes and more vines.

In stretches of open, weedy ground, I can see we're surrounded by steep mountains, and from the sun's position, I figure we're going in a westerly direction. If we keep going that way, I think we'll go down into the canyon I see far ahead.

Izel moves well, jumping over logs, dodging trees, and vine-covered bushes. As we climb up a valley slope covered with purple flowers and stunted trees with ferns all about, a cloud sweeps over us and she disappears into a thick, cool fog. Walking barefoot now, I like the wet, springy ferns on my feet. They remind me of the misty mornings in the forest when Father would take Mary and me to look for mushrooms.

"Izel!" I shout. "Wait for me! I can't see you."

I almost run into her but at the last moment I see her black huipil and head covering. I try to stop but end up leaning into her. To keep from falling, I embrace her. We hold on to each other, both of us breathing heavily, expelling our own puffs of tiny clouds.

"Open your mouth," she says.

I open and wait. When nothing happens I ask why I should open my mouth.

"For the water," she says. "On the tongue, can you feel it?"

"Yes," I answer. I lick the moisture from my lips. I expect her to touch them. We're still holding each other, my eyes closed. I'm not sure what she's going to do, but it doesn't matter. I like what I'm feeling.

Then she lets go and moves away.

For a while, I follow her closely through a forest that seems to float in the clouds. Among the shapes ahead of me, I follow the one that appears and disappears in the mist. She shouts a word that sounds like "cuaweetl," then my right foot hits something solid, and I have to step around a small pine tree, a sapling, a word Father taught me.

He called them baby trees and said that they should be given the chance to live.

He and Mother taught me a lot about nature but never about affection and how some emotions can overwhelm a person. I've seen the unions of dogs, pigs, and people in all sorts of places, but my parents never told me what I might feel in such an embrace.

"What was that word?" I ask Izel.

I can barely see her in the fog, but I sense she has turned around and is facing me. "*Cuahuítl,*" she says, and then pronounces the Spanish word for "little tree"— *arbolito*.

I garble the Náhuatl word and ask how to say "I like you" in her language.

"*Nemistli meki*," I hear. I try to repeat it, and she giggles and tells me this is no time for a language lesson and for me to speak *cristiano*. When I get to where she stands, she reaches for my hand and squeezes it before moving on.

Suddenly, as quickly as we enter the cloud, we leave it and emerge into sunlight.

Before us is a wide slide of broken rocks. Izel lets go of my hand and starts across. "Be careful," she calls back. "These rocks can fool you."

We've talked about hurting ourselves, breaking bones. She's so desperate to escape her devil savages that I believe she means it when she says she'll leave me if I ever injure myself.

We're thirsty and haven't eaten anything all day. I watch Izel cross the dry river of rocks, stepping lightly from one stone to another. She told me that when she went on raids as a translator, if she had tripped and broken a leg, her savages would have left her behind.

I see her black dress and head coils disappear into the weeds and brush. She's become a bobbing black mushroom daring me to catch up.

But I take my time crossing, careful where I step. Just as I reach the other side, she pops out of the bushes and raises a finger above her head. "Listen! You hear it?"

I stand still but hear only my own breathing and a few birdcalls.

She turns, and I follow her into the forest, picking my way through branches of pine and leafy trees. I've lost sight of her, but before long, I come to a wide, shallow stream. She's kneeling at the edge, scooping handfuls of water into her mouth. I drop down and start to do the same but lose my balance. I brace myself, forearms hitting the water first. The stones are smooth, and I stretch out, face down, immersed in the cool current. I swallow water, then I lift my head with a gasp and breathe. I roll over onto my back and shout, "Eureka!"

Izel motions for me to be quiet.

"Yes!" I shout again. "Eureka!"

"Lower your voice. We're not free yet."

"Eureka," I say softly.

"What?"

"It's what you say when you find something."

Izel nods, repeating the word. She stands, unravels the spirals of thick yarn on her head, and lets it all drop. Then she quickly lifts up her black huipil and pulls it off.

Only her face, neck, arms, and the bottom part of her legs are smudged with charcoal.

The rest of her coppery skin is bare and unmarked. I stare at the patch of hair below her belly and then watch her breasts rise when she lifts her arms to her head and shakes out her hair. With small steps, she comes my way into the stream and slowly settles herself next to me.

"A dream," she says, rubbing off the charcoal on her skin. "I'll never wear black again."

"What about your savages? Don't you need the disguise?"

"English, it won't matter."

"You don't know that. Maybe they gave up the chase."

"That's not how they are. To them, hunting us is like playing a ball game."

"But they're still afraid of you because you made yourself black."

"And you? You're white. They like white flesh."

"That's not funny."

"It's true."

"So let's keep moving."

"Not yet. I want to dream a little more."

For a while, we lie with our faces above the water's surface, seeing only bits of sky through the leaves. I turn over and start moving across the smooth stones toward the other side of the stream. Halfway across, the water turns warm. "Izel, come over here."

She crawls over to me, one side of my body in cold water, the other side in warm.

We switch positions, then switch again. I close my eyes and feel so relaxed I almost fall asleep. I hear her laugh and turn to watch her rub and rinse her face, neck, and arms. "Now we can go," she says.

I can watch her forever. Every moment feels normal. But she beckons with her hand, her small, beautiful hand. She waves and points ahead. I get to my knees and stand. "Let's walk in the water," I say. "Maybe they'll lose track of us."

She laughs. "No, they know that trick and many more."

Just then, we hear a loud noise like a ship igniting all its firepower at one time. Then the ground begins to move and we collapse in the stream. Around us the trees sway and branches fall. We try to stand but can't keep our balance.

I roll on top of her, thinking I'll shield her from whatever might fall on us.

"*Temblor*," she says, and for the first time I hear the Spanish word for "earthquake."

The movement slows and then stops. I'm still on top of her, part of us in warm water, part in cold. Her breasts press against my chest, her thighs against mine, and I sense a thickening movement between my legs. I'm excited. I know what I want to do, but I see the surprise and maybe fear in her eyes and do nothing.

"Tepeyolotl," Izel says. "It's him."

"Who?"

"He's the heart of the mountains and takes the shape of a jaguar. You respect him because he can be mean and dangerous."

I roll to one side, sit up, and look around. I'm thinking a jaguar might be looking at us through the leaves. I have no weapon except the little penknife under my loincloth. The blade would be useless against such a big cat with great powers.

Izel stands up, and I watch her move out of the stream. She tears a strip of cloth from the hem of her huipil and wraps it across her chest and then rips another piece to wrap around her waist, covering herself down to her thighs.

"English," she says, "we must hurry."

I get up and follow my vision of beauty downstream. We walk in the water and then on the weedy bank until darkness descends, and we have to curl up in a hollow next to a large tree trunk.

I need the rest because I've been shivering for some time and feel a fever coming on. Izel says it's because I had no protection from the cold, foggy air on the mountain. Whatever causes my fever and chills, I no longer think I can escape illness. I've crossed the sea mired in filth, crawled ashore starving and thirsty beyond belief, and lived the filthy life of a Guachi slave. In all that time, I was never seriously ill. Now I'm being brought down by a cloud.

Izel holds me all night. In the morning, she covers me with leaves, ferns, and moss. Then she leaves. I barely see her when she returns. I must be delirious. Her hands push what feels like worms into my mouth, and her voice tells me to swallow.

Then she helps me walk to the base of a cliff where she says she found a small cave. I stumble in and fall down on a mound of leaves. Before I close my eyes, I see Izel holding a spear.

When I wake, she tells me I've been asleep for three nights and three days, shivering, wet, and hot to the touch. I was able to swallow water, and I said her name and words in Spanish and English.

"I thought you were going to leave me," I say.

"Why would I do that?"

"To escape. You said so."

"José, it's no use running."

"I'm awake now, we can go."

"No, you must eat."

"What about your savages?"

"I think we're safe now."

I try to stand but can't. I'm dizzy and weak. I rub my eyes and listen to Izel tell me she will accept the inevitable. "All the earth is a grave and nothing escapes it," she says. I can't argue. We all die, dust to dust, as Deacon Brown used to say. We must accept the inevitable. But then Hassan swore to me that he'd never give up life easily, that as long as he breathed, he would fight to live.

"Here," Izel says, offering me a strip of roasted meat. "Rabbit."

"You made a fire?"

She nods. "I want cooked meat, no more raw."

She puts a sliver of rabbit meat in my mouth and I slowly begin to chew. I've grown so accustomed to tasting blood with meat that the fat from this cooked morsel gives me a pleasure in the mouth that I've almost forgotten.

Izel has been busy. Besides starting a fire, she speared a rabbit and collected seeds, nuts, more worms, and tiny fruits that are as sweet as honey. With grasses and reeds she also wove a small bag to carry our food.

After two days of rest I'm ready to walk. Whatever illness I had is almost gone.

We move through a sparse forest. I feel strong enough to make a set of arrows and a bow. Izel helps me collect the slender branches for the arrows, and she twists cactus fibers for the string. I have no feathers but hope to shoot birds at close distance. Then I can collect feathers to tie on to the ends of the arrows.

Over the next five days and nights, we make our way through the canyon to a wide expanse of rounded stones and boulders. The stream we've followed strangely ends or has gone underground. The air is now drier, the vegetation sparser. Then we enter a flattened landscape of brush, thorny trees, and cactus with long, pointed leaves. These are the magueys that give the Guachis a sweet juice that they take from the hearts of these plants.

We walk to the west. To escape the worst of the heat during the middle of the day, we stay in the shade of ravines and under mesquite branches. The sun drops down, and we pick our spot for the night. We collect broken branches to make a circle around our space to protect us against snakes and other creatures. Then we lie down to sleep, belly to back, under a moonless sky and a blanket of stars.

"Tell me what your land is like," Izel says.

"Well, it's not as dry as this," I say, then describe plowed fields, cottages, green forests and London streets filled with fishmongers, yeomen, milkmaids, soldiers, drovers, beggars, orphans like me, soldiers, even the Queen herself. I tell her who the people are and what they do. I mention Greyfriars, Deacon Brown, and my life by the Thames. I tell her about Bankside and bearbaiting.

"Dogs fighting bears?" she asks.

"Yes," I say, unable to come up with the Spanish word for amusement. I tell her it's like watching Chuckles clowning around for the other Guachis.

"They laugh at dogs fighting a bear?"

"Or a bull, sometimes it's a bull."

"That wouldn't make me laugh."

"It's what happens."

For a while, I stare up at the universe of tiny lights, close my eyes, then I hear her soft voice. "Good night, José."

"Good night, Izel."

The next morning we make our way down the middle of a sandy creek bed. We're leaving tracks, but Izel no longer cares. She believes the devil savages stopped hunting us after the earthquake. It's why she started making fires days ago.

"How do you know?" I ask.

"It's what I feel."

When the sun rises overhead, we rest, then doze under the shade of a mesquite tree. Then we climb out of the gully and head toward the horizon. The sun's now dropping fast and we'll soon have to look for water and something to eat, then make a ring of thorny branches around us before we sleep.

I don't know how Izel feels, but I'm content. Here we are in a dry wilderness, always thirsty and with no destination in sight. I've survived a fever that almost killed me, and our bodies are now kept alive on little more than cactus juice and a few lizards and snakes. Yet I feel joy just holding her hand.

"The earth shaking," she says, "remember?"

"I'll never forget it."

"Tepeyolotl saved us."

"The jaguar?"

She nods. "We showed him respect—there in the water."

"You mean—"

"Yes, that. He left us alone. And the devils hunting us—he scared them away."

Chapter 9 – Emilio

Two days later I see a giant eye. It's early in the morning and the shelter of sticks and leaves that we built begins to move. Everything shakes.

"Izel," I whisper, tapping her shoulder. "Something's outside."

The shelter keeps shaking, and the eye disappears from a hole above us, then returns.

"Just the wind," she says.

"No, look up."

She turns her head. "It's a cow. Eating the leaves."

"A cow?"

Izel stretches her arms. "Or maybe a bull."

For a while we lie on our backs, listening to the animal's munching, then we talk about who might have cattle.

I say Spaniards but Izel believes they could be natives, which is what she calls all Indians except her Guachichil savages.

"*We* look like savages," I say, thinking we're nearly naked, our hair is wild, and we're covered in grime, cuts and scabs.

"I'm going out," she says and sits up.

"No, wait. If the people are Spanish, I can't say I'm English."

"Why not?"

"I'm the enemy."

"So tell them the truth. Tell them what they did to you on the ship. Tell them you're an orphan. Tell them you were a slave of the savages. Tell them you escaped with me."

"What will *you* say?"

"The truth. My people were Totonaco and Nahua. I speak Náhuatl and Spanish, and that's why the savages let me live. I translate for them."

Izel leaves our shelter on all fours. I hear her greet the cow in Spanish, then listen to her coax the animal to be calm and still while she takes some milk. I crawl out into the early morning light and see her on her back beneath the cow. I watch, fascinated by the expert movement of a single raised hand. She's pulling on one of the udder's finger-like teats, squirting milk into her mouth with short pulls and squeezes.

"Now you," she says. "Get under and keep your mouth open." I trade places and she squirts milk into my mouth from two teats, one after the other, until there are only drops. Izel says she used to milk cows at the Spaniards' place. "They like to be milked.

This cow didn't have much, but she gave us something."

I mention the milkmaid at Greyfriars and all the milking she had to do every morning. "That's a lot of pulling!" Izel says, then tells me the word for milking a cow, *ordeñar*.

I hope I can someday write in Spanish. I wonder what the difference might be between spelling English sounds and Spanish sounds. I ask Izel if she thought I could pass for a Spaniard.

"I don't think so, but why would you do that?"

"In case I have to hide who I am."

"And telling the truth?"

"I'm now José Campos—from Spain."

"José, all I want to say is be careful. Lying can bring problems."

Izel often keeps me from stepping on "snakes and spines," as she likes to say. So after we talk more about telling the truth and improving my speech, I put the Spanish idea aside, at least for the time being.

I have to pee and turn away from Izel. I hear her doing the same thing, wetting the ground. But at the same time we also hear a rooster crowing. The faint, screeching calls seem to be coming from the north. In the distance, I can just make out the square, low shape of a hut or cottage. Izel stands, sees the same thing, and without a word between us we start walking in that direction—she with her spear and me with my bow and arrows.

Before long, we're approaching the adobe house next to a corral with a fence made of wooden stakes and long cactus tubes. We step past a two-wheel cart and creep along the fence toward the gate. Inside the enclosure are two mules, a calf, two goats, and a scattering of chickens.

The sound of barking comes from inside the house, then the door opens and a barefoot boy comes out with a skinny black dog. We stand still but the dog must have caught our scent because it runs directly to the part of the fence where we are. I can see the snarling, barking snout inches from my face. The boy comes up behind the dog and when he sees us, he yells, "Chichimecas!" and runs back to the house.

A man with a gray beard comes out carrying a curved sword in one hand and a kind of shield in the other. He races to the gate, opens it and, with the yapping dog at his side, rushes at us, waving his sword in the air. Izel drops her spear and raises her hands. "We're not savages," she yells in Spanish. "We escaped from them."

The man stops, lowers his sword and calls the dog back with a whistle.

"It's the truth," I say. "We were their slaves."

"Chichimecas?"

"Yes," Izel answers, "Guachichiles."

I plead with outstretched hands. "We're thirsty, hungry—nothing more."

The man looks us over, his gaze moving from our messy, bushy hair to our bare feet. "Welcome," he says and gestures with his sword to follow him. "Come."

We follow him along the fence and into the corral. His thick neck and muscled arms and shoulders remind me of Hassan. He's shorter and stockier than Hassan but is probably as strong as my African friend. And judging from his gray beard, I figure he's old enough to be my grandfather.

He pushes the calf to one side, then shouts to the boy to go get the goats that escaped through the open gate.

"The cow's over that way," Izel says, pointing in the direction from where we came. "We took some of her milk."

The boy closes the gate and leaves with the dog. "Luisito!" the man calls out. "When you're done with the goats, get the cow."

"Yes, sir."

"Eyes open!"

Our host introduces himself as Emilio Álvarez. We tell him our names and he points to a clay urn and ladle and says we can have our fill of water. Then he waves an arm at a wooden barrel with a block of soap on the cover, the first soap I've seen in years. "Clean yourselves there."

Emilio goes inside while we drink water and wash up at the barrel. We dry ourselves with strips of scratchy cloth that Emilio comes out to give us, then he hands me a pair of scissors he says he uses to cut hides. "For your hair."

When we're done, we look at our new selves. Izel pokes a finger into my side, then runs a hand up and down my ribs.

Emilio comes out of his cottage holding clothes in one arm. "Here, José, wear these," he says, handing me a pair of knee pants and a brown shirt. Then he turns to Izel and holds up a folded white garment that has an embroidered design at the bottom and around the opening at the top. "This huipil should fit. It was my wife's."

Izel grins and takes the dress in both hands. She opens it from the bottom, slips her head through the center and pokes her arms through the holes at the sides. "Thank you, Don Emilio. May God repay you."

"Not me. Thank the Chichimecas. They're the ones who killed my woman, my life."

"*¡Ay, no!*" Izel cries.

He wipes his eyes with the back of his hand. His wife was Nahua, he says, but it didn't matter to the savages. He shakes his head, then steps back to look at us. We're now clean, shorn, and properly dressed.

Emilio instructs us to sit on a wooden bench under the shade of a large mesquite tree. He disappears into his cottage and returns with a plate of food for each of us. There are tortillas, beans, and some kind of stewed meat.

"Eat," he says, pointing at the food. "You must be hungry."

We dig into the meal with gusto. It's been a long time since we've had such a variety of food, and everything tastes delicious. Emilio watches us eat, nodding in approval.

After we finish, Emilio beckons us to follow him into the cottage. Inside, it's cool and dimly lit. The walls are adorned with handwoven tapestries, and there's a simple but comfortable feel to the place.

He gestures toward a large wooden chest. "You can find some more clothes in there. Take what you need."

We open the chest and find an assortment of clothes. I select a couple more sets of pants and shirts. Izel finds a few more huipils, each with its unique design.

Emilio then hands us a pair of leather sandals. "These should help protect your feet. And here," he says, handing me a small knife, "you might need this."

I thank him, feeling a mix of gratitude and disbelief at our good fortune.

Emilio explains that he lives alone on this small homestead, tending to his animals and the land. His wife passed away several years ago, and his children have moved to the city. He seems content with his solitary life.

As the sun begins to set, Emilio invites us to stay the night. We express our gratitude, and he leads us to a small but tidy adobe building where we can sleep.

Inside Emilio's dwelling, a few candles light one side of the room; flames from the fireplace brighten the other side. There are also open slots in the mud walls that let in light. We step across the dirt floor, sit down on a bench next to a table of planks and watch Emilio tend a blackened metal pot hanging over the fire. Izel offers to help but he wags a finger at her.

"Don Emilio," I say.

"No, no *don*. That's only for the rich."

"Emilio," I say, glancing at Izel.

"Yes."

"I'm from England."

He stops stirring the pot and looks at me, nodding. "Go on," he says, and I tell him of my journey from London, coming to a strange shore, cast away with starving mariners.

"How long ago was that?" Emilio asks.

"Maybe two years."

"How many were there?"

"A hundred, maybe more."

"They were the English heretics. In Pachuca they were calling them pirates, English dogs selling slaves."

"That's true."

"And you left them?"

"As soon as I could. I had to get away."

Izel nudges me on the shoulder. "Tell him what they did to you, tell him."

I hesitate, thinking how to say it, how to describe men who saw me as an evil papist, worthless, no better than a bug on a rat.

"You don't have to tell me now—or at all."

I ask what happened to the English mariners and Emilio says they were arrested, put in harnesses and marched all the way from the coast to the city of Mexico. A trader in hides told him that once near the town of Metztitlán he saw the line of Englishmen pass through the valley. They were guarded by two Spaniards and many Indians. The guards beat the stragglers on the head and neck, leaving the dead ones for the vultures.

"And the men who lived?"

"They were sent to prison or given away as slaves and servants to convents and rich families."

I could have been one of those men. A servant, a slave of white men and women.

Any worse than being a slave of the Guachis?

From a plank of wood near the fireplace Emilio brings over two pewter plates, sets them on the table with wooden spoons and serves us what looks like chicken stew. Then he reaches for a small basket filled with something wrapped in cloth. "Tortillas and chocolate," he says.

We drink the foamy liquid and eat the flat corn cakes as if we're starving, which in a way we are. It's the first proper cooked fare that we've tasted since being captured by the Guachis.

"You're lucky, José," Emilio says. "They'll probably hang some of those men— or burn them. The Holy Inquisition is here now, and that's what they do to heretics."

Izel looks puzzled. Emilio tells her the priests of the Inquisition are like soldiers who look for heretics and all other enemies of the Roman Catholic Church—people like Lutherans, Moors, Jews, witches, anyone blaspheming or speaking with the devil.

"They burn them?" Izel asks.

Emilio nods and serves what's left in the pot. "Sometimes yes, sometimes no. Sometimes twenty lashes. I saw that in Seville. If they live through that, they spend years in prison. Or they chain a man to a galley bench, where he's got to row until he's too old or his body is too wasted to lift an oar."

Emilio finishes eating and is picking his teeth with a sliver of wood. He apologizes for talking so much. For months after the raid on his land, he's been alone, talking only to the María in his head. "Now I talk to the wind, to the animals, and lately to Luisito."

His son Antonio runs a mule-train business in Pachuca. He brought the orphan boy to his father as a kind of gift to help with the cattle. Emilio had been doing well selling meat and hides to the mines—until the Chichimecas attacked.

"They were on horses," he says, "and they painted themselves red. Their heads looked like heads of roosters. They killed most of my herd, and they cut some of the animals for the meat. María died with an arrow in her chest, and one of the savages ran at me with a club and knocked me down. By some miracle I didn't die."

I feel for the man, but he seems to have come through the worst of things without falling apart. He says he's Portuguese and worked for years in Seville. "I've seen the best riders on the best horses in Spain, but the barbarians who ride horses here are the true masters of the animal. And all without saddles."

"Señor Emilio," Izel says, "the savages we lived with had no horses but they could attack and kill just the same."

Emilio stops poking branches in the fire. "Well, pray you never meet the devils who killed my María," he says, sitting on the stool at the table. Moments later, Luisito enters and sits down next to us. He pulls out a tortilla from the basket, rolls it up in one hand and begins to push it into his mouth. He's quite dark and looks to be about eight or nine years of age.

Emilio remembers that when he first arrived in New Spain he had very little money and only the possessions he could carry. But he found work with a Spaniard who owned many of the mules used at the silver mines of Pachuca. A blacksmith from Spain taught Emilio to make and fit mule shoes. That's when he learned words in Náhuatl from the Indian workers and from María, a Nahua servant girl whose father tended mules. "She was still a kid," Emilio says, "coming around to watch us work. One day she asked if she could hit the iron and that's how I taught her to strike and shape things with a hammer. Imagine, a girl of thirteen doing that."

"Can you spare some leather?" I ask. "I want to make us sandals."

"Leather I have."

"Can you make me huaraches too?" Luisito asks.

"Of course, and yours will be the first."

Emilio gives me some strips and odd pieces from a cured hide, and I go with Izel and Luisito outside to the sunlit corral. With the scissors I snip and shape the pieces while Izel watches and

118

Luisito sings in Otomí. Luisito says his mother taught him before she and his father died of smallpox.

After he sings for a while, Izel follows with songs of her own in Náhuatl. When I finish making Luisito's huaraches, he ties them on, then goes off stomping and scuffing around by the chickens.

"Now us," I tell Izel and set to work cutting the leather.

Chapter 10 – Secrets

More than a year has passed and Izel now cooks our meals, washes our clothes and grinds the corn for making tortillas. All four of us sleep on reed petates and Izel is the first to rise in the morning. If I'm up early, I milk the cow or I wake Luisito to do the milking while I carry the water jugs from the well to the corral. We eat and then Izel and Luisito go off to the hills to collect wood.

When Emilio and I aren't tending the corn and vegetables in the field out back, we scrape and soak hides in barrels of brine. Emilio still has water in the well, but the pond he made by damming up a stream is almost empty because it hasn't rained in years. He's afraid he won't have water for tanning hides or for irrigating his field.

Today, Luisito asks me to teach him how to make a bow and some arrows. So we hike into the hills to the north to look for the best wood to use for arrows and a bow. And then we go to an ancient quarry to chip and gather chunks of obsidian to make arrowheads.

At Emilio's place I show Luisito how to make a bowstring with twisted animal tendons, then I give him his first lesson in how to shoot an arrow. Afterward, he runs off with a handful of arrows to, as he says, "hunt for our dinner." When he returns, he says he almost hit two birds and scared away an armadillo.

Luisito's enthusiasm reminds me of William, a skinny boy at Greyfriars, who was always the first with his hand up to answer a question from Deacon Brown. Luisito might fail ten times at using the bow, but he never loses the spirit to do it right. In the end, when he finally kills his first rabbit, he reminds me of myself when I finally learned to swim.

Lately I'm learning something else, this time under Emilio's eye. He possesses a single book, one he smuggled past the shipping inspectors looking for anticlerical books. Years ago, he read to his son the tale of the young rogue Lazarillo de Tormes.

Now the book is my guide for spelling and new words. I sit in the corral and write in the soft dirt. I read parts of the book to Izel and Luisito, who sometimes join me in my lessons with Emilio. And some days he slowly reads from the book and I write the words in ink on sheets of parchment he's made from calves' skin.

I feel I have a family again. We sleep, eat and work together, as we did digging and building a latrine this afternoon. Emilio and I dig the deep, squarish hole, while Luisito and Izel mix the mud with dirt, water and grass. Then we shape adobe bricks and let them dry in the sun so we can build the walls later.

Emilio loves physical work. Whether it's shoeing mules, tanning, making candles or mud bricks, he says he feels most alive when he's using his strength and his hands.

When we're finishing the latrine, I tell him I like physical work too and I'm ready to find a job in a town, maybe Pachuca. Emilio looks at me and nods. "You know you can stay here as long as you like."

"Thank you, Emilio. You've been good to us."

"Then why leave?"

"I want to see more of this land."

"And Izel?"

"She feels the same."

"If you must go, stay away from the mines. Only death and disease come from the mines."

"Another thing, Emilio. I want to marry Izel."

"It's about time. You're seventeen, yes?"

"Eighteen I think."

"That's a good time to marry. But, you know, priests only marry Catholics. And you're Lutheran."

"They don't have to know."

"Look, José, I won't say anything to anybody. I don't care. It doesn't matter to me what you are. But someday the secret just might jump out of the bag. Then what?"

I ask if I could pass for a Spaniard.

"Maybe, but you have to have a history, a Spanish family, some story of your blood going back to your father, grandfather and his father. We can invent something people will believe. Your accent comes from Seville, so we'll start there. We'll work on it so by the time you leave, you'll sound like a Sevillano and you'll have a story about who you are."

Emilio seems excited by the idea of inventing a life story. As he speaks I'm puzzled when I hear that "purity of blood" is what's most important to the church and to most Spaniards. I think the words have to do with our health, Izel's and my own. Then Emilio tells me blood purity is the Spaniard's way of separating people by the color of their skin and their appearance. He uses the word *casta*, which I understand to mean a person's line of ancestors.

But he scoffs at the notion of purity. He says he was born and raised by his parents in Portugal. For a time he also lived in Spain and then came to New Spain and felt himself to be a stranger to the Spanish order of things, especially after his marriage to María. "She was Nahua," he says, "and our son is a mestizo. You two remind me of María and me when we were young. Forget what they say about blood. What matters is purity of heart."

Emilio offers to let us sleep in the back room, where the leather is stored. "It'll make marriage in the flesh official," he says, "unless it's already happened."

"No, it hasn't."

"Well, the room is yours to sleep in."

Later, outside, I have to fight back nerves when I ask Izel if she would sleep in the storage room with me as my wife.

"Married?" she asks with a surprised expression.

"Yes, married."

"Husband and wife?"

"Yes, you and me."

She looks away. After a moment, she turns and smiles, her eyes and eyebrows raised to the clouds. "But you know," she says, "it's not official until we marry in the church."

"Whatever you say."

Ever since that day in the shaking forest under a jaguar's gaze, I have wanted to caress her and not just touch her—as Father might say. I trace my fingers on her breasts and follow my fingers as if she were a map, as if every dip and rise were smooth hills and hollows I could explore. I've dreamed of this map but never imagined how quickly all fingertip feeling dissolves into one pulsing, undulating movement gripping my entire body. It's a kind of blind wrestling of our bodies, both of us moaning until at last I race into the sweetest jolts of pleasure I have ever felt. Izel stays tense for a while, and then I feel her relax with a long sigh.

Afterward, in the dark on our petate, we lie side by side, sweaty, neither of us speaking, breathing hard, the room smelling of cowhide leather. I cover us with Emilio's second wedding gift, a blanket—the first gift being the silver wedding rings that he and his wife once wore. I don't know when Izel falls asleep, but I do as soon as my breathing slows and grows quiet.

In the morning, I open my eyes and see a streak of sunlight passing above our heads. It's coming from a hole in the wall. When I raise an arm to block it, Izel grabs my hand and pulls me to her. We are naked and she softly says good morning, first in Náhuatl—"*Cuallitlanecic*," then in Spanish.

"It's better than a good morning," I say. "It's the best morning of my life."

"How can you say that?" she says.

"It is."

"And the fleas?"

"So scratch yourself. There's not much else you can do."

"Yes, there is. We can get up."

I pull the blanket to one side and we stand. I embrace her. "Where do I scratch?"

I ask her, my fingers curved into little claws.

She laughs and steps back. "I'm going to go milk the cow," she says, pulling on her huipil. I quickly dress and follow her into the front room. Emilio is snoring, stretched out between Luisito and the fireplace, a few embers still glowing. Izel has already gone out to the corral, where a nearly grown calf is butting heads with one of the goats.

After the milking and our morning meal, Emilio talks to me about my plan to find work in Pachuca. "You can take a load of hides on one of the mules for Antonio to sell," he says. "Luisito can go with you. It'll take you two or three days and he knows the way."

We're seated on benches in the corral, and Emilio is watching me use my penknife to make quills with two of the rooster's tail feathers. When I finish splitting the tips to make proper nibs, he asks if he can see the knife. I hand it to him and he looks it over, studying the handle.

"Do you know what the mark on your handle means?"

"I was told it means 'life' in Hebrew."

"Where did you get the knife?"

"My father gave it to me before he died. He never told me the meaning of the mark."

"What do you know of your family's past?"

"Almost nothing. My mother and father never spoke of the family, never told me about my grandparents—only that they lived outside London and died years before Mary and I were born. But I always had the feeling my parents were keeping a secret from me and my sister. And then before my father died he told me to flee the country."

"Did he say why?"

"All he said was 'England likes you not.'"

Emilio glances around the corral and at the door behind him as if someone else might be listening, even though Izel and Luisito are off collecting wood. "If I tell you my secret, can I trust you not to tell anyone?"

"Of course."

"No one."

"On the memory of my dear parents, not a soul."

Emilio returns the penknife. "It's a dangerous thing to know. I never told María, and my son doesn't know. But if I tell you, it's only because my secret may help you understand your dying father's words."

He tugs at his beard, shakes his head as if to clear his mind, then leans toward me and speaks slowly, almost in a whisper. "We always knew we were Jews, all of us, for many years living and working in Seville, keeping our faith and customs. Then we were told to vanish. All Jews had to leave the kingdom or become Catholic."

Emilio says his great-grandparents escaped to Portugal, but after a few years they were again told to leave or become Christians. So they converted yet still practiced their Jewish faith in secret. Emilio's mother and father prayed to Jesus, Mary and the saints.

They went to mass and knelt for Communion. No baby male was circumcised. Emilio thought of himself as a Roman Catholic. But behind the walls of his grandparents' house, deep down he knew they and the entire family were Jews.

"How did you find out?" I ask. "How did you know?"

Emilio stands and steps to the door of the house. He pulls out the dagger from his waistband, digs into the adobe brick next to the right side of the doorframe at a spot about shoulder-high. After he stabs at the dried dirt a few times, he pulls out an object with his fingers and holds it up to the light, then places it in my hand. "It's a mezuzah. My mother gave it to me."

The reddish stone is as long and wide as my middle finger. One side is rounded, the other side flat with a long hollow space in the center. Engraved on the rounded side is what looks like a tiny tree with three branches pointed toward one end. Emilio says all he knows is that the piece was placed beside the door of every dwelling where Jews lived, and they would touch it before entering their homes. Because his grandparents were converted Catholics, his mother hid the mezuzah.

"And the little tree?" I ask. "What's that?"

"A Hebrew letter. It stands for a book called the Torah, or the teachings of Jews." Emilio says that as a small boy in a mountain village near the Spanish border, he remembers his mother and father would touch the doorway with one hand as if something were still there. "Before I left to find work in Seville, my father gave it to me so I would always know who my people were. But he said I should hide it and no one should know I have it. If a Catholic discovered my stone and denounced me as an infidel or secret Jew, I could lose my life."

I hand back the mezuzah and he returns it to its hollow. Then he mixes water and dirt to make enough mud to cover up his family treasure, using his dagger to smooth the surface. "I'm probably not supposed to hide it, but I want to live," he says. "What if the Holy Inquisition knew? People are burned for such things. But that little mezuzah is my only touch to the past, to my ancestors."

Because of the engraved mark on the handle of my penknife and what Father said before he died, Emilio thinks I could very well be a descendent of Jews who left Spain and Portugal. Jews had gone everywhere—to Greece, Morocco, Persia, the Indies, Amsterdam, some to London.

I pick up my knife and rub a finger over the mark etched into the horn handle. Did my own parents hide a mezuzah under the doorframe of our home in Greenwich?

What else could they have hidden from me and my sister?

Father told us he had been a Catholic, but after Elizabeth became queen he had become a Protestant, raising us as Protestants. But how could my parents have been Jews in hiding? What were Jews anyway? Is that why Father told me to seek Jacob the apothecary? All I knew about Jews was that Christians despised them as the people who killed Jesus. I'd heard this in church services and many times from my *Mynion* shipmates. They said Jews had tails and horns, drank the blood of Christian children and caused the Black Death.

Emilio is now telling me that the Inquisition hunts down Jews and Judaizers to torture and burn them.

"Of my secret," Emilio said, "not a word to anyone."

"Never."

"José, what you told me about your family—"

"Yes?"

"Careful, no one else can know."

Chapter 11 – A Reunion

We follow Luisito across a plain dotted with maguey spikes and clumps of brush. I lead the mule, loaded with the cured hides and a basket with our food and water bag.

Trailing behind, Izel stops and points to the north. "See them?" she says.

I halt the mule with a yank on the rope, then study the horizon. Two tiny figures on horses are moving toward us. We watch in silence—until Luisito asks if they are Chichimecas.

"If they are," Izel says, "what do we do?"

Luisito pulls an arrow out of the quiver on his back. "Kill them," he blurts.

"Fighting is hopeless," she says. "Maybe we should leave the mule and run, try to escape."

"They won't chase us," I say, "because they only want the mule for its meat."

"No," Izel says. "To them we're all meat."

She's right. They hunt for sport. Even if they don't want their prey for food, they'll chase us for nothing else but the thrill of hunting, especially hunting and killing a white man and two natives who don't belong to their tribe.

The three of us stand on the side of the mule where we can best defend ourselves. I hold my bow and two arrows in one hand and the rope to the mule's halter in the other. Next to me Izel grips her spear, and behind the mule's rump, Luisito squats, clutching his bow and arrows.

Our plan has been to stay in Pachuca with Emilio's son, Antonio. He'll sell the hides while I look for work and Luisito returns to Emilio's place with the mule loaded with the supplies he requested. That was the plan. Now we think only of fighting for our lives.

The two shrieking warriors rush at us. Their faces and bodies are painted over in red and yellow stripes, and the man on the black horse in front already has his bow out. At about thirty yards from us he shoots an arrow that hits the mule through the neck and the animal collapses. Izel raises her spear and is about to fling it when the same shrieking warrior shoots another arrow that pierces her hand. She cries out and drops the spear.

I pull back my bowstring and loose an arrow that strikes the man just below his neck. His head tilts back and he slides sideways from his horse. In that time, I ready another arrow, yank it back and let fly at the other attacker, who is in the act of shooting at *me*. But my arrow hits first, my target the man's open mouth. He slumps to one side of his horse, then drops to the ground, the arrow protruding from both sides of his head.

"Luisito!" I shout. "Get the horses!"

Izel's kneeling on the ground, crying, with blood spreading over her huipil. I kneel down and reach for the arm that has the smooth reed arrow showing on both sides of her pierced hand. Without explaining, I break off the arrowhead end and tug out the shaft. She's screaming and I tell her the worst is over. But there's more blood, this time in spurts.

Off the Guinea coast I saw tourniquets applied to wounded men on the *Mynion*. So using my penknife, I cut off the rope from the mule's halter, wrap it around Izel's forearm and tighten it with a knot Carlos taught me. Cries turn to whimpers and I tell her I'll find the plants that will heal her. Then I make a small ball from strips of my shirt, place it on the wound, and wrap more strips around her hand.

I remember the plants Hump used to treat open cuts, plants that I know from gathering them with the women. I watched the old healer many times apply certain ground leaves, cactus juices and mashed fruits to wounds. I'll do the same for Izel.

Luisito, who's already caught the two mares and tied them to a mesquite tree, has been watching. I tell him to put Izel's bloody hand in his lap and press down on the ball of cloth. "Sing to her," I say.

Later, when I return, I see that the singing must have worked some magic because Izel is sitting up and smiling. "It took you long enough," she says. "I thought you'd gotten lost."

"I found what I need."

I remove the strips of cloth and see that the bleeding is now a trickle. So after squeezing the cactus juice on both sides of her hand, I cover the wound with slivers of cactus and dry mesquite leaves, then I wrap it all again and remove the tourniquet.

Before long, the three of us are seated around a crackling fire, chewing pieces of skewered mule meat.

"What about them?" Izel asks, pointing her chin toward the two bodies.

"I'll bury them," I say.

"They don't deserve it."

"Hmm, maybe you're right."

After eating, with Izel in the middle, we lie down on two hides and cover ourselves with the wedding blanket. I hold her good hand and turn my head toward hers. Our faces must have been inches apart because she kisses me on the lips and whispers a thank-you. I like her touch and the sound of her voice.

The sky has darkened and I stare at the sea of stars, counting the brightest ones, watching for the tiny lights that move. I've never killed a person before. Now I've killed two people and would do it again to save our lives. I didn't give it any more thought than I would if I were shooting two rabbits. I wasn't scared of the men, thinking only of shooting and releasing each arrow.

I listen to Izel's and Luisito's breathing, regular and soft. I close my eyes and eventually the two warriors appear, standing over me. I'm afraid they're about to pound us with rocks, so I force myself to speak, to make a sound. I try to shake myself to wake up but I can't. After a while exhaustion takes over and the figures are gone.

I awake as the eastern sky begins to brighten. I sit up and feel the morning chill. I reach over and touch Luisito's forehead. When he opens his eyes I whisper that we have to bury the bodies in the dry streambed. Luisito nods, and without waking Izel, we get to our feet and step away. I tell him that even our enemies deserve a burial.

At the streambed we use our hands and sticks to dig long hollows in the sand. Then we return to the dead warriors and drag each body by the legs over to the troughs. I keep their bows and arrows and put the feathers, shells and strings of scalps into the graves. As we're covering the bodies with sand, Luisito asks if the savages have souls.

"Yes," I say.

"Do they have heaven and hell?"

"I don't know," I answer, wondering if Hump is floating about in a kind of pleasant afterworld, a reward for all her healing work.

Luisito slaps at some ants crawling on his legs. "I think these two are going to rot," he says, spitting on one of the graves. "Same as bugs."

When we return to Izel, she's sitting, cradling her bandaged hand.

"We buried them," Luisito says, "and they're going to rot."

Izel shrugs. "Good."

I take her hand and ask how it feels.

"It hurts but not as bad as yesterday."

I tell Luisito to tie the hides onto the black mare. "You ride in front of the hides.

You can ride a horse, yes?"

"Of course."

"Well, I can't."

Izel giggles. "You've never ridden a horse?"

"Never."

"You mean without a saddle?"

"With or without."

"It's the same as on a donkey."

"No donkey either."

"Well, don't worry, we'll show you."

"Sorry," I say, wiping my forehead with the back of my hand.

"No need to be sorry," she replies, her fingers running through my hair. "It's a good smell. It means we're moving, we're alive."

We share a quiet moment, looking up at the celestial display above us. The night is calm, and a gentle breeze rustles the leaves in the nearby trees. Luisito, curled up nearby, is already asleep.

"You know," Izel says, breaking the silence, "I never thought I would find someone like you."

"Someone like me?" I ask.

"Yes. Someone who understands, who cares."

"Izel, you saved my life more times than I can count. If it weren't for you, I'd still be a prisoner among the Guachis."

"And you've saved me too, José. We make a good team."

I can feel the warmth of her body next to mine. The hardships and dangers of our journey seem momentarily distant.

"What do you think will happen when we reach the coast?" I ask.

She sighs, contemplating the question. "I don't know. But I want to find a ship and sail far away. Start anew, where no one knows our names or cares about our pasts."

"I'd like that," I say, realizing that the idea of a fresh start holds a special appeal.

Izel leans in, and we share another kiss, sealing an unspoken pact of mutual support and companionship.

The nights pass, marked by the steady rhythm of hoofbeats and the occasional howls of distant creatures. As we journey toward the coast, our connection deepens, forged by the challenges we face together. Each day brings us closer to the unknown future that awaits us, but for now, we find solace in the company of each other under the vast canvas of the open sky.

"You too."

"We both do."

"We stink."

"No," Izel says. "I like the smell."

"You like it?"

"A little, yes."

"Well, I don't. Luisito, what do you think? Luisito? He's asleep."

"José, have you ever seen a horse born?"

"No, but I think it probably comes out looking like a puppy—or the size of a puppy."

"I've seen that too, but a baby horse is different. It's bigger and right away wants to walk. First, the feet and legs come out, then the body."

"Legs first?"

"I watched the man pull on the legs to get it out of the mother."

"Where was that?"

"At the *patrón*'s place. I was touching the mother's belly, getting wet in her sweat, and it was beautiful."

"The sweat?"

"Everything—the little horse, the mother, the sounds, the sweat."

"I remember the birth of my sister, Mary."

"You saw her come out?"

"More or less. I wasn't that close. My mother was on her bed screaming, and my father and two ladies were standing next to the bed. It scared me—my mother screaming like that."

"Well, it's different with horses."

As we're falling asleep, I nestle against Izel, breathing the odor of dried horse sweat and thinking that the smell isn't too bad. I imagine that if Izel were giving birth, I'd be holding her hand and both of us would be wet with sweat as our little creation came into the world.

In the morning, we get going at first light. There's no trail, just open country. When we reach the hills and start the climb up through the brush, Luisito says it'll probably take at least another day to reach Pachuca. He's guiding himself by a line of distant mountains to the south.

As predicted, two days later in the morning, we come to the narrow road that leads to Pachuca. The ruts make it obvious that wagon wheels, animals, and people have traveled on the road.

Before long we reach a native carrying a white man on his back. The bearded passenger is well-dressed and seated in a small wooden chair tied to the bearer's back. He's facing backward. Another native, toting a big bundle, walks behind them. They stop, and I greet the man in Spanish.

"My God!" the passenger says, laughing. "From far away I thought you were Chichimecas."

"Not at all," I say and explain who we are.

While Izel talks with the porter, I speak with the dapper man. He says he's a tailor returning to Pachuca from Metztitlán and that he's been watching us approach on horses for some time.

"You never know who you'll meet in these parts," he says. "Well, I must keep moving. May God go with you and keep you safe." The tailor touches the brim of his hat and nods.

"Goodbye, sir," I say.

He's sitting upright in his chair, wiping his face with a handkerchief, and orders his bearer and the porter to continue.

After they leave us, Izel says the Mexica man told her that a mountain peak called Popocatépetl threw fire into the sky, and in one village an old wise man, a *tlamatini*, saw a great evil coming to the Mexica. When I hear the prediction, I think of what Emilio told us about all the natives who had died of diseases after the Spaniards arrived. How much more harm, I wonder, could strike the people of this land?

For a long while we listen to Luisito sing in Otomí while the horses plod through a more desolate, drier land than the pastures and mountain forests we left behind.

I silently rehearse the facts about my imagined Spanish self, the one Emilio and I created. I was born José Campos in Seville about eighteen years ago. I don't know the year or if I was baptized because I came into the world an orphan. I was told my mother was a prostitute and died in childbirth. I never knew my father and was raised by the women of a brothel. I lived on the streets and eventually joined the servants and slaves belonging to a silk merchant sailing for New Spain. In the port of Veracruz, I came down with a kind of swamp fever and the merchant left me, thinking I would die. But I lived and for two years worked for a Spanish cattleman named Emilio Álvarez on land located far to the east of Ixmiquilpan. He taught me to read and write, enough to copy letters and documents.

141

That was to be my story.

I recite all this to Izel. She listens without interrupting, then asks why I have to invent a past.

"Because I can't say I'm English. Not now, not here. English people are the heretics."

"What does that mean?"

"It means I'm not Catholic." I don't mention my real parents, that they may have been Jews pretending to be Christians.

Far ahead on his black mare, Luisito signals with his arm and shouts, "Look! Slaves!"

Izel hurries the mare and we soon catch up to Luisito.

"Where the road turns," he says, pointing. "They're walking in a line. See them?"

I squint. "Barely."

By the time we reach the line of native bearers walking behind the Africans, I count more than twenty black men and four women. They're mostly naked with their hands bound and iron collars around their necks. Three white men, probably Spaniards, patrol the slaves with whips.

"Izel, I think I see Hassan."

"The big one?"

"Yes!"

Hassan turns and stares at us. Then his face brightens and he grins. I hold a finger to my lips and motion not to speak. I point ahead and nod.

We pass the guard at the head of the line and he stares at us. We must be a curious sight—raggedy, filthy figures on horses with no saddles. But then he raises the handle of his whip to his hat and greets us with a cheerful, "Good afternoon!"

I return the greeting and we keep moving. I turn around and see that my old African friend is smiling.

"Izel, I have to help him."

"There's nothing you can do. He's a slave."

"There has to be something."

"You said he was once a free man."

"That's what he told me."

"You believe him?"

"Yes."

"Maybe it's all a lie, like the story you and Emilio made up about *your* life."

"No, he didn't lie."

"How do you know?"

"I know it; I feel it. In that ship, Hassan was in chains and I was living like a rat. We had nothing but truth to talk about. That's what kept me alive, talking truth."

After a while, Luisito suggests I sit in front of Izel before we get to Pachuca.

"You'll look more Spanish that way, more in command."

"He's right," Izel says. "The gentleman always goes first."

Izel and I trade places. "Remember," she says. "You control the mare as if she were a donkey."

"I've never been on a donkey."

"Then just hold on. She'll follow Luisito's horse."

I take the reins in one hand and grip a handful of the mane. Izel slaps the mare on the rump and the horse starts forward with a jolt. Before long, I think of how to free Hassan. I turn my horse around and shout to Luisito to follow us.

"English, what are you doing?"

"Going back."

"Why?"

"You'll see."

Part of me wants to practice being Spanish, but mostly I want to bargain for Hassan. I used to go to the market with Mother, watch her haggle for fish. She was a champion haggler. If the fishmonger quoted five- or sixpence for dried and salted fish, she would end up buying it for four.

But she never haggled for a person, a grown African man. Hassan isn't a fish, but I'll have to pretend that my friend can be trafficked as easily as fish or bread, even given away to pay a debt.

Before we reach the slaves, I tell Izel and Luisito not to say anything. I'll do the talking.

We ride up to the guard who greeted us earlier. He pushes his hat back and raises a hand to halt the procession. I swing a leg over the mare's head and drop down to the ground. "I need one of your pieces," I say, using the word "pieces" because Hassan told me that the traders and customers in Seville used that word when they were buying and selling slaves, even white slaves.

The guard stares, frowning. "You don't look like a person of means."

"True," I say, "but I have a pile of fine cowhides." I point to Luisito and the mound of leather behind him. "See for yourself."

The guard steps up to the black mare and fingers several layers of the smooth, tanned hides.

"Ready to use," I say. "How many hides for the big piece over there?"

"Ten."

I chuckle and tell him I would trade no more than five hides for the big African.

"Eight," the guard says.

"No, sir," I counter, shaking my head while walking over to Hassan. I pretend to inspect him, giving him a smile the guard can't see. "This piece is damaged. There are scars all over his back."

The guard now removes his hat and wipes his brow. "Of all these Africans he's the finest *bozal* among them. You see, the stripes on his back have only made him stronger, able to bear the whip."

"I don't think so. He might say something else. If only I could ask him in his language."

"No good in that. He's deaf. Never talks and doesn't seem to hear."

"You see? He's damaged. Can't even speak."

I know I stumped the man. We haggle a bit more and then, turning away, I say,

"Four leather hides and not one more."

"Five!" he shouts.

I stop and turn around. "That will do."

"Fine," the guard says, "but I get to choose the hides."

"Luisito, untie them."

"Yes, sir!" Luisito snaps, playing his part as an obedient servant. He slips off the horse, and Izel also drops down to help Luisito remove the ropes cinched around the hides.

The transaction of leather for Hassan is completed with as much efficiency as Mother used when buying from the fishmonger. This trader takes the five hides, hands them to one of the bearers, then I step to where Hassan waits in the line of slaves. I undo the rope around his waist and unbuckle the iron collar around his neck. Then I ask the seller to untie the slave's hands.

"Are you sure you want him unbound? He's a beast."

"But he's my beast. I'll handle him."

"Very well, he's no longer my business," the trader says, pulling out a dagger from his waistband. With one deft motion, he cuts the cord between Hassan's hands and walks away. "Good day to you, young man," he says, tilting his hat and waving goodbye.

"Goodbye," I say, then whisper to Hassan, "Let's go. You'll soon be free."

Luisito waits with the hides that are again tied onto the rump of the black mare. "You get on first," I tell Hassan, who easily boosts himself up onto the horse's back in front of the hides, pulling up Luisito, who sits in front. I point ahead. "Go. We'll follow you."

Izel and I follow at a trot.

As soon as we leave the traders and their slaves far behind and out of sight, I shout for Luisito to turn off the road and look for a hidden place where we can stop. Luisito spots a dry gulley where we get off the horses. Hassan and I embrace. He kisses me on both cheeks, thanking me each time.

"I thought you couldn't speak," I say, and he laughs.

Izel hands him a leather bag of water. While Hassan drinks, she takes slices of cooked mule meat from a basket and waits for him to finish. Soon we're all seated on the ground, at first just watching Hassan tear at the meat and chew. After a while, he tells us what happened to him since he last saw me on the *Mynion*.

"In the fight with the Spaniards," he says, "the ship I was on had been hit many times by cannon balls and was sinking. I was chained. I thought I would die. But Allah had another plan."

Hassan's salvation came when the timber that anchored his chain split and fell away. He was suddenly free to climb up to the main deck, carrying his chain of iron links. Amid the screams and confusion of fighting, he crawled to the rail and dropped into the water. The weight of the chain pulled him under, but he kicked and struggled to get back up to the surface. He stayed afloat long enough for a Spanish sailor to pull him into a boat already filled with wounded or nearly drowned English captives. Taken to shore, Hassan was sold in the Veracruz slave auction for work on a sugar plantation.

148

At first he cut cane but because he spoke Spanish he was moved to his owner's house to work as a footman and caretaker of the carriages. He was free to roam the property, and when the time was right, he escaped on horseback to the mountains, joining other runaways.

"I was free again—all of us were free," Hassan says. "We had our own village, but it all came to a bad end when the Spaniards attacked and overran us."

He was returned to his plantation master, who had him whipped almost to the point of dying. Then he was sold to work in the Pachuca mines.

"Why did you stop speaking?" I ask.

"When they caught me I thought silence would be best until I could run again."

"You're free now."

"Thank God," Izel says.

"No," Hassan corrects, "thanks to Allah."

"Is that God?" she asks.

"Yes, my god, my lord."

After a moment's silence, Luisito says he thinks Hassan should also thank me, since I bought him.

"And for only five cowhides," Hassan says, laughing. "Is that all I'm worth?" "Well," I say, "if you had spoken, maybe six or seven hides."

***

With me riding in front of Izel and Hassan seated behind Luisito, the two mares amble along the road toward Pachuca and its silver mines. As we ride, I tell my friend about our time as slaves of the Guachichiles, about our stay with Emilio, about our marriage, about my invented Spanish self, and about being attacked.

Hassan congratulates me and Izel on our marriage and compliments me for my accuracy with a bow. "I hope you live a good life together and have many children."

"We're not really married yet," Izel says, "not by the church. Until then I'm still Izel Estrada."

"Estrada?" I say.

"The name of my *patrón*, the Spaniard."

"What's your family's Nahua name?"

"Tochtli. 'Rabbit.'"

A long time ago, she says, her family had that name. But her grandparents worked in the house of the encomendero. They were his slaves and they took his name. "So before Estrada you were Izel Rabbit?"

150

"No."

"Miss Rabbit?"

"Never!"

"We could have many little rabbits."

Hassan and Luisito are laughing when Izel shouts, "José! Stop it! I'm Estrada until we get married in the church."

"Good."

"Then I'll be a Campos."

"Perfect."

Chapter 12 – Pachuca

Despite my ragtag appearance, I sit up straight, trying to appear as much in command as possible. The smoke of burning wood and the smells of chili, corn and beans fill the air. Riding into Pachuca, with Izel's arms around my waist, I see no visible timbers in the mud walls, no pointed roofs of the English kind. I haven't been in a proper town since I left Plymouth on the *Mynion*. Around us is only a collection of shacks made of dirt, sticks and stones.

"Otomís live here," Luisito says. "Antonio lives near the plaza—where the rich live."

"And the Nahuas?" Izel asks.

"Over there by the hill."

Hassan wants to know where the blacks live, and Luisito says many slaves live near the mines.

"And free blacks?" Hassan asks.

Luisito shrugs. "I don't know. Here and there."

He leads the way, seated ahead of Hassan and the pile of hides. Our two horses make their way along a narrow dirt road between the dwellings. Barking dogs approach and everyone stares at us.

By the time we near the town's center, the sun has set and lights glow in windows. We're now moving on wider cobblestone streets where stone walls rise two and three floors above us. We stop at a small door built into a wooden gate. Luisito asks for help to get down and Hassan easily lifts him off, then dismounts himelf.

Luisito calls out, slapping the gate with one hand. "It's me—Luisito! With two horses."

We wait and then the gate opens, pulled back by an old man.

"Don Lázaro," Luisito says.

"Welcome," he replies.

Luisito leads the black mare by the reins into a large courtyard crowded with mules. Under several stone arches at one side, men are entering a room, flickering light coming from inside.

Izel and I get down off the brown mare and follow Luisito and Hassan into the courtyard.

"Luisito!" a man's voice calls down from the balcony.

"Yes, sir!"

"Who's that with you?"

I look up and in the shadows I see a man, probably Emilio's son. "José Campos,"

I say, "and my wife, Izel."

"Antonio Álvarez," he answers.

"I have leather hides from your father."

"I'll be right down. Amparo!"

"Sir?" a woman's voice answers.

"Three more for dinner."

"Very well."

Antonio Álvarez descends the wooden stairs holding a lantern. He greets us warmly, thanking me for the hides, ignoring our pitiful state, especially Hassan's almost-naked condition. He points to one side of the courtyard and tells us we can put the hides in the storeroom. He also offers us a place to stay, two rooms next to where his workers sleep.

Antonio resembles his father in his muscular size, although his skin is darker and he has the wide face and eyes of his Nahua mother. He's a mestizo, the same as any child Izel and I might have.

When we finish moving the hides, he has Lázaro bring Hassan a serape and tells Luisito to water and feed our horses.

Antonio then turns to me and asks how his father is.

"Well," I say.

"And the Chichimecas?"

"No attacks, not since we've been there."

Antonio says he begged his father to come and live with him

154

in Pachuca, but Emilio told him he couldn't leave his wife's grave.

"He talks to her every day around sunset," I say. "He gets down on his knees and just talks."

"How is it that you got to my father's place?"

"His cow woke us."

"Cow?"

I tell Antonio of our captivity and living as slaves of the Guachichiles and about our escape and waking up one morning to the sound of his father's cow chewing the leaves of our shelter.

"Come," he says, gesturing toward the stairs. "You must be hungry. We can do better than cow's milk."

We follow our host up to the second floor and enter a carpeted dining room with a long table and a large fireplace.

"You can wash up over there," Antonio says, pointing to a basin on a stand.

We take turns washing our arms and hands with soap, rinsing them with water we pour from a jug. Then we drink water ladled out of a tall clay urn. Afterward, we sit at the table, which is set at one end with only one plate, cup and spoon. From another room a gray-haired woman emerges carrying plates, bowls, spoons and cups, which she distributes among the three of us.

Two younger women in huipiles carry out a steamy pot of what smells like tamales as well as bowls of beans, tortillas and strips of meat. It's all spread out between us and Antonio, who's at the head of the table.

"Serve yourselves," he says.

Hassan is the first to reach for a *tamal*. "Thank you, sir. This is a dream."

Antonio gestures to the older woman. "Amparo's magic."

"Where's Luisito?" I ask.

"With the mule drivers. Amparo takes care of feeding him and everyone else." Antonio raises his hand. "Before we eat, I want to say a prayer. Thank you, Lord, for this meal and for bringing us these visitors. I'm honored. Amen."

We begin to eat and right away I hear sounds of pleasure from Izel and Hassan.

With each spoonful of beans, I'm also moaning with delight.

Antonio asks Hassan about his life, but I'm so absorbed in eating that all I'm hearing are bits of my friend's work as a pottery slave in Spain. I catch Hassan's loud, cheerful baritone: "I was sweet fruit and the English plucked me out of a tree." He snaps his fingers. "A slave again."

Antonio shakes his head. "But you're free now, no?"

"Yes!" I say, interrupting. "I bought him for five leather hides."

Antonio looks surprised. "Only five?"

"The trader wanted ten."

"Is a man worth so little?" Hassan asks.

I explain that Hassan was being sold as a mute with scars all over his body.

Antonio studies his big guest for a moment. "Well, if he had been speaking Spanish, he'd be worth at least four hundred pesos, or many more hides than five."

Hassan raises a hand. "I don't care what I'm worth. José gave me back my freedom."

Antonio asks me if the trader made a bill of sale, signed and witnessed by someone else.

"No. He took the hides and Hassan came with me."

"Well, that's not how you sell and buy a slave. You need a bill of sale, a legal account of what happened, even a description of Hassan."

"I don't think those men could write."

"Don't worry, I'll take care of it. I'll find the trader, and if he can't sign a document, I'll talk to the buyer at the mine where the slaves were going. I know him. I'll tell him what happened. And the man with the hides is proof enough that there was an exchange."

Antonio stands, picks up a pitcher and moves around the table to pour red wine into the cups that were set before me and Izel. Hassan waves away Antonio's offer of wine, saying he's a Muslim and is forbidden to drink spirits.

"Then drink chocolate," Antonio says.

Hassan smiles and nods.

"Amparo!" Antonio calls out. "One cup of chocolate, please."

"Coming, sir!"

Antonio raises his cup, waiting for everybody to be served and for the three of us to lift our cups. "To the joys of freedom," he says, "and may Hassan never again be a slave."

I watch Hassan swallow and set the cup down. "I pray that Allah will always keep me free."

"No, Hassan," Antonio says. "In this land you pray only to a Christian god or to Jesus Christ, the Virgin Mary or the saints. Anything else is very dangerous."

"Like being a heretic?" I say.

"Precisely."

"Or a Jew."

"Yes. And if the church finds out, God help you."

I add that Emilio described to me what the Inquisition does to heretics.

"Then you know the dangers," Antonio says. "The authorities will also have to know Hassan is a freed slave."

"Authorities?" Hassan asks.

"I'll take care of that. Just don't mention Islam. Tell them you're already a baptized Catholic."

"But I am. My owner in Seville arranged it."

"If you value your life, pray to Allah in silence; pray in the dark where no one can see you. The church has eyes and ears everywhere. I know the men who hunt nonbelievers. If they accuse you, all of us are involved."

Antonio tells us he knows clerics in Pachuca and elsewhere, and he has influential friends among merchants, mine owners, and military officers. Years ago, he himself was on a path to the priesthood, studying in the city of Mexico. But he changed his mind because he saw how most Spaniards and other white people treated natives, mestizos, Africans, and all those of mixed blood. "They looked down on me, the son of a Portuguese immigrant and a Nahua woman. Unless we come from noble Mexica blood, most of us are still treated poorly."

"You were going to be a priest?" Hassan asks.

"I stopped my studies."

"Stopped believing?"

"Not that. It was the lack of respect."

Antonio says he went home to Pachuca and took over his father's mule-train business after his parents moved away to raise cattle on land granted to them by Viceroy Enríquez.

Hassan asks what the mules carried and Antonio points to the fireplace. "First it was charcoal from the forests to the royal mines around here, then to towns like San Miguel and Guanajuato. But everything changed when they started using mercury to mine silver. Mercury was king."

"The remedy for the pox," Izel says.

"Yes. But the truth is that the real king should be Bartolomé de Medina. He's the man who brought us mercury." Antonio's expression turns serious as he tells us that quicksilver to separate the mineral from the ore comes from mines in Spain and Peru. His mule drivers hauled it in lambskin bags from the ports to the mines around here and in Guanajuato. "Then they discovered silver in Zacatecas," he says, smiling. "That made New Spain one of the richest lands in the world."

"Don Antonio," Izel says, "there's something else you should know. It's true that José and I live as husband and wife, but not yet before God. We want to be married in a church."

Antonio smiles and claps his hands. "I know just the priest to do it."

I made this promise to Izel but I'm a little nervous about it. I'll have to pretend to be Catholic, and Emilio warned me that if such a deception were ever discovered by the inquisitors, they'd surely condemn me. I'm still an Englishman with likely Jewish roots, raised as a Protestant, and now passing myself as a Spaniard baptized in the Catholic faith. I would face a death sentence.

I think of what Emilio said about never telling his son that his forebears were Jews. What would Antonio do if he knew his family left Spain for Portugal and was forced to be Catholic? Emilio said he never told Antonio of the old rituals, the secret prayers, the Friday night candle lightings, the changing of sheets for the Sabbath. And he never showed his son the hidden mezuzah.

I'm thinking of this while Antonio is speaking. "Help the miners," he says. "Too many are sick, too much death."

I want to applaud these words. He's a man who should be in my bag of good stones, except there's no bag and no more silly kid's game. Now I'm hearing that he wants to shelter us and find work for me and Hassan at the Purísima. "The mine," he says, "isn't what it used to be, but they still need people."

***

Antonio finds us work at the mine and arranges for our wedding to be held in a chapel where his friend the priest gives sermons in native languages. That's where we are now. He tells us that Father Juan is known as a one-arm Spaniard who speaks both Náhuatl and Otomí. They studied together to be Dominican friars and only Juan finished. Because he was learning the two languages, he was sent to serve the Nahuas and Otomís in Pachuca.

We're sitting in the first pew and I'm looking at Father One Arm, as they call him, trying to imagine what Antonio told me about the man's missing arm, that in place of an arm he has a small hand with tiny fingers that he keeps hidden under his cassock. Antonio believes his friend's birth defect brings him closer to the poor of his congregation, believing the natives accept him because they see him as a fellow suffering soul.

When Antonio told me this, he raised his right hand to his left shoulder and wriggled his fingers. "When we were students he used to read holding the Bible with the little hand. Imagine, he felt sorry for *me* because I had to hold mine with two hands. And he got out of a lot of chores I had to do, like washing pots and bowls, scrubbing floors."

I wish my parents could see Izel and me married. They would see how happy I am with my bride. Izel also misses having her mother and father here today. She whispers in my ear, "I know we carry them in our hearts. But it's not the same, not like the days when they used to hold my hand—or hold me in their arms."

"I'll do that," I say.

She pats my hand and we see Father One Arm point at us with his good hand and gestures for us to rise and approach the altar. As I stand, I look back and can see Hassan smile. In the pews behind him I catch the faces of Amparo, old Lázaro, and the mule drivers and their families.

Father Juan asks us to kneel and says something in Latin. I catch the word *benedictus*, thinking this is the most blessed thing that has ever happened to me. But now he's bending over to the side without the arm. He's fussing with his cassock.

What's that? Oh my, it's the little hand. He stands up and I hear gasps and cries of "*¡Ay!*" and "*¡Dios mío!*"

Father Juan's tiny fingers wave to the congregation and someone shouts, "Miracle! It's a miracle!"

His good arm nearly touches us. He's gesturing, telling everyone to settle down, that he was born with a deformity and is sorry to have hidden it for so long. "No better occasion," he says, "than to introduce my little friend to you at this happiest of occasions, the marriage of Izel and José."

He now has us both kneeling before him.

A man's voice comes from the rear of the chapel and I hear "*¡Amen!*" from others. The words sound like words spoken in

Náhuatl. I look at Izel and she says that Father One Arm is now Father Two Hands.

Father Two Hands marries us, but the ceremony is all commotion and outbursts by people in the chapel, shouting about a miracle from God. When we leave the chapel, women throw flowers before us, and the sounds of drums, flutes, singing, and barking dogs follow us all the way to Antonio's courtyard. We enter and are told to sit at the head of a long table of planks covered with bowls of tamales, tortillas, and grilled pieces of chicken and pork. At the other end of the table, our host, Antonio, sits next to a beaming Father Two Hands, his tiny fingers holding a cup to his lips.

Izel looks radiant in her white huipil. Her head is covered by coils of dark yarn and decorated with white and red flowers, and I'm wearing a clean tunic and white cotton trousers. Old Lázaro wishes us well, Hassan kisses Izel's hand, and before we begin to eat, Father Two Hands blesses our meal. "Amen," I hear from a chorus of everyone—mule drivers, their wives and children, Lázaro, Amparo, Luisito, kitchen helpers, and Hassan.

Under the table, I find Izel's hand. Our fingers intertwine as we watch porcelain plates piled with steamy meat-filled tamales placed before us, followed by bowls of beans, rice, and a vegetable stew. Izel raises a spoonful of the stew to my lips. "You first," she says, and I open my mouth.

***

Many months later, Izel's scream wakes me in the night. She clutches my hand and tells me the baby's ready to be born. I leave our bed and step into the next room to light a candle with a glowing ember I take from the kitchen fireplace. Returning, I find her hunched over on hands and knees by the side of the bed. "The midwife!" she shrieks. "Hurry!" I yank on my trousers and boots and Izel tells me her name is Micaela.

I light the lantern candle and step out into the courtyard. Izel's cries must have awakened old Lázaro too, because he's already at the front gate, opening the side door.

"Go with God," he says.

I can't run over the cobblestones or I'll trip, but I wish I could fly over the rooftops to where the Nahuas live. I'm walking as fast as I can without stumbling. I hold the lantern high, seeing flickering walls on my left and right. A dog barks, then more dogs. I'm closer to the Nahuas. A rooster crows. I follow the dirt paths between the shacks. I shout for Micaela, the *ticitl*. A man comes out of a doorway and waves to me. "Over there," he says in Spanish, "Micaela lives there." I call her name and wait. "I'm coming," I hear a voice say. Then I see a dark figure of a woman come out of a doorway. She's small and carries a bag under one arm. She knows Izel, nods to me, and we hurry along to Antonio's place.

165

Lázaro has the door open. "This way," I say to the *ticitl* and lead her across the courtyard to our rooms. I go in first and see Izel in bed holding the baby on her stomach. Amparo is kneeling by the bed with a knife in her hand. "A boy," Amparo tells me. She reaches for the umbilical cord, which looks to me like a dark, yellowish snake on Izel's belly.

"I'll do that," Micaela says and takes the knife from the cook's hand. "Bring me hot water."

"Right away," Amparo answers and hurries out of the room.

I wipe away the sweat on Izel's brow. "It's the same," she whispers, "just like with horses."

"Horses?"

"I'm sweating like a horse."

"Ah yes," I tell her, "my little mare—with my little son, little David."

Amparo enters with a pot of water and sets it on the floor next to the midwife.

"Move back," Micaela orders. "I have to separate mother and son." She says something to Izel in Náhuatl, dips the knife blade in the water, then cuts the cord in one quick motion.

***

I'm now a father and I work counting goods and ores at the mine. I also write reports for the *patrón*, Bartolomé de Medina. At this moment, I'm watching the fingers of a young man pushing and pulling thin, stiff strips of bamboo through a cross weave of what will soon be a basket, one that will be carried on the back of a man lugging rocks out of the mine. The weaver, Minoru Tanaka, works his basket magic in the open work yard of the Purísima. The mine is known for being the first in New Spain to use mercury to separate silver from the watery sludge of pulverized rock.

"Do you ever miss?" I ask Minoru.

"Miss?"

"Putting the bamboo in the right place."

I make a stabbing motion with a finger, then grimace as if I had pricked my finger.

Without stopping the weave, Minoru answers, "Yes, much blood."

"Well, blood or no blood," I say, glancing at the two finished creations next to Minoru, "no one but you makes baskets this strong, this good."

Like me, Minoru is also an orphan, or unwanted child—he was never sure which, since he has no memory of his parents. He told me he comes from a Japanese island called Kyushu. As a child he worked for a basketmaker before being given away to a Portuguese trader in exchange for a musket. The trader sailed to

Manila and in turn sold him to a Spanish merchant. He said he and a group of Chinese and Filipino slaves were chained together in the hold of a galleon. Many died during the voyage, and by the time the ship arrived in Acapulco he was almost dead himself, feverish and taken over by the bloody flux.

Minoru and the other slaves were taken by wagon to the city of Mexico, where they were led to a slave auction and sold one by one. He's a *chino*, purchased by the Purísima buyer for the price of two healthy goats. He heard the story months later that the buyer told the mine owner that the *chino* slave had "a quick eye and looked to be very clever" and would be good as a house slave.

His chores included errands to the mine. One afternoon he was bringing a basket of tamales out to some workers near the entry to the main shaft when he passed bearers emerging from the tunnel hauling sacks of rocks. With gestures and drawings in the dirt, he told me and other yard workers that he could make strong baskets with shoulder straps for the miners to carry loads more easily on their backs. He said he used to make such baskets in Japan.

I told this to Antonio and he spoke to the aging owner, Medina, who then asked to have Minoru make two baskets. He did and they worked so well that Medina had him make more baskets of reeds, bamboo, even strips of tree bark. With the help of an Otomí weaver, Minoru finished more than fifty of the sturdy baskets in a matter of months.

As a gift, Medina gave Minoru to Antonio to show his appreciation for bringing him such an inventive human treasure. Antonio then gave Minoru his freedom.

I can thank Antonio and his connection to Medina for keeping me out of the mine's tunnels and shafts. I only have to keep tallies of all manner of things—from the number of tallow candles used every week in the mine shafts to how much feed is eaten by the mules that plod around in the circular patios, mixing crushed ore with their hooves. And under Antonio's tutoring I'm improving my written Spanish enough that I can write reports on the mine's operations.

But Hassan chose to work for pay, hauling rocks as a free man. He's not like the other miners. They're either slaves or must work to pay off debts. Twice he nearly died in cave-ins, but because he was stronger and bigger than most of the miners, he recovered both times. Hassan also lives under Antonio's protection. He eats well and sleeps in his own bed. He says every night in the dark he prays to Allah that someday he'll have enough money to leave the mine and start his own business making pottery.

***

Today, I'm counting a shipment of mule shoes near the mine's corral. Izel, who helps Amparo in the big kitchen and shops for food in the *tianguis*, just left me my midday meal of tortillas and chicken. With little David wrapped in a rebozo slung on her side, she walks from Antonio's place to the mine. I watch her walk away, then turn to finish counting the mule shoes. I'll eat as soon as I finish the tally, but I hear a voice that stops me. I hear the word again. "Joey!"

No one has called me Joey since I left the *Mynion*. I look up and see the figure of the red-bearded gunner, the same man who threw a mallet at me. He's approaching from the direction of the main mine shaft, and he's holding a short whip in one hand.

I stand and move away from the corral post and duck behind a tethered mule. I lift the animal's left foreleg, as if I'm inspecting the iron shoe.

"Joey!" the man shouts, coming close to me. "Well, look at you," he says in English. "All cleaned up and in proper garb."

I let go of the foreleg, stand and look over the back of the mule at the scowling, ruddy face.

"The devil take me!" Red Beard says, placing the whip on the mule's back. "It's you, isn't it?"

We haven't seen each other in five or six years and both of us have changed. To me the gunner seems shorter, fleshier. I'm taller and my body is bigger. I also have a thin beard. I answer in Spanish, saying I don't understand the question.

"Joey, don't lie to me."

I shake my head. I haven't heard spoken English—other than Izel's imitations— since I was pushed into the sea and told to swim for my life.

Red Beard steps next to the mule. "You don't have to play weasel with me." In Spanish, I say I don't understand, then go back to inspecting the mule shoe.

"Go to the devil," I say under my breath.

"Alright!" Red Beard says in English. "I speak enough *cristiano* to know you think I should go to the devil. Well, good news, laddie! To you I *am* the devil! I'm the new overseer in the deepest shaft, taken on this morning by Don Bartolomé himself.

So stop pretending or I go straight to the Inquisition judges."

I get up, feeling weak and hollow.

"I know these gentlemen, boy. They heard me out and knew I wasn't a heretic like most of me mates. Just a good Irish Catholic still saying me prayers. It's why they set me free to work at this mine."

I tighten my fists, close my eyes and nod.

"We thought you was drowned, and here you are, hiding in plain sight. Well, no more of that. I found you and you'll work for me. Understand? Deep down below the mountain."

I open my eyes and glare at my former tormentor.

"Answer me, boy! Or have you forgotten the Queen's speech? You with all your reading and writing. Come on, just say, 'I want to work for you.'"

My lips quiver. I can feel the blood burning my face.

"Come, Joey, say it. 'I want to work for you.'"

When I pronounce the words in English, Red Beard snaps the whip and says, "That's me old Joey!"

Chapter 13 – Devil's Slave

Hassan and I work from sunrise to sunset, all days except Sunday. We wear loincloths, but unlike most of the barefoot slaves and natives, we protect our feet by tying on woven straw sandals Minoru made for us. When they wear out, we always have more to tie on.

Since my encounter with the red-bearded foreman, I work with the miners hauling up rocks weighing as much as a large man. Under the light of candles and pine-pitch torches, I follow Hassan and the others into tunnels until I reach the vertical shafts. We climb down rope-and-wood ladders until we get to the cold, wet bottom. This is where men with hammers and iron poles break chunks of rock off the tunnel walls. They load the rocks into our baskets and we climb back up to the tunnels and out to daylight.

Like many of the porters, Hassan chants or prays words that keep him to a steady pace. I keep quiet, trying to stay at a certain pace myself. Everyone listens for the first signs of falling rock or someone above us slipping and tumbling down, rocks and all. It happens every day. First come the shouts and then the rocks, and sometimes a miner falling to his fate. For us below there is no protection. All I can do is turn and lean against the rock and hope that whatever is falling doesn't strike me.

For months, I've endured this labor without falling sick or injuring myself. Now I'm starting to cough. At first, it was a shallow, throat-clearing cough. Every morning, I feel it coming from deeper in my chest.

Although we're both free men, we still work under Red Beard. I can tell from his laughs and grins that he likes giving me extra tasks, calling me in English "heretic," "maggot," "turd" and other vile names. He orders me to haul water and food down to the rock-breaking crews or shoulder heavy timbers into the tunnels for ceiling supports.

"I'm the devil's slave," I tell Izel. It's evening and we're sitting at a table in the room Antonio lets us use. A single candle burns on the table. We're speaking Spanish, but Izel uses the Náhuatl word for demon, *tzitzimitl*, when talking about Red Beard. "You have to run, José, or the *tzitzimitl* will kill you." She's serving me a bowl of *pozolli*, a meat and corn stew she brought from Amparo's kitchen. "He won't stop until that happens." She imitates her view of the monstrous demon, making a menacing expression, growling and raising her hands as if they were claws. I love watching her imitations, some she learned from Chuckles.

"But I can't," I say, turning and looking through the gloom. I see David, asleep on our bed. "I can't leave."

"If you don't escape," she says, "you won't see our son again. And you won't see this one." She pats her stomach.

I stop eating and smile, then begin coughing. It's now a wet cough that comes and goes at all times. The hacking stops and I rise, come around the table and bend down to kiss Izel on the forehead and caress her belly.

"I didn't want to tell you until I knew for sure," she says.

Suddenly, I begin coughing again, doubling over with each heaving eruption.

"Ay, José! If the *tzitzimitl* doesn't kill you, the mine will. I beg you, get out of there!"

I straighten up and catch my breath. "I can't. I'm trapped, same as on the ship." I clutch the table edge, sit down and start eating again. "If I run, I want you and David to come with me."

"No. It's safer here—for me and Davidcito."

"We'll run together."

"Wherever you go, send me word and I'll find you."

What she says makes sense, and I see a way I might escape. I stand and step across to the door. "I'll be back. I want to talk to Hassan and Minoru."

I go to their room and ask my friends to come with me to talk with Izel. Hassan rouses himself from his bed and Minoru stops cutting strips of bamboo. They rise and follow me across the courtyard to my doorway. We enter and sit on stools around the table. I stand behind Izel and announce that I have to escape from the mine and the foreman before I become too sick to work.

"I'll go with you," Hassan says.

Minoru raises a hand. "Me too."

Izel shakes her head. "What do I tell Antonio? All of you leaving at the same time."

"The truth," I say. "Tell him I'm English, tell him about Red Beard, why I had to leave. He'll understand."

"You tell him."

"She's right," Hassan says. "Antonio should hear this from you. He's been very good to us."

"Fine, but in the morning."

Izel reaches up and takes my right hand, caressing it with her cheek.

Hassan says that one of Antonio's mule trains is about to leave for Acapulco and maybe we can join the line.

"I'll talk to the *patrón*," I say.

Izel drops my hand. "José, are you crazy? Telling Antonio the truth is one thing, but telling Don Bartolomé de Medina who you really are is dangerous. What are you going to tell him? That you're English and not Catholic?"

"He knows."

"What?"

"He knows."

"My God! Now the church will take you away."

"That's not going to happen."

"How do you know?"

"I trust the *patrón*. He won't throw me to the dogs."

Minoru mutters something.

"What are you saying?" Hassan asks.

"Fall down seven times, stand up eight. It's what my master in Japan used to say."

Hassan shakes his head. "Not when you're a pile of ashes. I've seen the bodies of men and women burn in Seville. No one gets up from that."

I'm gently gripping Izel's shoulders, telling her not to worry. "The *patrón*'s a good man. I spoke to him when I was writing reports. I told him the truth. And look, I'm still here; I'm fine."

I look down and see Izel roll her eyes. "Barely," she says.

***

My truth telling with Medina occurred one morning before Red Beard made me his slave. The old *patrón* entered the mine's work yard and stopped to watch me make a quill with my penknife. Antonio had told me that the man who made the wealth of New

177

Spain possible by using mercury to mine silver had been spending more of his time in the city of Mexico and less at the Purísima. When he did visit his property, he almost never left the big house inside the hacienda's walls. But some days, early in the morning, he would walk to the mine's work yard.

Years ago, Antonio said, Medina arrived in Veracruz from Seville with a plan to use mercury to recover silver from the ore. Granted land on a mountainside above Pachuca, he tried out his method. He vowed that if he was successful, after the King got his due in silver ingots, he would give a quarter of his wealth to a charity to shelter and educate orphan girls in the capital city. And that's what he did when he became rich.

On the morning Medina stopped to watch me, he asked me how I made good nibs and about the best bird feathers to use for writing quills. "I wanted to meet the scribe Antonio sent me."

I told him my name.

"Campos," he said. "From Seville?"

"Yes."

"Where did you live?"

"Triana, sir."

He smiled. "No one writes in Triana. They're all illiterate sailors. Tell me, who taught you?"

"A scrivener."

"And your family name is Campos?"

"Yes, sir. I never knew my mother. I was told someone found me in the fields.

So they named me Campos, José Campos."

"Why don't I believe you?"

"It's the truth, sir."

"Who really taught you to read and write, to cut quills and make ink? I can't believe a scrivener by the river, so busy with all those ships, had the time to teach an orphan boy."

After a pause I nodded and said I only watched the men with quills scribbling on paper. "The truth is, sir, I came to New Spain as a cabin boy for Emilio Álvarez, Antonio's father. He taught me."

"And that knife, who gave you that knife?"

"Uh . . . I found it."

"Really? Let me see it."

I handed the penknife to the *patrón*. He examined the blade and the bone handle with the Hebrew *chai* mark, then gave it back. He said the mark reminded him of his ancestors. "They were Jews. Now, tell me the truth—and no lies—do you know what the mark on the handle means?"

I looked around and into the sun, blinded by the light.

"Answer me, son, in all confidence."

What would Father have answered? Medina was waiting for me to speak. So I spilled out my tale—from my English birth and my father's gift of a penknife, to my time with the slaves on the *Mynion* and with the Guachichiles as a slave myself, and to my suspicion that I was a descendant of Spanish Jews.

Medina laughed. "So your ancestors are from Seville after all!" He gestured for me to continue my work. "Don't worry, your secret's safe with me."

"Thank you, sir."

"No, thank the Almighty. He's the one who gives us life and takes it away." Medina removed his wide-brimmed hat, wiped his brow with a handkerchief and moved a hand over his gray hair. Then, as if speaking to himself, he talked about missing his dead son, a young man about my age, who died on a voyage from Seville to New Spain.

"I cannot judge you, young man. You may be Lutheran or you may have Jewish blood, as I do, or you may pray to Indian idols behind altars. That's not my concern. I can only judge your work, your tallies and lists, your reports."

Medina turned and faced the yard's storage rooms and workshops. "On that, you do well," he said, stepping away. "Keep to it, José Campos. May it go well with you." I stood and said goodbye, watching the stooped figure walk away toward the orecrushing area, where men were leading mules walking in circles. Then I picked up my knife and kissed the handle.

***

In the morning, I speak to Antonio and he wants to know why I didn't tell him what was going on. He could have done something.

I cough and clear my throat. "I'm also English."

"What?"

"Called a heretic."

I trust Antonio with my life and I believe I have no choice but to tell him the same story I told Emilio, omitting only my likely Jewish ancestry. Antonio listens and afterward embraces me, telling me that of course I can ride in the mule train. "Get away, anything to break that man's hold on you."

I'm coughing and this time the deep hacking makes me bend over. Whatever is trying to get out settles down. "Hassan and Minoru," I say, straightening up, "want to go with me."

Antonio nods. "And Izel and the baby?"

"If it's not too much to ask—"

"They'll be safe with me."

181

"Oh, and we have another child on the way."

"Wonderful!"

***

After three days riding toward the capital city, I trade the mule's back for Hassan's back. On Antonio's advice and to avoid pursuit, I am to play the part of a properly dressed gentleman being carried by a slave. And we'll be followed by Minoru and Oreja, Antonio's best and oldest muleteer, both acting as my porters.

Our small group has left the line of Antonio's pack mules to trek south along a trail leading to the road that will take us to the Tacuba causeway. I'm still sick, strapped to the chair, rocking and swaying, dozing and coughing.

It's early in the morning as a shimmering lake comes into view. Hassan says the city across the water appears to be floating. I open my eyes and ask him to turn around so I can see.

He's right. The water's surface is bright and white, and the island looks like a floating sheepskin. I catch my breath, then start coughing again, a fit that leaves me wheezing and tired.

"Don't talk, it only makes it worse," Hassan says, turning around and moving forward. Plodding behind us are Minoru and the mule driver, a Mexica man with a distorted face and one overly large ear. He's thin, older than the rest of us, and is my Náhuatl translator and guide.

"Young man," he tells me, trotting forward. He offers me water from a leather bag. "You need water." I lift the bag to my lips and drink. He says he knows someone in the city he believes can cure me.

When I finish drinking, I give him back the bag. "Thank you, Oreja."

The English word for *oreja* is "ear," and it's the name everyone uses for this man. He's cursed with a face that looks to have been squeezed and pushed to one side of his head—the side with the big ear. Antonio told me Oreja understands people as well as he knows the ways of mules, and he can tell a lot about people by their expressions when they first see him. "Everyone stares at a monster," Antonio told him, "but some people stare softly. They stare with their hearts."

As an infant, Oreja had been given the Nahua name Moquatlahuitec, or He Hit His Head Against Something. But a friar baptized him as Juan San Martín because he was born on that saint's feast day. As Juan San Martín grew, other kids would call him "Oreja"—not always in ridicule but with some affection for the smart but oddlooking boy. They especially tried to get him to smile or grin because that's when his face would shift to the center. If it weren't for his enormous ear, he would look almost normal. The friar who christened him was so taken with the boy's intelligence and good nature that he taught him church duties as well as how to read and write Latin and Spanish.

183

On this day, Oreja's smile is practically permanent because he's going home. He grew up on the streets of Náhuatl-speaking natives along the city's south shore, and he says he was happiest when working with his father on the two chinampas that their ancestors had built. These floating gardens were made with mud, sticks and tree roots. Oreja tells me he likes nothing better than passing the days tending to the rows of corn and vegetables with his dog beside him. For him it's a world of birds, butterflies, caterpillars and flowers, a world where no one stares at him.

***

As we near the water and the causeway, I'm struck at the lush growth spreading around us. After spending three days crossing a plain withered by years without rain, I welcome the change with a kind of silent reverence. I cough and cough and then I stare overhead at the clusters of flowers with violet petals. Alongside us on the trail are sunflowers, and farther on is an enormous tree Oreja calls *ahuehuetl*. Passing under its shade, I breathe in the sweet smells of flowers and other plants around us. I hear birds, the clicks of insects and voices coming from the many small boats on the water.

Not even the cool, mossy forests beyond Greenwich can compare with this. It's a tonic for my ailing senses. I wish Izel and David could be with me, wish Mother, Father and Sister Mary could see and smell the blossoms. In London I heard the town crier shout about a marvelous new world. Was this what the crier meant? Another time Deacon Brown looked at me and said I might sail someday and reach a land of riches. Was this the Bible's Eden that he described?

When Hassan steps onto the causeway's stones, we join the traffic of natives and slaves bent under loads. A cart pulled by oxen and loaded with goats passes us. I'm coughing, and when I finish I look up to see a well-dressed man greet me with a nod and a tilt of his hat. "And the same to you, sir," I answer. He moves on and I tell Oreja and Minoru that my disguise in Antonio's silk and brocade clothes must be convincing.

"We'll see," Oreja says.

"You heard the man."

"He felt sorry for you."

"What?"

"You weren't on a horse. A real gentleman rides a horse."

Hassan laughs. "I'm his horse!"

Minoru shouts, "Then carry me too! I'm a weaver, not a mule!"

We start on the causeway at a point just beyond a hilly area called Chapultepec. The road is straight and level and runs alongside an aqueduct. Dressed in my finery, I sit in the chair tied to Hassan's back, nodding to travelers passing us on horses, in carts and on foot. To our left and right the lake's surface is crowded with long, small boats carrying corn, fruits, vegetables, chickens and pigs headed to markets. It's not much different from the loaded boats on the Thames in the early morning. The difference is that most of the natives with paddles and poles are women.

We leave the causeway and move onto a wider street. Hassan veers to the side out of the way of traffic. "I want to rest a bit," he says and stops. Minoru and Oreja untie me. They set down their burdens and help me to my feet. Hassan slips out of his ropes and sits on the ground next to a squatting Minoru.

Before us is a parade of black and native porters, people on horses and mules, carts and donkeys draped with bags of charcoal and clay jars. I stare at the wide avenue with an open waterway down the middle. On both sides of this spacious passage rise stone-walled homes, some several stories high. In the canal, traders and vendors paddle the slender boats in both directions, some with fruits and flowers, others with caged birds, chickens and baskets of fish.

"Welcome to Tenochtitlán," Oreja says with a sweep of an arm, "home of the Mexica—and just about everyone else!"

Chapter 14 – Floating City

Minoru says he's never seen so many people, and a wide-eyed Hassan can only repeat what I just said in English—"Splendid!" He doesn't know what the word means and looks puzzled. "Beautiful," I say in Spanish, remembering that Deacon Brown once called the city and its canals the "Venice of the New World."

"Let's go," Oreja says. I sit in the chair that's roped to Hassan's back. I tie myself in, then Hassan stands and we're on the move again. Nearing the cathedral in a sprawling plaza, we stop and make way for groups of what look to be wealthy women dressed in brocades and lacy mantillas. They hold rosary beads in both hands, reciting prayers. Behind them comes a large group of black and native men and women in their own finery. At the head of one group walks a Mexica woman with her own servants. She's dressed like a Spanish woman of wealth and has loops of red beads around her neck.

"Who's that?" I ask Oreja, whose face creases into a normal-looking expression.

"Granddaughter of a Mexica prince. She's a descendent of Moctezuma. They're on their way to Mass." Oreja grins. "What do you think, Hassan? You could have your pick of these flowers."

"Not when I'm hauling around His Majesty."

I elbow Hassan in the ribs. "Careful, slave."

187

"Ah, forgive me, master."

"What do you all think of my full name? José Campos de Medina."

"Sounds like a gentleman's name," Oreja says.

"Why Medina?" Hassan asks.

"Bartolomé de Medina. He was good to me."

Hassan whirls around so I can see the entire line of bedecked women. "Very well," he says, "Don José Campos de Medina. Enjoy the view."

Hassan plods alongside the causeway to the cathedral and across the plaza— Oreja calls it the zócalo. We pass by a big *tianguis*. It's busier and more crowded than any market I've ever seen. Mostly natives are buying and selling fruits, vegetables, blankets, hats, baskets, chairs and so much more.

We cross over a canal filled with boats heading in both directions. Even with my coughing, I smell enough of the flowers and foods carried by the loaded boats that I close my eyes and breathe deeply. My thoughts drift away as I hear Oreja announce that we've come to the city quarter where the Mexica and other natives live.

When we arrive at Oreja's family home by the southern canal, Hassan lowers me to the ground. I untie myself, step away and start coughing. When I finish my fit, I thank Hassan for playing the part of a porter.

"Thank Antonio," he says. "He's the one who wanted me to carry you."

"I'm sorry to be such a burden."

"I'll do anything to save your hide, but the journey is over, my friend. We're here." He laughs, drawing the attention of someone inside.

"Who is it?" a woman's voice says.

"Sisters!" Oreja shouts. "It's me, Oreja! I come from Pachuca with friends."

When the sisters appear, Oreja presents them affectionately as "my little spinsters." Xuchitl and María, the taller and older of the two, embrace their brother. "Thank you, sisters," Oreja says. "If only our parents were here to bless you."

"They are," Xuchitl, says, touching her chest. "Here."

Oreja smiles and for an instant his happy expression resembles María's.

She unrolls two petates and tells Oreja and Minoru to put down their loads.

"Wash up outside," she says and points to the doorway at the back of the room.

I step out into a courtyard, look around and see the water jar next to a copper basin. Across the hard dirt two ducks waddle away from us.

After cleaning up, we're told to go to the table that's in the sunshine at one side of the courtyard. I sit on a stool and feel the afternoon warmth on my face. Just then María and Xuchitl come out from the blackened kitchen doorway with bowls and plates of beans, tortillas and green chilies.

Soon we're eating and drinking atole, a thick, sweet corn soup. I'm coughing but not as much as on the walk from Pachuca. "My friend at the hospital," Oreja says, "is only a student, but I believe if I ask him he'll come to see you."

"José needs rest," María says. "Good food and rest."

I stifle a cough so I can hear Hassan elaborate on his dream of someday making pottery again, even owning his own business. "Clay is my friend," he says. "When I worked in Seville, the earth would come alive in my hands. I want that feeling again."

Minoru says he wants to weave baskets to sell in the *tianguis*.

"And you, José?" Oreja asks.

"Maybe a scrivener again."

Hassan's eyes and eyebrows rise.

"Antonio taught me, so at the mine I could write reports."

Oreja wags a finger. "Not you, José. Your business is here, resting, healing."

I feel my lungs are about to explode again. I wait, trying to catch my breath and calm down. But I can't hold back. Out comes a deep, rattling cough. Another breath and I nod. "I can do that too."

***

Oreja's friend Domingo examines me—looks at my tongue, listens to my chest and has me open each eye as wide as I can. He's a small man, much shorter than I am, and he asks me to sit on the bed so he can see the eyes better. He's nodding. Maybe I'm beyond help, maybe I'll cough myself to death, maybe I'll die in this very bed. I don't know but it's hard not thinking about dying.

Domingo tells me to lie down. "I have to prepare a medicine." He leaves and I'm dozing when he returns with a cup of tea that tastes like grass. It's bitter but I get it down. "Now rest," he says. "The women will give you more later. It will take time but I believe you will be healthy again. Goodbye, sir."

I wave and watch him leave. Maybe I won't die after all.

Later, the sisters bring me more of the medicine. Again and again. Finally, they bring me food—beans, tortillas, squash and some goat meat. I wish Mother could see how kindly these women tend to me. It reminds me so much of how she cared for me whenever I was sick.

In time, my hacking ends and I begin to recover my strength. Every day that passes I thank the sisters and Oreja for their attentions, though I wish Izel could take on that duty. I miss her and our little David so much that my heart aches.

Days later, when I'm well enough, I join Oreja and his sisters in their narrow boat as they pole across the water to their chinampa. To me it's a magical green garden. I rest in the shade with my back against a willow tree. I watch my hosts weed and water the young cornstalks and other plants, like tomatoes, chilies, and the squash they call *chayotl*. Then they haul up mud in buckets from the lake bottom and spread it along the rows of plants.

It's perfect here. No more slave ship, no more running from Guachichiles, no more living in Red Beard's hell. Now I can sit back against the tree and gaze across the water at two mountain peaks, white against the blue sky. I'm listening to the chirping of birds and buzzing of bees. The air is warm and I smell the wet earth. A grasshopper lands at my feet, flies away, and I can only breathe, watch and wait.

***

I'm well now, well enough to begin looking for work. Oreja takes me to see Domingo at the hospital for natives. The medical student who first saw me says he thinks there might be a need for scriveners at the hospital. This is because some years ago a visiting doctor from Spain, Francisco Hernández, along with a group of scriveners and artists, began using part of the hospital to compile a book on medicinal plants native to New Spain.

At the hospital, I talk to a young Spanish doctor and he hires me for a modest salary. My tasks will be to register patients, write letters and petitions, and take dictated notes for physicians when they examine patients.

I settle into a routine and finally feel safe from any pursuit by Red Beard. So I ask Oreja if he can send word for Izel and David to join me.

"I'll bring them," Oreja says.

"I'll pay you."

"No, I brought you here as a favor to Antonio. Now that you're on your feet, my mission's over. Remember, on the road we're all mule drivers."

"What?"

"On the road we're all mule drivers."

"You sound like my father, with all his sayings."

"And why not? What I know is best said with a few words."

"I suppose."

"It's true. For example, what would be your advice to someone about to go on a long journey? Something in only four or five words."

"I don't know. Watch out for thieves, take plenty of water."

"No, that's the obvious."

"What, then?"

"Long way, short steps."

***

During the time I am healing, my two friends also find work. Hassan moves to Puebla and is making vessels at a pottery workshop. Minoru stays here with me and the sisters, making baskets to sell in the big *tianguis*.

When Izel and little David arrive in early 1576, I'm outside in back watching Minoru weave a basket. I hear Oreja's voice and then María, who is welcoming them. Before I can cross the courtyard, I see David running out the open doorway. He's in my arms and I'm hugging him. I set him down and now I feel a hand on my shoulder. I turn and Izel buries her face in my chest. When we let go of each other, I smile at seeing her very large belly.

"Soon," she says, patting the mound, which is the size of a pig's head.

"My brother, José," David announces.

"And if it's a girl?" I say.

David giggles. "Quetzal."

"Three years old," Izel says, "and he's already naming the baby."

Xuchitl, María and Minoru have been watching and we're all laughing. Just then Oreja enters the patio leading a mule loaded with a leather bag and a basket, just behind the space where I figure Izel and David probably sat.

María says something in Náhuatl to Izel, then the two walk around the mule and move across to the room where I've been sleeping. David runs after the women. He's bigger now and talks a lot. Watching him, I'm thinking he'll be my helper, my little man, the same as I was to my father. I can still hear him. "Little Man, fetch my quill, knife and ink horn."

One morning, as I'm about to leave the house for the hospital, I hear the sounds of drums, flutes and shouts coming from the street. Then I hear a man's voice shout words in Náhuatl.

"What's he saying?"

Izel's sitting at a table in the front room cutting cooked squash on Davidcito's plate. She looks at Xuchitl with a puzzled expression.

"Auto-de-fé for the heretic," Xuchitl says in Spanish. "This afternoon in the

Plaza Hipólito. They're burning someone."

"Who is it?"

"An English dog. That's what he's saying."

I follow the two sisters outside, where they're watching the musicians retreat down the street, followed by people and dogs.

"Why burning?" I ask.

"The Holy Inquisition," Xuchitl says. "They want us to see the autos. You can go and see for yourself. It's a big thing. The viceroy and his judges and all the priests—everyone goes, poor and rich. Last year they led a long line of these Lutherans through the streets. They were on horses and some men were hitting them with long whips."

At the hospital near the Plaza Hipólito, I ask for permission to leave my chores to watch the burning of an Englishman. I push and squeeze my way through the mass of mostly short natives and taller blacks and mestizos. Near the front of the crowd across what looks like an empty ceremonial space, I see a single post erected over a pile of brush and firewood, all of it set before rows of seated figures on a wide, raised platform under a canopy. These are the dignitaries Oreja told me about. They're dressed in garments with sashes and lace collars. The clerics are dressed in red, brown and black robes, and at each side of the platform there are more people standing.

I hear a short blast of drumbeats, then some horns. Over the crowd I see a barechested man seated on a horse. His hands are bound behind him at the waist and I can't yet see his face. His head is bowed and he moves slowly. People step back to make way for the horse and rider. They're striking him with sticks and branches, shouting, "English heretic! Lutheran dog! Devil's dog! Enemy of God!" Just then, the man raises his head and I recognize the face of Cornelius, the *Mynion*'s barber and surgeon.

Poor devil, barely hanging on to the saddle, slipping to the side. Why burning? Why? Cornelius is Irish Catholic. I asked him why he knew Latin so well and he said you don't forget words the friars beat into you.

The two priests beside him, they're shouting, calling for him to repent. "Save yourself! Save yourself! Repent!" They're pulling him to the ground, then they hold him up. I want to shout in English, "Cornelius! Why are you going to die? You're a Catholic."

On the platform, the priest points to Cornelius and speaks. I can't hear the words. Another man in a black robe stands and reads from a scroll, then shouts an order to begin. They push him to the pyre. They tie him to the post and a rope is looped around his neck. The rope is pulled, and his arms and legs tremble. His head jerks back and then falls forward. I feel a weakness in my stomach. He shouldn't die like this.

They're tossing lit torches onto the pyre. Flames rise out of the wood and brush, and the body burns. I hear shouting, cheers and then horns and drums.

I already knew from Antonio that other Englishmen had faced the Inquisition's judges. Some were whipped and put in prison or sent to Spain to row galleys for years.

Others had to wear yellow tunics as penance. And there were some Englishmen who avoided torture and punishment by convincing the inquisitors that they had never abandoned their Catholic faith.

The sky is darkening and I head to the sisters' place. I keep seeing the barbersurgeon struck by sticks and whips, wondering why he died at the stake, why he died if he was Catholic. It seems so wrong to me that my former shipmate would be killed at the stake for being a Lutheran when he really wasn't. At least I didn't think he was.

Going out to the courtyard, I see Izel sitting outside on a stool next to the door.

"How was the burning?" she asks.

"Sad. I knew the man."

"Well, you're safe, no?"

"Yes."

"You're sure?"

"Stop worrying."

Taking both my hands in hers, she places them on her big belly. "You feel it?"

"Yes."

The bump moves again and we wait. As darkness falls, a rooster breaks the silence.

"Are you hungry?" she asks.

"No."

"Well, you have to eat." She grips my forearm and stands up. "Come," she says and pushes the door open.

Chapter 15 – Pestilence

It's December, the storms have gone and now the rats, mice, squirrels and other small creatures are everywhere. They're out of their holes and hollows, eating whatever they can. We hear them at night, scurrying in the dark, chewing, squeaking, having their way.

At the hospital, patients talk of the many villages that have been swept away by rivers and moving mounds of mud. They say the crops are gone and what's left is a land that's alive with little scavengers, as if the rains had awakened them from their long sleep during the dry years.

Izel and I have our own new life. Our baby girl's name is Yaretzi. In Náhuatl the word means "you will always be loved." We tell David we can't name her Quetzal because that's the name of a bird—and birds fly away. Right then he begins calling his sister Yetzi. We laugh and start calling her that.

Perhaps because she was born when the rains stopped, Izel and the sisters see Yetzi as a gift from God or from Tlaloc, the giver and taker of rain. That she is mestiza is never mentioned. Only census takers and tribute collectors and most Spaniards would ever call her a "mixture." But everyone, as I'm learning at the hospital, fits into some name or class of people. Spaniards will see Yetzi as a mixture, just as all natives are called "Indians."

Besides the arrival of our daughter, we receive another gift, this one from Minoru, who gives Izel a bamboo basket he made in which to keep her. "Let's hang it next to the bed," I suggest, remembering the suspended wooden box my sister Mary lay in after her birth.

Izel is in bed nursing Yetzi. She looks up at the ceiling beam. "Good, but hang it over here on my side."

I leave the room and return with enough rope to loop one end over the beam and hang the basket at a height where Izel can easily lift Yetzi or set her down in the basket. Xuchitl and María begin visiting the room to hold her. They pace by the bed or go outside to sing and let the baby's mother sleep.

***

I am to work as an assistant scrivener in a group of mostly native artists and writers supervised by Dr. Hernández. He's a physician to the King's court with the title protomédico of the Indies. His mission for the past six years is not only to study the medicinal uses of plants and animals in New Spain but also to produce illustrated volumes on the subject. Much of the manuscript has already been written in Latin and will be translated into Spanish and Náhuatl.

I learned that on their travels over the central valleys and plains, Hernández and his group talked to healers and villagers who'd been struck by one illness or another. He and his assistants, along with his son Juan, have installed themselves in a large room on the second floor of the hospital. There he has space for his collection of plants and is able to question and examine many Nahuas, Otomís, Purépecha, Tlascaltecas, and other natives.

When I first enter this room, I speak to the head of the plant collection, who tells me the protomédico has not yet arrived for work. In the meantime, I should look around to see what the artists and scriveners are doing. I'm quickly drawn to what the native illustrators are depicting with such delicacy in line and color. I talk with one of the men finishing a painting of a cacao pod hanging on a leafy branch. The artist tells me he was taught by his father, who, in turn, was schooled in the craft of picture writing by his father. Same story as mine.

When Hernández arrives, I'm sitting at the end of a long table with veteran scriveners, who are all Spaniards or sons of Spaniards. Hernández dictates to one of them in Latin while the others are busy copying the corrected first drafts. Now and then the doctor nods to me and dictates a side note in Spanish, or he sends me away on errands to fetch a particular plant or to ask one of the doctors a question and write down the answer.

Unlike the older scriveners and artists, I'm an all-around helper for Hernández and the other doctors, who probably see me as a capable young man from Seville. But I'm also willing to take on all manner of chores—like trapping snakes, rats, and large insects found in the hospital, especially among the pots and boxes of medicinal plants. Hernández says I'm fearless. Once he even asked me where or how I learned to catch such creatures. I shrugged and answered that in a previous life I had been a Guachichil savage.

***

I sit up in a sweat, shouting, "No! No! No!"

Izel stirs and asks me what's the matter.

"Nothing, a bad dream."

She pats my arm.

"I saw a rat," I say and look around in the dawn's glow. Light is filtering in from around the door and window shutters.

"A rat?"

"Yes, climbing out of Yetzi's basket."

Izel pushes up on one arm, peeks in the hanging basket, then drops her head back onto her pillow. "She's here, José, next to me."

"It was one of the rats on the ship. The one I told you about."

"The one you talked to?"

"Yes, and he was in Yetzi's basket."

"I told you, she's fine."

"Sorry I woke you."

"Please, English, no more rats."

"No more, go back to sleep."

After a moment's silence, Izel asks me how I could tell it was the same rat.

"Don't most rats look alike?"

"No, there are differences. This one smiles a lot."

She punches my arm and turns away from me. "Now I know you're dreaming."

For a long while I remain seated on our straw mattress. I think of the rats and their hiding spots on the *Mynion*. I remember the three rats climbing up the mooring line when we were on the Guinea coast. It seems so long ago. More than ten years have passed since that awful time, yet I can instantly return to my life as a rat myself, crawling around belowdecks in near darkness, ever the watchful rodent.

At the hospital the next day, I'm writing on paper bought from the city's new paper mill, the first in New Spain. The white surface is much smoother than the rough bark paper I've been using. My pen strokes are now fluid and steady. Father would find this paper much to his liking.

I'm writing words spoken by one of the older doctors, a short, bald man examining a new patient. She's a young Nahua woman dressed in a dirty huipil. She's writhing on a cot beneath the physician's gaze. I sit at a table, dipping the quill into a pewter inkwell, then writing the words for the patient's symptoms. "Burning fever, black tongue, yellowish skin, diarrhea, delirium, pale-green blood coming from her nose, ears, mouth and vagina."

She moans and shrieks, and I jot down the words that remind me of the miseries suffered by my parents and sister before they left this world.

The young woman's own parents, after giving an account of their daughter's illness, have been waiting outside the door of the examination room. They've been squatting on the floor with their backs against a wall, and now they murmur prayers, staring into the courtyard and its jumble of plants collected by Hernández.

"José," the doctor says, turning to me, "go tell the *protomédico* that I have a new patient with something he should see."

I set down my quill and am about to leave when the woman begins to shudder and arch her back. "Tell him to hurry," the doctor says, raising a hand. "It's urgent!" I bolt out of the room and move past the courtyard columns, skirting around the many patients and others waiting to see a doctor or feed a meal to a patient who's a relative. I skip up a wide stone stairway, three stairs at a time, nearly crashing into a woman sweeping the floor at the top. I swerve around her and run down the corridor to the big hall where Hernández is dictating a sentence to one of the scriveners. Seeing me rush in, he stops and gestures for me to speak.

Gasping, I blurt my message. "Dr. López says to come! It's urgent!"

Hernández gives me a quick nod. "Come with me," he says and hurries to the door.

Downstairs where the young woman is still convulsing, López, the attending older doctor, apologizes to Hernández for the interruption but says he thinks he should see this in person. "It's back!" the older man announces.

"What's back?" Hernández asks, stepping close to the writhing young woman.

"*Cocoliztli.*"

"My God."

"I've seen it before. About thirty years ago."

"Not smallpox?"

"No. The fever's the same, but all the bleeding? Everywhere. Black tongue, yellow skin. And look at this." López, who's holding a candelabra with lit candles, passes it to Hernández. Then he leans forward and grabs the woman's head with both hands. "José?"

"Yes, Doctor."

"Hold her arms down."

I reach over the patient's body to keep her hands and arms still. López sweeps the long black hair to one side and Hernández looks closely behind the left ear. Three pink nodules the size of peas stand out brightly against the creamy brown skin. Hernández steps back and López lets go of the woman's head. I release her arms.

"We have no name for it in Spanish," the shorter physician says, "but the Indians call it *cocoliztli*, sometimes *huey cocoliztli*, the great pestilence."

Hernández looks down at the pitiful figure on the cot, still writhing and twisting but no longer bucking and arching her back. "Like the pestilence from years ago."

"The same," López says. "And the nodules behind the ears mean the end is near.

She will soon die. That was the way it was the last time it hit us."

"Us?"

"Well, the Indians, almost always Indians. And millions died, as you and His Majesty know."

"How long is the course of the disease?"

"Three days, five days, maybe a week but no more."

Hernández sighs. "Any others like her?"

"She's the first I've seen."

"What's the treatment?"

"We tried various things but in the end nothing helped."

"Always fatal?"

"Almost always, but there were a few who lived. For some reason the very young and very old managed to live."

"And this poor creature?"

López takes back the candlestick and moves his head from side to side. "The nodules. Death is coming."

***

It's the end of summer and *huey cocoliztli* appears to have skipped over the central parts of the city, where most of the Spaniards and fair-skinned people live. It's settling into the native neighborhoods and spreading to surrounding villages like a windblown fire. I know I'm probably immune to the disease, since I'm healthy despite working among so many of its victims. And Minoru also feels safe from the scourge. After weeks of seeing fewer and fewer Nahuas showing up at the *tianguis*, he feels fine. Those natives who don't come to the market either are sick with the affliction or have already died.

Izel and the two sisters are afraid that they and the children will be struck down by *cocoliztli*. The sisters are also worried about the sickness reaching Oreja, who returned to Pachuca weeks before the pestilence struck. I hear them talking outside with a shrill fear in their voices. We're seated at the table on the patio and I'm watching David walk circles around the ducks.

"We can't leave," Xuchitl says. "Where do we go? This is our home."

"Pachuca," María suggests, "with our brother."

"*Cocoliztli* is there too," Minoru says. "In the *tianguis* I hear all the news. Traders come from everywhere. And I hear it's killing people in Pachuca."

Izel shakes her head. Yetzi is hanging on her mother's side in a rebozo. "My children have their father's blood. They'll be safe. Right, José?"

I shrug. "I don't know. Perhaps. But what's certain is that *cocoliztli* kills Nahuas and other natives. The only Spaniards I've heard of who died of this plague are friars from outside the city, the ones who care for the sick and bury the dead in the villages."

There's a loud knocking on the front door. "José," Xuchitl whispers. "Don't answer. It might be the husband of the woman who died this morning."

"They think I can heal," I say. "Everyone knows I work at the hospital."

After more knocks we hear a man's familiar voice asking to be let in. He promises he doesn't have the pestilence. "What I have are gifts!" the voice shouts.

And then, a laugh we all know. I hurry into the house and open the door to see Hassan's smiling face. His large frame fills the doorway. "Hassan! Come in."

My friend ducks his head to clear the doorway beam, then sets down a large sack he carries on his back. We embrace while Izel, Minoru, the sisters, and David gather around Hassan. He hugs them all but holds on to David, raising him and then setting him down.

"I've got something just for you," he says and bends down to open the sack. "Here, a little friend." He hands over a cloth-covered doll of a boy wearing pants, a shirt, and a tiny brimmed hat. David holds the doll up to his face and stares at it. Izel touches her son on the shoulder. "What do you say?"

"Thank you," he tells Hassan, then runs out to the patio.

"And here are some things I made for all of you," Hassan says. He lifts two straw-wrapped bundles from the sack and unwraps one. It's a ceramic pitcher decorated with wavy blue lines on a white glaze. He hands it to María. "For both of you, for your chocolate." The sisters giggle, then María promises they'll always think of him whenever they use it. "It's beautiful."

"In Seville, I made the same kind of pieces," Hassan says. He opens the other bundle and removes three white-and-blue bowls, one each for Izel, me, and Minoru.

After the gift-giving, then hearing screams from the street, Hassan says he worries about all of them, especially Izel and the sisters. "I've seen a lot of people die. Almost all are natives."

"And you?" I ask. "How safe are you?"

Hassan smiles. "I'm good. *Cocoliztli* has jumped over me."

He says where he works, seven native potters were taken by the disease. He could leave the workshop because there's no demand for pottery in the *tianguis* and shops. People with money buy only what they can eat. Everyone else buys petates to roll up their dead for burial.

Minoru says he's seeing the same thing. "But white people are afraid food will run out, that the sellers will die. I saw one lady and her servants—a black woman and a mulatta—get out of a carriage and walk around to have a look at what there was for sale. A lot of us, like me, sit on the ground behind what we sell. When she walked by me, she stopped and looked at my baskets, then at me. 'Listen, *chino*,' she said. 'If you and your kind brought us this plague, then you should burn in the fires of hell.'"

"What did you say?" I ask Minoru.

"Nothing. What could I say?" "That you're not really Chinese."

Minoru laughs and shakes his head.

"Where does *cocoliztli* come from?" Izel asks.

I tell her that no one knows, not even the doctors.

"Why does it like killing common people, us *macehuales*? Why, José?"

"I don't know, but so many poor souls are dying. At the hospital we have many beds, all of them with people sick with *cocoliztli*. And there are more bodies on the floor, alive and dead."

"Maybe God is punishing us for something," María says.

Remembering that Queen Elizabeth fled to Windsor Castle to escape the Black Death, I say, "All I know is that you have to run from it. All of us."

Xuchitl pulls at María's huipil and says they have to finish preparing dinner. While the sisters are leaving the room for the kitchen, Izel shifts the weight of her rebozo so that she can see Yetzi. I see her glistening black eyes. After touching the tiny face, Izel glances my way. "She feels a little hot."

I place a hand on the baby's forehead. "No fever. But this is why we must leave— before it's too late."

"Where will you go?" Hassan asks as he sits down at the table.

"North. It might be the safest direction. But I don't know."

"What's there but the mines?"

"And land."

"Yes, but full of Chichimecas. Don't forget there's a war going on with them.

And you and Izel walking with two babies? No, too many dangers."

"I've faced worse. Remember the ship?"

"Well, if you go north, stay away from the silver roads. A lot of thieves there."

"I already asked. The doctors tell me all roads lead to Zacatecas."

"Just stay off the royal routes."

"I thought we should go over the mountains on trails, then down to San Juan,

Querétaro, San Miguel and beyond."

"Walking?" Hassan asks.

"I have enough pesos saved up to buy a good mule or an old horse."

"My friend, I'll give you my horse. He's young, strong."

"I can't do that."

"You will. I insist."

Izel, who's pacing about with Yetzi cradled in her arms, asks Hassan how he will return to Puebla.

"I'll walk or ride with one of the wagons going to Veracruz. I know a few of the drivers."

"Where's the horse?" I ask.

"At the baker's place near Plaza Hipólito. He's got stables.

RON ARIAS

I'll go with you so he'll know you're the new owner."

"I'll pay you back."

"When chickens grow teeth."

I turn and embrace my big friend.

Hassan holds me tightly. "Listen, José. For Izel's and the children's sake, stay clear of the black clouds."

"Clouds? Black clouds?"

Just then María and Xuchitl enter, both announcing dinner and carrying clay pots that trail wisps of steam. "Sit, all of you!" Xuchitl orders, setting down the pot of beans on the rough planks of the table.

Hassan whispers in my ear, "I'll tell you later."

Chapter 16 – Black Clouds

I turn around to see Izel rocking back and forth on the old mule, which we've named Mula. David looks snug sitting in front of her, with Yetzi hanging to one side in the rebozo. Izel yawns, then her head and body tilt forward. Suddenly, her head jerks back and she sits up straight.

"Careful, Mamá. You fall and they fall."

"I'm fine."

"Why don't we stop here and rest?"

"No, let's keep going or we'll never get anywhere."

"I'm sorry I got us into this disaster."

"It's not your fault."

"At least they didn't hurt you and the babies."

"Maybe they felt pity for us."

"I don't think so. Those kind of men don't have hearts."

For a long while we move in silence under the morning sun, following a worn trail bordered on both sides by thin stands of pine, juniper and oak. I've been leading Mula by a rope tied to the halter. Yesterday we were ambushed by three men with whips and daggers. Izel and the children were on Hassan's fine black stallion, and I was leading the mule that carried our possessions. So sudden was the attack that I only heard the crack of the whip, then I felt the sting of the leather strip circling my arms and chest. I stumbled and fell to the ground.

We lost everything—our food, clothes, a petate and a bundle of pots, bowls, spoons and knives. Also Hassan's horse. We were left with only Mula, two raggedy blankets, the clothes we wore, and my penknife. So we pushed ahead, hoping to reach a village, maybe a farmer's hut, anyplace where we might be fed. Izel had almost run dry of her own milk and she worried for our daughter's life. For now, all we could do was stop at streams, hoping the water might replenish her nearly empty breasts.

I hear sounds of crunching twigs and leaves. I tell Izel to wait for me, then drop the rope and slowly move in the direction of the crackling sounds. From my shoulder I slip off the bow and two arrows tied together. Yesterday I made the arrows and then used my sandal straps to make a bowstring for the pine branch that would do for a bow.

I move between the trees, following the noise for some time. I step as quietly as I can, but the fox or whatever it is makes a thrashing sound and escapes through the underbrush.

I tell David that it was a fox that pleaded for his life. "He was so smart," I say, "that when I listened to his cries and didn't shoot, he ran away into the forest. I think I heard him laugh. Imagine, a fox laughing at me."

David claps his hands and giggles. Then he returns to his collection of pinecones lined up in a square with one in the middle. "Papá, look—a house!"

Izel's on her back on a patch of grass next to Yetzi, who's spread out on the rebozo.

I lift David up and hold him in one arm. "Is it a house for all of us?" "Just for me," he says, shaking his head.

"Well, let's go look for a bigger house—big enough for all of us." "A house with food," Izel says. She rolls over and gets to her feet.

We fold the blankets and put them on Mula. I help Izel and Yetzi up onto the mule and then place my son on his spot behind the withers. "Let's go," I say and lead Mula back to the trail. Since the robbery, we haven't seen a soul. This is odd, since the trail appears well traveled by human feet and the hooves of mules and horses.

About noon, we see a curl of smoke rising slowly over the trees ahead. "What do you think?" Izel asks.

"People," I say. "Let's get a little closer."

"Smoke," David says.

"That's right," I say, "but now you must not talk, not even a little sound. Let's all be quiet."

Before long we emerge from the forest and stop at the edge of a wide, treeless swath of land studded with tree stumps. On the other

217

side of the clearing, about the distance of a good arrow shot, two plumes of smoke rise over what appears to be an encampment of some sort. Men are moving next to a huge pile of wood. Off a ways to one side stand dozens of mules. "Burning charcoal," I say. "*Carboneros.*"

Izel shakes her head. "They cut so many trees."

"The mines need charcoal, lots of it," I say. "Day and night the fires have to burn."

"And the forest becomes this."

David turns around and pulls at his mother's arm. "Do the trees grow back?"

"I don't think so. No, these are probably dead."

"Why do they kill them?"

Before she can answer, I turn and whisper that we should go off the trail to our left in order to avoid the camp. "It wouldn't be safe for us. Those men are probably all Otomís."

"José, they could give us food."

"And *cocoliztli*. No, we have to stay away from them."

We trudge on and reach the end of what has been a forested plateau, now broken by clearings. We find a trail that leads us down a brush-covered mountainside to a sloping, cultivated plain. The trail is now a wider path that skirts a stream, then continues through land overrun by clusters of grazing sheep and cattle. Here and there, gophers, rabbits, squirrels and other small animals move about.

I stop to scan the rolling lowlands. "I don't see anyone."

"Look," Izel says, pointing to a dark smudge beyond a hill. "More smoke."

I squint, studying the spot. "I don't think so."

"It's a cloud!" David blurts.

"No," I said, "it's not a cloud."

"Then what, José?"

"Death."

"What?"

"Vultures."

"So many?"

"Hassan called them black clouds."

"Is it *cocoliztli*?"

I nod. "They're probably over a village."

After drinking water in the stream, we begin following a path between low walls of piled-up stones that separate us from the cattle and sheep. "English," Izel says, "when are you going to use your arrows and the bow you made? We're dying of hunger."

I was thinking the same thing when she spoke. "Yes, my love, we will eat," I say and drop Mula's rope. I remove the bow and quiver of arrows that hang on my shoulder, set an arrow on the string, pull back and let go. It strikes the rabbit in the side and it collapses. In one breath I have a second arrow out, draw back and release it, toppling another rabbit. Then I climb over the stone wall to retrieve the two animals.

Meanwhile, Izel swings a leg over Mula's rump and drops to the ground. Then she lifts David, sets him down and says they're off to gather branches and twigs alongside the trail.

When I reach the dead animals, I set my bow and arrows on the ground and use my penknife to skin the two creatures. Izel builds a fire in the middle of the path and we roast the rabbits on sticks. We sit on the blankets, devouring everything but the bones. Yetzi cries much of the time but David happily chews and swallows every morsel we give him.

"Izel, we need things. I want to see what I can get from that town, the one beneath the black cloud."

"Don't go, José."

"I'll be safe."

"Take the mule."

"No, it's better that Mula eats. There's plenty here."

"Then, go with God."

David rushes into my arms. "No," I say, "stay with your mother." I kiss him on the forehead, turn him around and nudge him in her direction. Izel is shuffling in circles, trying to quiet the baby. "This one's hungry," she says, looking at David, then at the cows and sheep. "Come, Davidcito. Let's go find a mother with milk." In one hand she carries the rabbit skins, which she'll use to catch the milk for Yetzi.

After climbing the hill, I start down a path leading to the first houses. Until now I've been smelling the odors of plants, animals, dust and dung. The air is warm, still, and the cloud of swirling black birds rises and dips over the town. Suddenly, I step into another kind of cloud, an invisible, instantly familiar cloud heavy with the same sweet stench of rotting bodies that I smelled in London.

I walk between the adobe dwellings, one hand holding my tunic over my nose and mouth. I see fly-covered bodies to my right. Rats and mice are poking about, along with feasting birds. At one point the sky darkens for a moment and all I can hear is a shrieking chorus of calls from above.

Reaching the church, I stop before the open doors to watch the rodents scurry and vie for space among the vultures, crows, and other birds, all picking, pulling and tearing at what could have been a last gathering of infected natives praying for salvation.

221

I can no more imagine their final, desperate thoughts than I can make sense of Father's dying wish that I flee England. But I need no imagination to picture what this disease does to its victims. I saw this at the hospital, from their first feverish sweats to their final agonies as they bled to death.

I'm thinking of some of these patients when I'm startled by a deep voice from behind. "Can you help me?" the deep, raspy voice says.

I turn to see a bearded, hooded man with a scarf that hides all of his face but his eyes. He wears a stained brown robe, sleeves rolled up, and he holds a shovel in one hand.

"I need help with them," the man says, gesturing inside the church. "I dug a pit in back and have to drag them out."

I stare a moment at two birds tugging at a man's entrails.

"Excuse me, I'm Brother Dionisio. I won't touch you because my hands are covered in pestilence."

"José," I say, nodding. "I can help you."

"Good, but first, take this shovel to scare away the animals. They think they're the new kings of the town."

Dionisio hands me the shovel, then I use one hand to wave away flies. "Are you from Seville by any chance?" he asks.

"Yes."

"I'm the only Spaniard left here. The other friar was Otomí, Brother Sebastián. The scourge took him right away. The Indians call it the great pestilence, but it doesn't seem to attack many of us *peninsulares*."

From under his robe, Dionisio pulls out a long swatch of cloth and gives it to me, telling me to cover my mouth and nose.

"What brought you to this place?" the friar asks.

I tell him I was traveling from the city of Mexico with my family, intending to reach Zacatecas. But no sooner did we lose sight of the city than we were robbed of all our possessions. "My wife is Nahua, so she and the children are waiting for me outside the town."

"I pray for all the Indians," Dionisio says, still waving at flies. "A few are still alive, hiding in their homes. But let's bury these bodies now."

With a shovel in my hand, I follow the friar down the nave between rows of benches.

"I'll pull the dead out," Dionisio says, "and you chase the vultures away with the shovel."

The bodies are near the altar, and the friar lets me go first so I can scare away the birds, rodents and dogs. "Away!" I shout and start swinging the shovel. The vultures hop off a ways, the smaller birds fly up above the ceiling beams, but the rats and two dogs stay close. I keep swinging the shovel at the big birds, and they keep hopping back to their feast if I move away.

"Go on!" I yell. "Get, get!"

I look over at Dionisio as he's pulling a child by the legs, dragging the body out through an open door to the left of the altar. When I turn, the vultures are at it again. I hit one and hear a squawk. Dionisio's back and reaching for another body. "Father, let me do that."

"Very well," he says and takes the shovel. I reach for the legs of a woman whose body covers a child. Dionisio is shouting at the animals as I drag her across the hard dirt, through the doorway and outside. A few more steps and I'm at the edge of a shallow trench. Face up, face down, curled up, straight across—the lifeless figures are in a tangle. I shove the woman over the edge and look up at the cloudless sky. I'm blinded by the sun and shut my eyes, turn around and walk back to the church. It seems incredible that I'm doing this, pulling out these unfortunates, these people who only days ago were alive, talking, walking, eating, laughing. All I can do now is shake my head and breathe through my mouth.

In this way we finish the gruesome chore of moving many bodies into the pit. Dionisio addresses their souls with a prayer, then we cover everything with dirt. I use the shovel and he uses his hands.

As we leave the burial place and walk along the side of the church, I say I want to take things from the houses of the dead for my family.

"Take what you want," the friar says. "They won't miss what they had in this world."

Both of us are soaked in sweat, and now he walks slowly and stumbles, almost falling. "Yes," he says, "whatever you can take. I'll show you. Come."

"Brother Dionisio, I can see you are tired. We need water. Let's sit for a while."

The friar yanks down the scarf from his face and waves a hand for me to follow him. We walk toward a cluster of trees. He's old. Fifty years? Sixty years? Bald and the skin dark and wrinkled. Poor man. What's it like to be the priest of the dead?

We get to the well near the trees, pull up water and drink. Then we sit on a stone bench. He mutters something, waves away flies and clears his throat. "I tire of asking you, oh Lord," I hear him say. "Why did you take these souls in such cruel ways? Why? And me alive? Why, sir? Why?"

Dionisio begins to mumble. He looks away from me. He's crying. What can I say? Sit and wait, I suppose. Ah, he stands up and so do I.

"Go, son, go into the homes where people are no longer alive. Take what you need. God will forgive you. He must. Go now."

"Thank you," I say and walk away. Poor fellow, abandoned by his congregation. Where is his faith? Will it die too? Does he want to join the dead in the afterlife?

I know from the sun's place in the sky that I have to hurry, have to get back to Izel and the children, have to look inside each dwelling, each adobe hut, every corral. I go from door to door. There, in the shadows something moves. I squint and see a man, squirming on a petate. I back away, close the door and go on to the next door. I push it open and step inside. I call out and hear nothing. Around me I see clothes and bags hanging on the walls and a fire pit in the center with two pots on stones. From outside I hear a clanking noise and something snorts. I open the back door. In the corral, three burros stand beside a water trough.

I take from this place and others only what I think we will need for the journey north. In the end, this amounts to three male burros, one clay pot, wooden plates and cups, spoons, knives, more blankets, and a bundle of homespun clothes.

It's late afternoon when I leave the town and its stench. I'm wearing a woven hat with a wide brim that I took from a dead man. I'm seated on one of the burros, with the other two tethered behind and loaded with my new possessions. My legs almost touch the ground, but my sturdy little mount carries me away from the town at a trot. Not far away I see Mula standing near Izel and David. They're dropping sticks into a fire.

Izel looks up. "Well, look at you! A hat, burros and all those things! How did you—"

"I'm not a thief."

226

"Good."

"And everything has the blessing of the church."

"Davidcito, help Papá with his things."

I stop the burro and get off. David is running up to me but suddenly stops and backs away. "Papá, you stink."

Izel waves me away. She's standing by the fire, still feeding it with branches. "I can smell you from here. You know what they say—the man who reeks can't smell his own stink." She pinches her nose. "José, love, please go wash yourself."

I drop the rope to the burros, toss my hat to David, and walk off along the trail.

"Take care of them, son."

When I get to the stream, I step in where the current eddies. I submerge myself into the cool water, so that only my face stays above the surface. I feel the weeds and pebbles on my back. I think of all the dead that Dionisio had to bury. He was right to ask God why the natives must die. What did they do to deserve such an end? It's getting dark and my mind is drifting. Must get going. Rise. Hurry.

***

I see Izel by the fire. "All clean?" she asks.

I'm still shaking off the water. "And very wet."

"Davidcito, you smell him."

RON ARIAS

David steps close to me and sniffs. Before he can give an answer, I reach down, lift him up and swing him around and around by the arms. He laughs.

"Enough, José. You'll make him crazy. Sit, both of you. Let's eat."

I stop and set David down on the blanket where Yetzi is sleeping. I take off my shirt and pants and wrap myself in another blanket. "What are we eating?" "*Cordero*," Izel says, using the Spanish word for "mutton."

"In English we call that 'mutton,'" I say.

"Muh-tahn."

"Perfect. So let's eat some—"

"Muhtahn!" she shouts.

I tickle David, saying his mother's English is correct— "more or less." Then

David perfectly pronounces the word "mutton."

Izel cuts pieces of meat and hands them to us.

"How did you kill the sheep?" I ask.

"You left the bow and arrows. And I found a good knife when I was unloading the burros."

For a while we chew and swallow in silence, then Izel asks me what I saw in the town.

I want to say I walked into hell. I want to tell her that death was everywhere, but all I can say is that I saw many sick natives and one very old and sad Spanish priest, and he let me take the three burros and the things I brought back.

I look at my sleeping daughter. In the rippling light of the flames she squirms for a moment. I look up at the stars, then look at my children. I think of the girl I pulled from the church. Unable to stop seeing her, I begin to cry.

"José, the dead are in heaven," Izel says. She probably knows I saw something horrible.

My throat thickens and I'm wiping away my tears. "But first they went through hell," I say. "They were living in hell."

Izel hands me another sliver of mutton on the end of a stick. "Here, eat. Don't think about that."

Fat drips off the meat. I place it in my mouth and slowly begin to chew.

"Mutton," David says in English. "I like mutton."

Chapter 17 – Silver Road

With all of us on burros and the old mule trailing with our things, we come upon a white man driving sheep from a field of broken cornstalks. The young shepherd greets us with a cheerful, "Good day." He says that his flock has been feeding on what's left in the field because the farmers are no longer farming. "The plague is killing the Indians. I've seen it in the village up ahead. It's horrible. The devil has cursed these people."

The man picks up a chunk of dry dirt and throws it at a patch of crows. "If my sheep don't eat some of the crop, the rats and birds will finish it all."

He says the flock isn't his and he only takes care of them for the owner, who lives in Mexico. "You know, I'm from the mountains near Bilbao and we have good land for raising sheep. But this here is the best there is. If it weren't for this disease killing the people, it would be paradise."

I ask him about the way to the silver road north and he points his staff toward the hills to the north and west.

"José," Izel says, "a black cloud."

The shepherd looks at Izel and nods. "Stay away from that town. Take the cut on the side of the hill over there, away from the birds. See it?"

"Yes," I answer.

"Follow the trail over the hills to the valley on the other side. Keep going for about two leagues where it joins one of the silver roads. But where are you going?"

"As far away from *cocoliztli* as we can."

"It's moving everywhere."

I thank him and we move on. When we're some distance away I look back and see that he's watching us. "Go with God!" he shouts. "But hurry!"

We reach the trail and climb into the hills. Mula is slowing down, looking wobbly under the weight of our things. The animal veers to one side and then collapses to the ground. We get off the burros and watch the poor beast. David sits on the ground close to Mula's head. When there's no more movement from the chest, no more quivering of the nostrils, he says, "I think Mula is dead."

Izel reaches down and puts a hand on the long, still neck. "Yes, Davidcito, Mula died."

"Why, Mamá?"

"Everything dies sooner or later. Mula was old, very old."

"Why?"

"Everything grows old, Davidcito—Mula, burros, birds, trees. Everything that lives gets old and dies."

David pats the mule and pulls on its mane.

"Mula's spirit is now free," Izel says.

While loading our things onto one of the burros, I tell David, "Mamá means the mule will never again have to carry things. Mula can rest; Mula can sleep forever."

David strokes the mule's long ear. "When people die—"

"Yes," I say, "the same thing happens. Now, enough questions. We have to get going."

"Where do we—"

"Ask your mother. Let's get going."

I pick up my son and set him on the burro in front of Izel. Then I pull the ropes to the other two animals, and we get moving along the trail into the hills. Lots of cactus and only skinny, thorny trees spread out on both sides. I look back at Mula's dark shape on the ground. I didn't want to cut meat from our friend, and I think Izel felt the same way.

All morning and afternoon we skirt villages and avoid people. We are so hungry that we stop to pick red cactus fruit and look for snakes, grasshoppers, lizards, anything edible.

We start across a wide valley that slopes down toward a distant line of hills.

"Look, Papá," David says, pointing ahead.

I see a dark line across the middle of the valley. I'm thinking it's the silver road, then David shouts that something is moving.

"He's right," Izel says. "People moving."

I stop and shift the bow and arrows tied on my back. I shade my eyes, squint and make out the tiniest of figures.

"My little man has the eyes of an eagle," I say.

We spend a long time crossing open, trackless land until we get close enough to the parade of people and beasts. The afternoon wind has stirred up enough dust along the road so that the line of wagons, carts, animals and people now looks like a caravan of slow-moving dun-colored ghosts. The figures shield their faces with blankets, scarves and hats. The convoy is heading north, so we turn in that direction.

Izel easily spots the Nahuas, Tlascaltecas and Otomís, but she can't tell from their clothes who the other natives are. The men and women walk behind the oxen and wagons. Children are walking and some ride on the wagons and carts. At the rear just ahead of the pigs and sheep, a line of black slaves are tied together and watched over by men on horses.

We're on the road now in the line of travelers bound for Guanajuato, Zacatecas and Durango. We're almost in Chichimeca territory, but we're told that we're protected from attacks by the soldiers and native warriors strung out along the length of the caravan.

By late afternoon we're moving alongside an oxcart loaded with barrels of wine and jugs of olive oil. I'm talking to the pink-faced driver holding the reins. I ask him about any cases of *cocoliztli* among natives in the caravan.

"Don't worry about Indian diseases," he says. "The real danger is the savages. North of Querétaro they're in control. So if you and your family want to live, stay with the soldiers."

"The war goes on?"

"Yes, sir. Maybe you don't know it because you're young, but we've been fighting the Chichimeca tribes for many years. They kill soldiers, farmers and the Indians who fight with us. They kill anyone on these roads. They steal what they like and burn the rest. And now some are attacking on horses!"

He asks where we're going and I tell him Zacatecas.

"Then you'll be going through land of the Guachichiles. They're a terror, the worst. So we stay together with the soldiers. You don't want to be alone when those devils attack."

"I know."

"No, you don't."

"But I do. I know how the Guachichiles are."

"How would you know?"

"I lived with them."

"Impossible! A Spaniard like you? And still alive?"

"It's true. I swear it."

The oxcart driver laughs and calls out to someone up ahead. A man in armor steers his horse over to the oxcart. As the horse comes to a halt, the man flips his helmet visor up.

"Captain, listen to this man. He says he's never traveled a silver road, never been through the Gran Chichimeca. But he swears he knows the ways of the savages. Says he lived with the Guachichiles."

Izel has been listening and says she's also lived with the savages.

The soldier removes his helmet to reveal shoulder-length blond hair and a strawcolored beard. He's frowning. He studies us, then looks at my huaraches, at my raggedy shirt, stares at Izel in her dirty white huipil, one arm around David, the other arm cradling Yetzi in the rebozo.

"Tell him what you told me," the oxcart driver says.

The soldier introduces himself as Captain Alejandro González, commander of the unit protecting the caravan. "And you are?"

Maybe I shouldn't have said anything about the Guachis. I talk too much. What would they do to me if they knew I was an English heretic once captured and enslaved by a Chichimeca tribe?

235

"Well," the captain says, "speak up, man!"

"Sorry, sir," I answer, raising my head. "I am José Campos de Medina, and this is my wife, Izel. Both of us were captured by a band of Guachichiles and lived with them as slaves for more than two years. And we escaped."

Captain González begins asking questions, with me answering and Izel sometimes adding details about the lives and habits of "my savages," as she still calls the Guachis. The captain seems especially interested in the movements of the tribe and how they mount raids on Spanish settlements. Then he asks how far we're going.

"To Zacatecas," I answer.

He points to my ragged huaraches. "In those?"

"Yes."

"Zacatecas is many, many leagues away. Weeks and weeks of walking through danger. Your sandals won't last a week."

"I'll make more," I say.

"Well, what you know about the savages could be useful."

"Absolutely!" the oxcart driver says. "I had no idea, and to think that you combed their hair!"

"Only the women," Izel says.

Captain González asks for my complete name again, then wants to know what I do for a living.

"I'm a scrivener."

"I see. Well, I can use your services—but not as a scrivener. I want you to be a scout."

"Captain, I can't leave my wife and children."

"No, no, we'll take care of them too."

Captain González wipes the grime from his face, then offers to give me a good horse to ride and a mule-driven cart for my family and our goods, as well as a modest payment, food and water—all in exchange for our three burros and for my help as an informant on how the Guachichiles fight. "We can do this in a few days when we get to San Miguel. Think of it as work for your King and for Viceroy Enríquez. We'll even give you a proper weapon."

"No need, sir," I say, pointing to my bow and arrows.

"Are you sure?"

"Yes."

"A good musket can save your life."

"A well-placed arrow can do the same."

"We call it a war of blood and fire for a reason. We fire our weapons to kill them."

"But they believe it's their land," I say.

"Not anymore."

"They even fight each other for the land."

"Look, son, the first Spaniards fought hard to bring a Christian way of life to the heathen. We haven't stopped."

"I know that."

Captain González looks at the passing line of black slaves and shakes his head.

"Someday we will prevail."

"And them?" I ask, nodding in the direction of the slaves.

"We need them in the mines. If we don't have enough silver, we can't afford to wage war. And then where would we be? Even with the Chichimecas that we take as slaves and put to work—it's never enough. No, Campos, everybody has a part in this. What's your part?"

I hesitate, thinking of my roles as husband, father, scrivener, and now a soldier's aide in enemy territory.

I'm mulling this over when Izel speaks. "Sir, all we want is a home where we can live and work in peace. I pray for this every day."

The captain nods, still looking at me. "Well, do you want to help us?"

I look at Izel, who's smiling.

"Well, Campos?"

"Yes. You can count on me."

Chapter 18 – Chichimecas

I'm sitting at the rear of a natives' church in San Miguel in the last pew with Izel and the children. It's quiet and people are returning to their seats after receiving Communion.

I hear a loud voice say, "He's got to be the ugliest man alive!"

"Looks like a bunghole," another voice says, followed by laughter.

The voices taunt and jeer, then a calmer, familiar voice asks, "Sir, why do you insult me? I've done you no wrong. Please, let me go."

"And what will you do if I don't?"

"Please, sir, you're hurting me. Stop!"

"It's Oreja," I whisper to Izel. I reach down to the floor and pick up my bow and arrows.

"Be careful, José. Those men sound drunk."

I head to the open doorway. Outside, I see a group of men gathered in the street around a tall man berating Oreja, then striking him once in the face and knocking him down.

What can I do? I'm one against many. Looking to one side of the group, I see a line of about ten barebacked mules. Oreja was probably taking them to pasture somewhere outside the town.

I move to the front of the drunks in the crowd in time to see my friend being kicked by another man. Others, whites and mixed bloods, are calling for more blows.

Before I can yell at them to stop hurting an innocent mule driver, the tall man raises an arm and asks for quiet. He drinks from a jug someone hands him, then tells his victim that for two of his mules he will forgive his "monstrous" appearance and let him go. "What do you say, ugly Indian?"

Now or never, I'm thinking. "*¡Orejón!*" I shout. "*¡Orejón!*" The drunks around me start shouting the same word, meaning "big ear."

"So what do you say, *Orejón?*" the tall tormentor asks my friend, who's now standing and holding a hand to his bloodied mouth. When he recognizes me he smiles.

"Look, he's human!" someone yells.

"Still ugly," another voice says.

"Listen to me!" I shout. "Now that we know he can look like a Christian, what do you say we treat this man with a little justice? Let's make him a target. Let's stand him over there by his mules. Then I will shoot an arrow through his big ear. If I do, you let him go with all his mules. If I miss, then this gentleman here gets to take his two mules."

"What if you kill the Indian?" asks a fat man with a patch over one eye.

"We take all the mules!" another man says.

"But is that just?" I ask.

"You're the one who should worry about justice," the tall man says, drinking from his jug, then handing it off to the one-eyed fat man. "It's you they'll arrest for murder."

"So what do you all say?" I ask in my loudest voice. "Can I go ahead and shoot the arrow?"

Shouts of "Yes!" and "Shoot!" come from all around. Then I hear wagers on whether or not I can put an arrow through the ear.

I want to clear some space and wave at the men to stand back. Behind them I see people leaving the church and joining the crowd. Oreja is now being pushed toward the mules. "Silence!" I yell, then tell Oreja to close his eyes and not to move.

When all is set and everyone is quiet, I reach back and pull an arrow out of my quiver. I quickly fit the bowstring in the cut at the arrow's blunt end, raise the bow and pull the bowstring back as if I were sighting a rabbit that suddenly stops and is still. I release the arrow. As soon as it passes through the big ear, there's a moment of silence, then I hear cheers, whistles and hands clapping.

I look around, smiling, and see Izel rush up to Oreja with a cloth for his wound. He looks stunned as he presses the cloth to his ear. Another Nahua woman gives him two tamales from her basket.

Someone hands me my spent arrow, and after a few men collect on their winning wagers, the crowd breaks up and the rowdy ones leave. The young priest—not Father Two Hands—approaches me and my family. "It's God's will."

"Excuse me," Izel says, "but my husband also helped."

"Of course, but God directed the arrow. I only want to congratulate the shooter. From the looks of it, you saved that poor fellow's life. Those men were in no condition to be charitable."

I nod and we walk away. In the distance, I watch Oreja lead his animals into a corral behind the inn where I figure he's staying. I walk over to the corral with Izel and the children. Oreja is setting down a bundle of cornstalks for the mules and he looks angry. He asks me why I shot him with an arrow.

"As my father would say, 'Well is him who ends well.' And this ended very well indeed."

"You could have killed me."

"But I didn't."

"How did you know you wouldn't miss?"

"I just knew."

"Oreja," Izel says, "José learned to shoot with the Guachis. He got very good."

"I don't care how good he is. He was playing with my life."

"How is your ear?" I ask.

"I'm alive."

"But how is it?"

"There's a hole."

"It's all I could think of to do."

"If your sisters were here," Izel says, "they would be thanking José."

"I suppose I should be grateful. So thank you, José."

"I'll be back," Izel says and walks toward the inn, Yetzi hanging on her back.

"Watch your son."

Little David pulls on Oreja's tunic. "Can I see your ear?"

Oreja squats down and turns his head to let David stare at the dried blood on the ear.

"Does it hurt?" David asks.

"A little."

"Can I touch it?"

"No," Oreja says, wagging a finger as he stands.

"Please."

"After it heals."

Izel calls David to come and eat at the inn, then signals to me and Oreja. "Gentlemen, you too!"

After David skips off toward his mother, Oreja shades his eyes from the midday sun and turns to me. "Where are you staying?"

"At the presidio. The captain in charge of guarding the caravan hired me to help him understand how the Guachichiles fight. I'll have my own horse and Izel and the children will ride in a cart."

"Be careful, José. The offer sounds too generous. Your captain may have you doing more than talking about savages."

"We'll see, but let's go eat."

"No, food can wait. I have bad news."

"What?"

"Let's sit down over there."

I follow Oreja to the shade of a large huisache tree. He sits on the ground and I squat next to him.

"He's still after you," Oreja says.

"Who?"

"The foreman, the one with the red beard."

"Damn!" I mutter in English. "Damn that man!"

Oreja looks at me with a puzzled expression. "I'm sorry, but your life's in danger.

He's denounced you to the Inquisition."

"What can I do?"

"Well, stay away from churches and priests. No more Mass. You shouldn't be in that church anyway. That's for us natives. *Cocoliztli* is finding too many of us and it's not safe for Izel and the children."

"And you?"

"The way people stay away from me," Oreja says, chuckling, "it's the same with the pestilence. It's one advantage of being born as I was."

"Be serious."

"I am. It's true, most people stay away from me. Listen, how long will you stay here?"

He's waiting for an answer but I'm staring at a line of red ants crossing the dirt in front of me. Oreja touches my arm and repeats the question.

"My God!" I blurt. "Why does that man hate me so much? I am nothing to him!"

"You're wrong."

"Nothing."

"You're everything."

"How's that?"

"You're everything he's not. You're free of his control, free of the mine, free to hide, free to have your woman and children. My God, you're free to feel love!"

"How do you know this?"

"It's true. Red Beard may be jealous of you."

"What exactly does he know?"

"Only that you escaped with your family and Hassan."

"What about you?"

"Don Antonio protected me and Minoru. He told the church investigator that you left only with Hassan."

"Is Antonio in trouble?"

"No. They suspect nothing. As far as they're concerned, you left without telling anyone. You're not the first mine worker to escape."

"What about the *patrón*, Don Bartolomé?"

"He's safe. Antonio said the *patrón* told them he knew nothing of you."

"I have to think about this."

"Think later."

Oreja gets to his feet and waits for me to stand. "Listen, José, no one says you're not free to eat. Come."

I don't want to but I rise and I follow Oreja to the front door of the inn. "You never answered my question," Oreja says. "How long are you staying here?"

"In two days we leave with the soldiers for Zacatecas."

"Good. The sooner you leave, the better."

"And you?"

"I'm going south to Mexico with silver."

Oreja nods with a big smile. He says he and his mule drivers already delivered wheat, wine, tools and other goods to buyers in Guanajuato. But before he could return to Pachuca, one of the smaller mines hired him after an axle of its sole wagon broke from the weight of silver bars. Oreja agreed to transport the shipment to the mint by pack mule.

"That's a lot of silver," I say. "What about thieves or Chichimeca attacks?"

"José, it took us two days of travel from Guanajuato to San Miguel. That's the most dangerous part of the journey because the Pames have been attacking settlers and wagon trains more than ever. But my mules had a royal escort! Soldiers all around my mules. So I'm not worried."

Oreja opens the door for me. "I have soldiers because that silver is going to the King."

***

Two days later, Captain González apologizes for being unable to provide a twowheeled cart for Izel and the children. They'll have to continue on a single burro with the two pack burros trailing behind. But

247

I got the horse I was promised, though it was an aging nag that would never do in a skirmish with the Chichimeca warriors. "That's the best I can do for now," the captain said. "You have no idea how stretched the treasury is these days. But I promise you'll have food and shelter every day and night until we reach Zacatecas."

As we move north from San Miguel, I realize with increasing dread that the escort is pathetically short of men to protect such a long, slow-moving convoy of wagons, carts, animals and people. At least most of the travelers, unless they're slaves, carry swords, harquebuses and muskets of their own. Even so, if we're attacked I reckon that fifteen mounted soldiers and three dozen or so armed Tlascaltecas, Purépecha, Mexicas and Otomís will not be nearly enough to defend our cumbersome caravan.

The landscape is changing. Drier, hotter, no more villages, no more sheep, no more crops. The procession is now snaking through a land of brush, mesquite and cactus, passing barren hills and dry ravines.

Unless we are spending the night next to or near a presidio, we usually make camp before nightfall by the side of the road. Wagons and carts cluster together; animals are fed and watered. We light fires, prepare our meals and eat. After long, hot days on a dusty road, sleep is easy.

On such a night, resting against our saddles by a fire, Captain González asks me if I think we have enough soldiers and Indian friends to fight off the savages.

"No," I say, "not nearly enough."

"Of course, it's never enough. I thought you might say that."

"Captain, from what I know of the Guachichiles—and you say we're now crossing their land—it's not so much a matter of numbers. I think it's a matter of knowing how they attack that might help us."

"You mean ambushes?"

"Yes, but it's more important to know how they move."

"You mean from one place to another?"

"No, no. How they move their bodies."

"I don't follow you."

"They're like jaguars, quick and quiet until they surprise you with their screams and hollering. By then it's too late because suddenly they're upon you with only death on their minds."

Captain González scratches at the dirt with a stick. "I've made two trips like this. Each time the savages came at us where the road runs through a canyon or cuts below a place where they can see us, where we can't run or defend ourselves."

"How many warriors in each attack?"

"Maybe fifty or sixty."

"On horses?"

"The first time only three or four on horses. The second time many more."

"How many died?"

"Well, each time they came directly at us, charging like devils from hell. We finished off some of them before they got to us. Then the rampage started. We lost cattle, horses, a shipment of fine fabrics—"

"But people, how many people died?"

"Counting the Indians and slaves, we lost eight. On the second trip twenty-three people died. Some were still alive with arrows in them or left with half a scalp. We had no doctor, so the barber and a Nahua healer did what they could."

I use my finger to draw a typical route between two low hills. Then I suggest that far off to each side of the caravan, out of sight, one mounted man should ride ahead to search for Guachichiles. If one of the scouts sees them in the distance, he should return to the caravan. And then the captain and his force should attack them with as much surprise as possible.

"Will we have to use most of our men?" the captain asks.

"Yes, but we'll have the advantage."

"Have you ever fought the Guachichiles?" "Once— defending myself against two attackers."

"So you don't know if your plan might work?"

"Not for certain, but I believe their ambush party would not expect us to surprise them."

After a long, thoughtful pause, the captain agrees to the plan.

"Captain, I'd like to be one of the two scouts."

"Of course, I assumed that."

"But I need a better horse."

"You can take mine—I'll trade you."

"But, sir—"

"It's fine, José. I never leave the column anyway."

***

Morning comes soon enough. Under the dim light before the sun rises I sharpen my penknife on a smooth, small stone I keep with my quills and inkhorn. Father's penknife is the only treasure I have from my life in England.

David and Izel watch me as I move the little knife across my skin to shave off the shadow of a beard. Then I remove my clothes and ask Izel to help me rub rendered pig's fat all over my body.

"Why?" Izel wants to know.

"You'll see."

When this is done, I lie down on the ground, telling David to smear dirt on my skin. He starts slowly, then begins spreading handfuls of dirt on my chest and stomach, as if it were a new game, laughing, telling me I'm a big, dusty lizard. When I think I'm dark enough, I tie on my buckskin sandals, take my bow and arrows, then complete a running jump up onto the bare back of the captain's bay stallion.

"Be careful, English," Izel says as my mount trots off into the brush.

The other rider chosen to scout ahead is a Spanish veteran of many skirmishes with different tribes of Chichimecas. He rides fully clothed, protecting himself with a metal breastplate and helmet, boots and leggings. Besides a sword, he also carries a musket and bull-hide shield.

By late morning, I haven't sighted anything of interest beyond the usual movements of small animals. I'm scanning the horizon over the scrub of cactus and spindly shrubs when a flock of birds bursts into the air less than a stone's throw ahead of me. I stop the horse and listen. Faint voices. Off the horse and on the ground, I wrap the reins around a branch, then step away as if I were stalking a deer.

I pull an arrow out of the quiver and place the feathered end on the bowstring. I hear the voices again but louder. I stop, and through the branches of a mesquite tree I see two figures. Young men or boys, one black, one brown. Their faces and bodies are

252

painted with red streaks, painted for attack. Knives are on the ground and they're eating bloody parts of something they've probably just killed. Now they're talking again and I'm catching some words. But a black Guachi? Maybe he's a runaway slave, or was he captured in a raid? The boys have no horses, so they must be sentries for a raiding party nearby.

With my bowstring still drawn, I move one foot back. But no! My foot cracks a twig. The boys stop eating, cock their heads and slowly rise.

"Down!" I shout in Guachichil and step into the clearing. It was the first word I learned from Hump. Whenever the old lady wanted out of the chair on my back, she'd yell the word and I had to kneel so she could untie herself and get off.

The boys stare at me, not moving, mouths open. Again I say the word for "down" and move the bow and arrow up and down. The boys lower themselves into a squat and then I say "knife" in Guachichil. I kick the dirt sideways, gesturing with the drawn bow for them to push their knives away from themselves.

Then with grunts, gestures and a few gruff words in Guachichil, I get them to lie face down on the ground. Then I collect the knives and their bows and arrows. When the black boy reaches for a rock, I shoot my arrow so that it glances off the rock and knocks it farther from the boy's hand. In the moment he pulls his hand back,

I have another arrow in place on the bowstring. They are still and I back away and find my stallion. I toss the knives and bows into the brush but keep the arrows.

Back at the caravan, which is now moving ahead, I report that I came across what I think are two Guachichil sentries of a war party. Captain González takes back his horse, gives me another mount, then with most of the soldiers and native fighters we go looking for the enemy.

When we reach the area where I surprised the two young warriors, we search in vain for signs of a large force of attackers. All that I find are my own footprints and those of the boys.

On our return to the caravan, the captain asks me if I thought the boys took me for a Spaniard disguised as a savage.

"I don't think so," I say. "They were too scared. And I behaved like a Guachichil."

"Too bad we didn't find the main bunch."

Later that night, I lie next to Izel. David and Yetzi are sleeping between us. I tell her I didn't have the heart to harm the boys. "I could have but I didn't."

Izel leans over the children and kisses me on the lips. "José," she says, settling back with her face to the stars, "you showed them mercy."

"I was going to leave them but that's when I made a noise. I had to do something."

"Remember Chookles?"

"Chuckles."

"Well, I liked him and I think you did too."

"I did."

"What if he had been one of those boys? Would you kill him?"

"No."

"To me Chuckles seemed like a child, always playing and laughing. Well, maybe there was something of him in those boys."

"Maybe, I don't know."

We're silent for a while, then Izel reaches over and touches my arm. "Sleep, José," she says softly.

"I'm a savage," I say with a growl.

"You don't fool me."

"Because you know me."

"I know all your secrets. You're not even a Spaniard."

"Oh my God," I say and laugh.

"And not Catholic."

"Shh!"

"Don't worry, your secret is safe with me."

"Yes?"

"If you clean off all that dirt."

"In the morning."

***

As the first light begins to brighten the eastern sky, I look toward the horizon and see the figures approaching on foot. None cry out, none shout.

My skin is still dark with grime. I lie under part of a blanket next to Izel. She's sitting and nursing Yetzi while David plays nearby in the dirt with the daughter of a Spanish tanner and his mulatta wife.

As the silhouettes come closer, I reach for my bow and quiver but can't feel them. Then I try to rise but can only get to my knees. I want to say the word "Chichimecas" but can't. I want to tell Izel before it's too late. I want everyone in the caravan to wake up. I want to cry out that we are about to be attacked. I want the soldiers to begin firing their weapons. I try to shout but can't open my mouth. I can only watch as the wave of screaming warriors sweeps over everything.

That's when I see the same black warrior from the day before about to bash little David with a stone attached to a handle. "No!" I yell. "No!"

In the darkness Izel reaches across the sleeping children and touches my chest.

"José, what's the matter?"

"Nothing."

"You're sweating."

"It's nothing. Go back to sleep."

"Well, cover yourself."

I hear her sigh. Then I stare at the twinkling canopy above. For some time, I remember the attack, watch the silhouettes appear against the early sky, see them approach, and finally see the two boy warriors run past me and my family. For a while I listen to the quiet of the night, drifting into a dreamless sleep.

Chapter 19 – Zacatecas

In Zacatecas the pestilence kills natives in the mines by the hundreds. We'll have to flee again, this time to Durango or beyond to the frontier. But we have no money, no burros. When we arrived here, I traded our three animals for a shack and a flock of chickens. Izel sells eggs and I barely make enough as a scrivener on the steps of the town hall to keep us fed.

I sit with my box and wait. The black word *ESCRIBANO* is burned into the wood on one side. A sheet of paper, my quill, inkhorn, a vial of tree resin and a blotter are spread out before me. Only one customer so far today.

If only Captain González were here. I could use his counsel. But he and his troops left weeks ago with wagons of silver going south. He's years older than I am, but when I was his scout we grew close. And we were alike in one way. We were frauds. I found this out when I told him about my disguise as a Guachichil. He said I must have cast a spell on the two boys, and I told him it was just a disguise, nothing more. We'd been talking about missing the kitchens and other pleasures of Seville. He would mention certain foods and places and I would nod and agree.

Then he frowned and turned serious. "You don't fool me," he said.

"What?"

"You say you're from Seville and when I told you where you could eat the best grilled sardines in the city, you didn't know where the Tower of Gold was. Anyone who's ever been to Seville has seen the tower. It's right there next to the Guadalquivir."

I couldn't answer. He'd caught me in my own lie. He said the tower connects everyone who's sailed to the Indies or who's come from the Indies because all of Spain's silver and gold is unloaded by the tower.

"Who are you?" he asked me. "What are you?"

I think I decided to tell him the truth because he had told me he never wanted to be a military man, that he only "pretended" to be a soldier. I didn't hold back. I told him everything about my past, everything but my suspicions that I might be Jewish.

"So you're a fraud too," he said and smiled. "Ever wonder why so many of us here are inventions? Most of us come for a new start or to improve our lot in life. But because it's a world full of new people and new lands, it's easy for some of us to leave our past behind, walk away from our crimes and debts, even escape a bad marriage and start a new family. I know such men, José. So cover your tracks well. Go on inventing yourself."

"What about you?"

"I'm stuck being a soldier. But I've been lucky—they keep promoting me!"

I could use some laughs now—and his advice. We've been here for more than three months and customers are few. My one request today was from a Spanish woman who had me write a letter to her sister in Seville. She begged her sister and brother-in-law to come to Zacatecas. She insisted I write that the town was a place where fortunes are made as easily as plucking apples from a tree. *Come, sister*, she had me write, *as soon as you can. Treasure is everywhere. And make sure your husband brings all his shoemaking tools. There's great need of good footwear in the north.*

Not a word about the plague, but then why would she mention such a killer of natives? She painted Zacatecas as a kind of paradise with streets paved in silver. Who was I to change her words? Such letters are not about telling the truth. No, they're meant to persuade. So I write without questions, my mind elsewhere, my thoughts only about saving Izel and my children from *cocoliztli*. How can we escape? Beyond Izel's prayers, what can we do?

Ah, here's a man coming my way. He's dark and wears shabby clothes. A customer? He's looking at me. "Please, sir, a favor," he says. "Would you write me a letter to my uncle?"

"Of course," I say. "Sit." He squats next to me, then admits he has no money.

"How's that?" I say. I lean away from him, looking at the grimy face, the quivering, pouty lips, and the trembling, prayerful hands.

"I lost everything in a gamble last night. I'll pay you when I have the money. On the grave of my dear sainted mother, I swear I'll pay."

I pity him, but maybe if I write his letter he'll attract someone who *can* pay. Lid down on the box, my tools on top, and I'm ready. "What's your uncle's name?" I ask him.

"God bless you."

"His name?"

"I'm not a charity. I'll pay you someday."

"His name?"

"Bonifacio Durán."

"Title?"

"Mister."

"You call him uncle?"

"Yes."

"My dear uncle?"

"Oh, yes! My dear and most beloved uncle."

"What's *your* name?"

"Ignacio Torres."

"So I'll begin. My dear uncle—"

"Most beloved uncle."

"Ignacio, if you begin with those words, he might think you're just trying to flatter him with sugary words."

"But it's true, I am."

"Ignacio—"

"Nacho, please."

"Fine, Nacho. You want him to send you money, no?"

"Yes."

"Then you have to sound sad, desperate."

"I am."

"So let's not write anything too sweet or you might sound false. Keep it sad and desperate. Do you understand?"

"Yes."

Before we start, he tells me about his beastly work hauling rocks out of a flooded mine and about his gambling losses. "You know," he says, "most men have three weaknesses—women, drink and gambling. For me it's just one."

From my time at the Purísima mine I know that the miners, if they're not slaves, can keep a few of the rocks they carry out. Any silver dust or nuggets they can get out of the ore, they can keep.

Ignacio says he found a good nugget, had it refined and sold it for a treasure, for more money than he's ever had. "Then the devil's little worm got into me," he says. "In one night I lost it all!"

"Nacho, giving money to a gambler is risky."

"Then we must tell him I'm giving up my vice."

"Are you?"

"I'll try."

"Then that's what I'll write. Your uncle can judge whether or not you tell the truth."

"Why so much truth? He won't know what I really do."

"Nacho, truth and oil always come to the surface."

I sound like Father, always giving customers a bit of wisdom. This man before me, what else should I tell him? And who am I to give advice? Look at what's happened to me, to my family.

The miner touches my arm. "Young sir, my letter?"

"Yes, yes."

I write the letter, then tell Ignacio to make his mark. I pat the squiggle with the blotter, fold the paper and slip it into an envelope. I write his uncle's name and address on one side, then seal it with a drop of resin. I tell him I'll send the letter with the next caravan going south.

"Sir," he says, "thank you a thousand times. I will pay you back."

"Don't worry about it."

"I swear I'll pay you. On the grave of my beloved mother, I swear—"

"Nacho, you already told me that. And you're speaking sugary and false again. Forget the fee. It's only one real anyway."

"But wait." He raises a finger. "I think I can help you find customers."

"How's that?"

"If you permit me, I want to take you to La Tempestad. I think your services could be used there."

"La Tempestad?"

"A woman . . . and a tavern."

"Why would I go to a tavern?"

"It's really a *pulquería*, but there's more than just drinking *pulque*. I told you about the three weaknesses men have. Well, they can satisfy all three desires at La Tempestad. She takes care of that."

"She?"

"The owner. That's her name."

I first heard the Spanish word for "tempest" from Hassan. It's what he called the first big storm to hit the ship after leaving Africa.

"Why do they call her La Tempestad?"

"You'll see. Come with me."

Should I leave my place on the steps? Looking around, all I see is a cluster of men standing near the entrance to the town hall. In the street a woman and children beg with their hands out. And coming my way is a barefoot man leading two horses over the cobblestones. "Very well, Nacho. Let's take a look."

I put my things in the box and Ignacio leads me through back streets and footpaths to a long adobe place with few windows and only one entrance. It's a narrow doorway covered by a burlap curtain. In the light of late afternoon, above the curtain, I can just make out the shape of a curved spike from a maguey cactus. I hear a mix of many voices, laughter and the sound of a flute, drum and a woman singing. I follow

Ignacio, but before he enters, he tells me, "Everyone calls her La Zamba or La Zamba Tempestad."

"Zamba?"

"Like me—African father, Purépecha mother. Come, you can meet La Zamba. Then maybe we can throw a few dice."

"Nacho, wait," I clutch my box and step aside to let a man stumble out to the street. "I thought you were asking your uncle for help because you had no money."

"I don't, but you do."

"Nacho, I don't throw dice; I don't gamble. And you shouldn't either. You promised your uncle, remember?"

"Everyone gambles. Maybe not with dice or cards, but we all gamble."

"I told you, I don't gamble."

"But you do."

"What are you saying?"

"Gambling's in our blood.'

"No, it's not."

"But it is. You wake up every morning. Do you get up or go back to sleep for a little longer? It's a gamble—because what if you decide to get up and you stumble, fall and break a bone? Well, that was a gamble and you lost the bet."

"That's different."

"No, that's life. We decide to do one thing instead of another. It's all a gamble.

You came with me. That was a gamble. I quit my work in the mine, another gamble." "Alright, I see your point."

We step inside and a large, big-breasted woman says, "Good afternoon, my dear Nacho." She waves a handkerchief in one hand and holds a kind of club in the other.

"And who is this handsome young man with a box?" "He can tell you."

I make a slight bow. "José Campos, at your service."

"José, I am La Tempestad. But you can call me Zamba."

She laughs loudly. "As you see," she says, smiling and gesturing with one hand. "I can offer you many things—all the *pulque*, beer and wine you want to drink, all the cards and darts you want to play, and over there, sitting on those benches, all the love you can pay for. They are my girls. You choose. Any one of them."

Across the cavernous, smoky room, lit by candles and oil lanterns, I can barely make out the row of women, although at the tables all around I can better see a throng of men and some women— from dark and grubby to fair-skinned and well-dressed. They are drinking, smoking, eyeing cards or throwing dice. And near the entrance, off to the left, I notice a black man slapping the top of a box, which he holds under one arm. Next to him another man is playing a flute and a woman in a huipil is singing a kind of chant.

"Come, boys," La Tempestad says, then shouts, "Make way!" She moves through the crowd, waving the white handkerchief and poking people in her way with the club. "Move!" she orders again as she opens a path to a serving counter that's cluttered with pitchers, jugs, cups and mugs. She turns to me and with a cackling laugh announces, "The first is on me, José. But Nacho—he pays for his own."

La Tempestad speaks to the man behind the counter. He's pouring a whitish liquid out of a clay pitcher into a pewter mug. When he finishes, he looks at his boss and waits for her order. "Wine for the Spaniard, right?" she says, looking back at me.

"Excuse me," I say, "but I didn't come to drink."

"Then women."

"No."

"Well, if you're with Nacho, you probably want dice, right?"

I glance at Ignacio, who tells her that I'm a scrivener and would like to offer my services to her customers. "For all of us who can't write," Ignacio says, "José can write down our promises to pay off the bets we lose. He can write letters, love songs, wills, whatever we want—and for a very small fee."

La Tempestad is frowning. Then she slaps the handle of her club in the palm of one hand and says, "Very well. Go work your magic, José. I'll tell everyone what you can do for them. But you don't get a taste of my girls unless you pay."

"That's not going to happen."

"Well, we'll see. What if you write something for one of my lovelies and she wants to pay you with herself?"

"I'll refuse."

"Listen, young man . . . if it does happen, you pay me."

"La Tempestad—"

"Zamba."

"Zamba, I'm married, content with my wife."

"That's good, José. But look around you. Many of these men are also married. They come to let go, to be what they can't be at home. Or they have no woman, no home. In a way, this is their home. Games, drink, a bit of friendship in one of the back rooms."

She turns from me and whistles. After all but a few drunks oblivious of others quiet down, she points her club at me and announces my name and that I'm a scrivener offering to write letters, love songs, poems, promissory notes or whatever a customer wants.

"Write me a love song!" a voice cries out.

"Who could love you?" another says.

"Shut up!"

"Or what?"

"Or a blade under your ribs!"

"Boys!" Zamba shouts. "Enough! Behave yourselves or out you go!"

***

I work at a small table set outside the back door in a passageway to the rooms of the "Zambanada,"—or Zamba's herd, as everyone calls her group of prostitutes. Away from the babble and racket occurring in the tavern, I sit with my materials in front of me, candles to one side. My first client is a mestiza prostitute who asks me to write a letter to her mother in Puebla. "You can't say what I do," the young woman tells me. She jabs a finger at the sheet of paper on the table. "Just put down I'm working as a domestic."

"Yes, but let's start at the beginning."

"Oh, and how is my daughter? Put that in there."

"The beginning, miss . . . ?"

"Cristina."

"Cristina what?"

"Just Cristina."

"Something more?"

"Put Amada. Yes, Cristina La Amada."

"The Loved One?"

"It's true. The men all call me that."

"Fine, Cristina. Let's start at the beginning."

I finish her letter and within minutes other people are waiting. Before I start, I tell each person that I'm not a lawyer or notary, in case they want me to write something to do with laws, petitions and decrees. I write only what they tell me to write. And if they can't think of how to say something, I can help.

One customer after another sits before me. By the time I run out of paper, I've written more than a dozen letters, five promissory notes, one last will and testament and—for free—one word on a scrap of paper for a young mine worker who just wanted to see his Zapoteco name written in Spanish.

I get home that night tired but my mind filled with all that I saw and heard at La Tempestad. Izel greets me with tales of her own—the rooster chasing David, David chasing the hens, Yetzi's new moves crawling around, and news about *cocoliztli* deaths.

When I tell her that I'm now earning good money working at a tavern, she jumps up to embrace me. Then we lie on a petate next to where the children are sleeping. I tell her the place is run by a very large *zamba* who carries a club.

"Does she use it?"

"I don't know. I work in the back and don't see what happens in the big room."

"José, you smell of tobacco."

"Does that bother you?"

271

"No, I like it."

"So many smokers there."

With only one candle burning in the room and as quietly as we can, we remove our clothes and embrace again, this time both on our knees. "You still smell," she whispers.

"And you?" I say and sniff around her neck.

"Yes, what do I smell of?"

I bow my head, nuzzling and sniffing in the mass of long black hair covering one of her shoulders. "You smell of—no, you *taste* of something sweet."

I run a finger across her lips, slowly zigzagging across her chin, throat, breasts, stomach, stopping just above the part that is, as I tell her, "sweeter than honey."

She giggles, then lowers herself onto the petate, arms spread out. "English," she whispers, "come here."

***

I learn that despite the clergy's condemnation of gambling and prostitution, along with viceroyal decrees against these practices, money games and whoring flourish on the frontier. In Zacatecas and the mining camps farther north, life so far from the center of power is lawless, dangerous and deadly, especially now that the scourge is taking so many native workers and their families.

But for some people, even if they are not employed in the mines, profits are high. And this includes me.

I get in the habit of leaving some letters unsealed so I can read parts to Izel before sealing and sending them in the postal bags of soldiers, traders and others traveling south.

Cristina La Amada tells the other women I can be trusted, so the prostitutes seem to like asking me to write their letters, songs, and poems. Most cannot read, but that doesn't matter, since they now have paper with their thoughts, desires and dreams written in words they can recite from memory.

I never spoke of these women to Izel, afraid I'd upset her or stir the pot of jealousy. Father would tell customers with roving desires—it's best not to stir such a pot. So I never read the letters of the prostitutes to Izel. But all the rest of what I write for others she can hear. Today for amusement I read from a letter by the owner of a small mine.

"Very desired and beloved wife. I want to tell you how much I miss you. If God permits, as soon as you read this letter, I beg you to sell everything, all our property, our house and furniture, and make arrangements to come to this new world to join me in a better life than is possible in that wasteland of want that is Spain today. Bring linens and our paintings, saffron, five cured hams from Ronda, and at least ten pounds of rice, and do everything in your

273

power to bring with you a candlemaker and two masters in weaving woolens, for they will profit us greatly. Food is plentiful and cheap, and I have a house full of silver and you will have blacks, a man and a woman, to serve you. They are fine specimens and the male already speaks Spanish quite well. I bought them together at a good price. And you'll find no fault in my Indian cook, who prepares excellent meals. You will lack for nothing. I implore you to come as soon as you can. I love you more than my life."

Izel asks me to read the letter again. Afterward, she asks me if I think he's telling the truth.

"No one really tells the truth," I say. "Most people want something, so they want me to write words that will get them what they want. This man wants his wife. Maybe he wants her to bear his children. He didn't seem that old."

"I don't like the way he talks about slaves."

"That's how they are. They have no idea what it's like to be a slave. This man even lied about his two slaves. He never bought them. He won them in a bet."

"Did you tell him you were once a slave?"

"No, and he wouldn't believe me if I did. They all accept me as a common Spaniard, a scrivener. And that's all they need to know."

"Why did he want so many hams from Ronda? Wherever that is."

I fold the letter and insert it into the envelope. "I asked the same thing and he was surprised that I didn't know that the best hams come from Ronda. I told him I left Seville when I was a boy and didn't know much about hams."

"I like ham," Izel says. "When I lived in the Spaniard's house we ate pork almost every day. We had our own pigs."

"I didn't eat pork until I got to the orphanage, and that wasn't much at all."

"What's a Ronda ham?"

"The miner says it's darker than other hams and cured on the bone. It's so delicious that sometimes when he first puts a very thin slice on his tongue and begins to chew, his whole body tingles and he feels like making love."

"Really? He said that?"

"That's why he was in La Tempestad."

"What kind of husband is that? How can he say he loves his wife?"

"He's probably eating too much of that ham!"

"Well, none of it for you."

"Never, love of my life."

"Good."

I seal the envelope with the man's letter, then tell Izel I have some bad news.

"One of my customers," I tell her, "got a letter from a cousin in Puebla, informing him that *cocoliztli* has already killed more than eighty thousand people in the province of Tlascala. At the hacienda where the cousin works, the disease has taken more than two hundred natives, some blacks and even a few Spaniards."

Izel clutches her throat.

"We have to leave soon," I say. "We have the money now. I can buy a good horse and a cart."

The next day, I buy supplies for my scrivener work and for the trip, then with Ignacio's help I return home with my goods. For the horse and cart, La Zamba can point me to the best seller. She knows just about all the merchants, craftsmen and traders in Zacatecas. I also want to say my goodbyes to her, to Ignacio—who's now serving drinks behind the counter—and to many of my customers who might be in the afternoon crowd of patrons.

I enter without the box under my arm. La Zamba probably guesses that I'm leaving for the north. I already told her about the fear Izel and I have of the pestilence.

"You're joining the caravan to Durango, no?" she says.

"We leave in two days, but I need to buy a cart and horse first."

276

"My Spanish scribe, you're in luck. See that white man over there? Alone in the corner?"

"I see him."

"He's been here two days. He pays to sleep with one of the girls. We feed him and give him wine. He likes watching the dice. He came to Zacatecas with a horse and a cart and now wants to sell them. I think he's a tanner by trade and wants to settle here, but I can't be sure if that's what he actually said. He barely speaks Spanish." "I'll talk to him."

"Good luck. He's English. I think that's why he sits alone."

"Well, I'll try to talk to him. I know some English."

"Ave María, what don't you know?"

"A prisoner of English pirates taught me."

"José, we're going to miss you. *I* will miss you, my friend."

"You've been good to me, Zamba."

"Go, go talk to the man."

I walk over to his table and greet him in English. His broad face is a ruddy pink and he looks to be well above thirty years of age.

"Well, I'll be hanged! Is that English you're speaking?"

"It is, sir."

He extends a hand. "Put her there, mate. And sit your arse down. Roger Brown's me name."

"Joseph Fields."

"You the second chap speaking English to me since I left Mexico. First fellow was in San Miguel. Big red beard he had. Was with a priest but only the red beard spoke English."

"Excuse me, sir," I say and stand up. "I have to be somewhere."

"Don't go."

"I have to. I'm sorry."

"And here I thought we'd talk a bit of the Queen's tongue."

I turn and wave to my friends. "Goodbye, Nacho! Goodbye, Zamba! Goodbye, everyone!"

"And the horse and cart?" La Zamba yells above the din.

"Not from him!" I shout and hurry out into the street.

Chapter 20 – Fugitive

"Run!"

"Why should I?"

"They'll burn you."

"No, they won't."

"They will."

"They haven't burned an Englishman in years."

"They'll arrest you."

"Alright, I'll go."

"Now, José—run away!"

"Yes, Mamá. I'll run; I'll hide."

The flame from a single candle in the room catches Izel's glistening eyes. I pull her close and we hold each other.

"I'll be back."

"Don't let them catch you. We're not leaving our home. I have the Rarámuri boys helping and the children do so much more now. David's almost a man and Yetzi's no longer a little girl."

"I'll tell them," I say and cross the room to the courtyard door. I step out into the morning sunlight to see David and Yetzi sitting on the ground shucking corn. Green husks lie scattered to one side next to the ears of corn. Nearby, a black hen moves about pecking loose kernels. In the years since we came to the place we and the other settlers call Los Olivos, corn is what we grow, along with vegetables, fruits and olives.

I grab a green ear of corn and squat between my children. I peel back a strip of husk. "I have to leave," I say.

They stop shucking and look at me.

"I told you someday I might have to leave this valley."

Yetzi tosses an ear of corn at the black hen, missing as the bird runs away flapping its wings. "Why, Papá?"

"You know why."

"Why now?"

"Someone went to the church in Santa Bárbara and told them. Remember what I said about a man with a red beard, a man from England? He knows I was never Catholic. To him I'm a heretic, a Lutheran. He must have reported me to the Church. If they find me, I'll be taken away and punished, maybe executed."

My children listen with wide-open eyes. They look confused and frightened. I stand up and step over to one side of the doorway where Izel is now standing. "David, get me the machete over there."

He rises and retrieves the machete that's hanging on the far wall. He places it in my hand, handle first. I begin poking the blade tip into a crack between two of the mud bricks. When I've widened it to the width of a finger, I give the machete to David, then remove the leather pouch from around my waist and pull out the penknife.

"As you know, this was given to me by my father. It's all I have of my family in England. I'm going to hide it here and cover it. It'll be our secret."

I put the knife back in the pouch and start pushing it into the crevice.

"Don't go," Yetzi says, crying and hugging me from behind.

"I'll be back, Yetzita. Think of my little knife as me, as my life. Wherever I am, I'll also be here with you."

"No, Papá!"

"Don't worry, sweetheart."

"When are you coming back?" David asks.

"I don't know, son. Soon, I hope. Until then, you'll be the man of our home."

"Children," Izel says, waving them away, "Papá has to get his things together. David, go get Mancha ready. Yetzita, bring in the blanket that's hanging outside."

As David and Yetzi hurry across to the back door to the corral, Izel starts mixing dirt with water and a handful of dry weeds. Then she plops a clump of the mixture in my hands for me to cover the pouch. Afterward, facing the wall, I close my eyes. I pray to Izel's Virgin Mary and to my collection of spirits and forces beyond my understanding, pray to them to keep my family safe.

"English, enough," Izel says, holding out a bowl of water. "Here, wash your hands."

I open my eyes, pat the mud one more time, then turn to dip my hands in the water. When I finish rinsing the mud from my hands, Izel hands me a strip of cloth to dry them, then tosses the water on the dirt. Silently, we look at each other and embrace. Before long I'm hugging and kissing Yetzi and David.

I remove the silver wedding ring from my finger and hand it to Izel. "Until I return," I say, then hop onto the mule. I sit on one of my two blankets—the other for keeping warm. The only things I carry are a dagger, a leather water bag, a bow, a quiver of arrows, and a woven sack filled with tortillas, a few chili peppers, goat cheese and dried goat meat. Everything's hanging off my waist and shoulders. I look at my children and tell them not to let their mother carry water from the river.

Yetzi is crying but she and her brother nod.

"And David, give the Rarámuri boys a hand with the irrigation ditches."

"Yes, Papá." I know he will because he likes to be with them, run with them whenever they race with the ball. He reminds me of myself when I was running with the Guachichiles.

I pull the reins to the right and Mancha, our mule with one white spot on its forehead, starts moving. When we're at a steady trot, I turn to see my family. They're all waving to me. I raise an arm and keep it raised until I move into the brush and can no longer see them.

Mancha and I climb into the hills to the east. I look back to see the cluster of houses one more time. With an ache in my chest, I vow to return home as soon as it's safe.

I'm not afraid of a journey into lands where Chichimeca tribes are still at war with the Spaniards. I will avoid people and make my way east and south, away from the frontier and into the center of New Spain. I can hide until they think I'm dead. Maybe they'll forget me or I'll no longer be of interest to the inquisitors. They won't bother me as long as I hide my origins and profess to be Catholic.

Hiding is my plan. I'll change my name again, stay away from others, maybe work as a shepherd, maybe hide with Emilio. And when the time is right I'll return to my family.

My trail ends. It's not really a trail but a winding dry creek bed that's hidden in weeds and rocks. I have to pick my way up through the brush, cactus, trees and enormous, rounded rocks. I get off Mancha and lead the mule into a trail that I hope is passable. Sometimes it is and sometimes it isn't and I have to turn around and backtrack until I get to a cut in the boulders. It's slow but I'm going up the slope. The climb seems easier because I can see more of what's around me. And there are signs that tell me things, show me where water runs, where it collects, which plants store water.

Father taught me to read and write and how to live in a city. But the Guachis taught me how to live in the wilderness. With them I learned to shoot an arrow, to hunt, to feed myself and to fight. And with the Rarámuri I picked up something very different, something like kindness.

I first met three Rarámuri in the river valley of Rosario, where we settled after leaving Durango and Santa Bárbara. I'd been stalking a wild pig in the reeds along the river when something startled the boar. It looked up and started to run away, but I was ready and dropped him with a single arrow. Before I could retrieve the animal, three natives stood up from the reeds, and we stared at each other. I wasn't afraid, thinking they were just curious. Though my skin was fair and a beard covered half my face, I dressed as they did. A headband held back my long black hair and I wore only a loincloth, which was how I went about with the Guachis. With a few gestures I invited them to share parts of the pig, which I butchered on the spot with my dagger.

What I didn't know then was that these men live their lives by sharing whatever they have. So my first gesture stirred in them the beginnings of a friendship. I didn't know their language but it didn't matter. We were soon hunting together, and in time they joined me in tilling and seeding my field while Izel traded fishhooks, chickens and eggs with Rarámuri women for their baskets and clay pots.

***

I reach the top of a mountain pass and stop. This long and slow climb would be child's play for my Rarámuri friends in the mountains to the west. They would run to the top without a stop. As it is, I've been leading Mancha slowly on foot across broken granite. There's no vegetation here—only a steep slope of rocks and, beyond that, a sweeping view of a wide valley and more mountains. I've never seen anyplace as vast as this. It reminds me of the realm that Father said was a homeland for pilgrims, searchers and wanderers, a wilderness he called the Land of Nod.

I'm now thirty-two years of age—years enough, I think, to stop running and wandering. I have a family, work and a home. Yet I'm on the run again. I could have joined two expeditions into the land that Coronado saw, even if no one ever found the seven cities of gold. But I wasn't tempted. I had found my haven, the place where we can live, as Deacon Brown used to say, "free of want and full of goodly purpose."

I found my garden in Los Olivos, found it in the house we built, in the land we farm, in the water the river gives us, in the hills and mountains where we hunt. My garden is in the arms of Izel, in the voices of our children. Izel tells them she was a blackened slave of the Guachis, and when she saw me for the first time, I was covered in giant leaves. She thought I was a spirit of the forest. And I tell them about climbing the mainmast of the *Mynion* with Nicky or when I lived like a rat in darkness with Hassan and the other Africans.

But enough about my garden. I have to cross this wilderness. "Let's go, Mancha. We can do this."

***

In the days and weeks ahead, I straddle Mancha's back as we cross valleys, hills and a stretch of dunes. We skirt mesas, ford streams, and climb up to a scrub-covered mountain pass. Several times I see native groups and move away from them. I avoid making fires for fear of discovery, and I eat raw whatever game I kill. I get through the chilly nights in brush shelters, hollows, ledges and caves, with Mancha either hobbled or tethered nearby. In daylight I go south and east. As always I keep an eye out for patches of green where Mancha can forage and I can look for water.

I speak to my companion as if the mule understands me. As a distraction similar to my long-ago habit of looking at faces and collecting make-believe stones, I speak only English, addressing my family, Deacon Brown, my classmates, even the Queen herself. I speak of my time at Greyfriars, followed by fresh memories of life in Los Olivos. I tell my mute, big-eared friend that I taught David how to strike certain stones to make arrowheads, Yetzi how to cure leather, and Izel how to massage a pregnant woman's back the way I'd seen Hump use her hands on women before childbirth. Two times Izel has helped neighbor women give birth. She's become a midwife for the pioneer families in Los Olivos.

Though the conversations with Mancha are one-sided, I like the tongueloosening exercise in English. Today, as the mule is finding a way through scattered brush and I'm reliving the swim to shore from the *Mynion*, I hear what sounds like a loud crack of a whip. Suddenly, Mancha makes a guttural sound and begins to lean to one side and stumble. I'm falling to the ground and my head strikes a rock. I can't move. I open my eyes and squint. Against a cloudless sky, I see the silhouettes of three figures.

"Savage?" a voice asks in Spanish.

"Maybe," answers another.

"Kill him?"

"No. He's one more slave we've got."

A third voice speaks. "I know him." I shudder when I hear the accented Spanish.

I watch the red-bearded figure in the middle, now coming close. He seizes my arms and pulls me to my feet. "That's right, mate," the man says in English. "It's me."

***

I'm now Red Beard's prisoner, my hands bound by a rope attached to a caravan wagon traveling south. I know that if I stumble and fall, I'll be dragged along until I can get to my feet. But I do fall, and two of the Mexica behind me hurry to lift me up. The second time I fall, Red Beard rides by on a pinto stallion and sees me stumble and fall face down in the dust. He shouts to the wagon driver to halt, and when the pair of oxen stop, I get to my feet and wait for the rope to pull me again. "Water," I say in English.

"What's that?"

"Please, water."

"Louder! I can't hear you."

"Water."

"Water is it?"

I make a guttural sound and my tormentor looms above me, a coiled whip in one hand and the reins in the other. With a helmet and a metal breastplate and leather leggings, the gunnery seaman looks imposing with his sword dangling from one side of his waist and a musket in its sheath on the other side.

When the wagon starts moving again, I begin walking, repeating my pleas for water.

"You get water," Red Beard says, "if you tell me where you were hiding since you left Zacatecas."

I nod and he orders one of the natives trudging behind the wagon to give me water. After drinking my fill from a gourd, I give it back to the young man. "*Tlazocamati*," I say in Náhuatl, the thank-you word Izel taught me years ago. Then in English I tell Red Beard that I found work tending cattle near Durango.

"Me own English heretic!" the Irishman says, exulting. "I'll turn your hide over to the friars, I will. And what's me reward? To see you burn at the stake? No, I ain't that bloodthirsty. I'll turn you in and old Red will be walking with the rich! Oh, you didn't know? Inquisition knows about you—and I'm going to give you over like a gift and get a goodly reward."

Red Beard rides ahead, leaving me to berate myself for letting my guard down, for not watching the surrounding landscape, for spending hours lost in the past, babbling when I should have been silent, cautious, alert to sounds and signs of danger.

I'm sorry, Mancha, but you died because I'm a fool.

Red Beard returns and orders me to climb up onto the pile of sacks in the wagon. "I want you alive when I turn you in."

I pull myself forward, grabbing the topmost wooden plank with both bound hands. I raise myself and clamber over the planks at the rear of the wagon. I fall on the corn-filled sacks. After catching my breath, I lean back and soon fall asleep.

I awake after sunset and stare at the ceiling of stars. Without a moon in the blackness, the only light comes from the several fires and torches blazing alongside the cluster of wagons. Among the shadows come faint voices, even laughter. Feeling the night chill, I try in vain to burrow between two sacks. Then one of the escort warriors, while holding a lit torch in one hand, gives me a blanket. Later, the same young man returns with a strip of charred beef and a hard biscuit.

After eating, I begin to wonder how I can escape. It might take hours, but I reckon I can cut through my tether if I rub the rope on the corner edge of the post. Moving to the rear of the wagon, I begin the back-and-forth chore. Soon the twisted sisal fibers begin to spring apart until the entire rope is severed close to the knot near my hands. Though I'm still bound at the wrists, I'm free to escape. I figure I can always find a big rock with an edge to cut through the rope binding.

When the fires die down to embers, I can only see the silhouette of one sentry, who is standing near the mules and horses on one side of the wagons. I slip over the side of the wagon that the sentry cannot see. Then I step away and quietly move into the brush.

Not long after sunrise, Red Beard finds me beyond a rise, running across a plain of scattered brush and cactus. My hands are now free. He trots up to me on his stallion just as I'm about to jump down into a gulley. The whip catches me around the legs and I fall forward. I roll to a stop and slowly get to my feet. I pick up a fist-size rock and face the man standing at the gulley's edge, whip in hand.

"That ain't going to do you no good," he says, raising the whip handle. Then he snaps it and the snakelike end catches my hands, and I'm yanked up and out of the gulley. I lie stretched out in the dirt, naked except for my headband, tunic and loincloth.

"Now for a few stripes," Red Beard says, gathering the loose length of the whip.

"Take off that rag of a shirt."

I raise my head. "Go to hell," I say in measured English.

"As ye wish," he says, chuckling. He grips the handle in his right hand and raises the whip. In that instant, I hear a slight whistling sound and suddenly all his motion stops. I watch as blood begins gushing in spurts from the front of his throat. After a gurgling moan, he drops the whip and collapses.

I stay still, thinking whoever just struck my nemesis is about to kill me too. There was no gunshot, so I figure it must have been an arrow that passed clean through Red Beard's throat.

I'm still on the ground. I hear footsteps and turn to see a long-haired native wearing a dirty red shirt and clutching a bow in one hand with an arrow drawn back.

"Who are you?" he asks in Spanish.

"A man," I say, "like you."

"But you're white."

"Yes."

"Under the dirt you're white."

"I am."

"What happened here? He was going to kill you."

"Maybe," I say, rising to my knees, then slowly to my feet.

"At first I thought you were Guachichil," he says.

"I'm not, but I once lived with them."

"Well, I am a Guachichil."

"And you speak Spanish."

"I was a slave. I ran away."

"That makes two of us. I ran from this man."

I notice that my savior, who is about my age and height, has no thumb and first finger on his right hand. I know that such amputations are a common punishment for captured Chichimecas— so they won't be able to use a bow and arrow. I point to his three-fingered hand. "I see you still shoot a good arrow, even like that."

"I learned to use my other hand."

I nod and introduce myself. "José Campos."

"Indio Juan. It's what the Spaniards call me."

"Then, Juan, right?"

"Yes."

I look around and see that the horse is foraging by a mesquite tree. "What do you think? We take the horse and ride together?"

"Good."

"And him?" I say, gesturing to the bloodied body.

"Leave him."

"But they'll find him."

"It doesn't matter."

"They already want me for heresy."

Juan cocks his head with a questioning frown.

"I don't belong to the Spaniard's church," I say. "They kill people for that."

"You're not Spanish?"

"No. And now they'll want me for murder."

Waving a hand, Juan walks away to get the horse.

I stare at the crumpled figure on the ground. A fly crawls toward the open mouth. I look up and search the sky. I wonder how long it will be until the first vulture sees the body.

Chapter 21 – Friends

I pull the pinto by the reins, coaxing him into the river's deeper middle. Suddenly, the horse lurches, then falls, saddle and all. For an instant, I see a wild, frightened eye as he disappears beneath the muddy water. Then he comes up and is swept away. The current takes me too, but I begin swimming hard toward the opposite bank. When I can touch the bottom with my feet, I stand and move onto the rocks.

Juan is waiting. He's already made it across upstream by crossing on the tops of boulders. I was supposed to lead the stallion through the floodwaters where there were no boulders.

"We lost the horse," he says, extending a hand to help me up the steep bank, "and the rope."

"I'm sorry," I say.

"Blame the mountain spirits. They decide who lives, who dies."

"I hope they let him live. He was a good horse."

I peer downstream and see nothing of the pinto. The storm clouds are passing and the afternoon sunlight suddenly brightens the water's surface.

"We don't need the horse," Juan says, "not in the mountains."

Silently, we climb up the jumble of stones to get out of the ravine. Then we start hiking to the foothills ahead. By the time we reach a sandstone cliff, the sun has set and the sky is darkening. We find shelter beneath a ledge, then gather enough sticks, leaves and tumbleweeds to make a barrier for the night.

Many days have passed since my rescue. The pinto carried us across mostly flat, dry lands of brush, nopal cactus, and spindly trees. With Juan in the saddle and me behind, the two of us bounced along as one, seldom speaking, listening for sounds and movement, looking for prey, watching for pursuers or natives who might attack us for the horse.

All this time, I carried our only bow and quiver and hold myself close to Juan. When we do speak, it's usually when we spot certain plants, insects or animals— anything edible, from seed pods, fruits, berries and flowers to birds and small animals—or places where we might dig for groundwater.

It's only while climbing into the Eastern Sierra, after we lose the horse, that we talk of ourselves. We usually speak this way when we stop for the night, darkness all around, eyes to the stars. Tonight, Juan describes how he and his band of mounted warriors attacked a mining camp to take horses. But instead of riding off with the others in the attack party, he was knocked off his horse, captured and later held down for the amputation of a thumb. He speaks calmly of this and other parts of his life.

The Spaniards used him to haul ore out of the shafts. Then— because a foreman noticed he was good with the burros that pulled loads in the tunnels—he was put in charge of the mules that worked in the ore-crushing patios. Eventually, he was moved to duties at the mine owner's place. He improved his Spanish to the point where he could understand conversations. Once he listened to the mine owner tell a Spanish visitor that he had "tamed Indio Juan." He was described as an obedient and respectful slave and servant. In that way, Juan got to tend to all the animals and to mend carts and was trusted to run alone into the town on errands.

But he yearned to return to his people. Finally, on a moonlit night, he escaped on foot, using every trick he knew to evade pursuit—brushing over his footprints, walking in streams, hiding during the day, then walking backward or zigzagging toward the high peaks to the east, asking the mountain spirits to help him. He was still heading across the arid wilderness when he came upon me about to be whipped by Red Beard.

"You saved me," I tell him.

"The mountain spirits wanted you to live."

I hear him talking to the mountains around us. He says they are the guardians of life, the spirits that let us pass into a garden of plenty.

Just then we see a shooting star. After a long silence, Juan speaks. "When I ran away, I had to make a bow and some arrows. I had to learn how to shoot again."

"And you did."

"It wasn't easy changing hands."

I told him how Guachichiles had captured me, made me a slave but also taught me how to shoot and hunt with a bow and arrows. With practice I sharpened my aim and timing so that by the time of my escape from them, I could hit a bird in the air.

"Sometimes," I say, "I dream I can hit the stars."

"Only the ones with wings," Juan says, and we both laugh.

"I never dream," he says. "I see nothing when I sleep."

"I thought everybody has dreams."

"I don't."

After more silence, I ask if he thinks spirits dream.

"Yes, I think so."

"These mountains, do you think they'll let us pass?"

"When mountains dream," he says, "anything is possible."

***

For two days we climb up through a pine-and-oak forest that gives us little shelter from the chilly nights. I cover myself with the deer hide I wear during the day, while Juan wraps himself in rabbit and fox furs. We've been guiding ourselves by the sun, moon and stars and by what Juan heard from traders, soldiers and other slaves about a way over the mountains and down to the wet and warm lands.

I tell him my pursuers appeared to me in a dream. They're giving up the search and turning around.

"Yes, they're gone," Juan says, chewing on a strip of dried deer meat. "But we still can't make a fire."

"Why not?"

"The Huastecos. We're in their land."

"And your Guachichiles?"

"Maybe them too. I don't know."

"Where are we going?"

"To the river the Spaniards call Pánuco."

"And your people are there?"

"Maybe. We went to that river many times when I was a boy."

I'm twisting the deer sinew that stretches from one end of my bow to the other.

When I finish I signal I'm ready to begin the day's trek.

"We need more arrows," Juan says.

"I have two."

"You need more."

"Why?"

"Not just for hunting."

"Huastecos?"

Juan nods and opens a leather pouch that hangs from his waist. He pulls out a handful of narrow obsidian stones. In his palm they gleam in the early sunlight. "Let's go. We can make arrows later. The Huastecos live in the valleys, not up here."

We reach the snow-covered pass, but we also hike down to the lowlands—never having to shoot an arrow at a Huasteco or anyone else. Whenever we see smoke, we move away. Several times we see villages that appear to be abandoned and overgrown with weeds. *Cocoliztli* or some other pestilence could have killed the inhabitants, but Juan says *Guachichiles* also could have attacked and killed them. We agree to avoid villages and farmland, no matter how tempting it is to steal corn, vegetables and fruits.

As much as possible, we keep to the hillsides where we think Huastecos are not living. One night, long after we fall asleep, Juan cries out. I can't see in the darkness.

I'm silent, hearing nothing but his breathing—as if he's been running. He whispers that he saw *Guachichiles* about to attack us. "I wanted to tell them who I was, but I couldn't speak."

"So you do dream."

"I wasn't sleeping. I saw them and they were going to kill us."

"Well, it didn't happen. Just a nightmare with open eyes."

Juan's breathing quiets and he asks me if I've spoken to the spirits.

"No, I was dreaming of Izel. We always kiss before we sleep."

After a moment of silence, I ask if he has a woman. "Someday, maybe. If I find my people I will."

***

After many more days, we leave the forest underbrush and stop at the rim of a canyon.

Looking down at the strip of water far below, Juan tells me he's leaving.

"What?"

"I have to leave you."

"Why?"

"I have to do this by myself. If I find them or other Guachichiles, they'll see I'm alone. They won't shoot and I can talk to them. If I'm with you, a white man, they'll shoot first."

"Where do I go?"

"That way," Juan says, pointing across the canyon. "The people you want to find are beyond those hills."

"And you?"

"I'm going to where the river is born."

I look to my right, where the water comes out from between the canyon walls. Then I look down and to my left, squinting at the silver snake that disappears into a crevice of vegetation. Climbing down will be dangerous if not impossible. I'll have to hike farther along to find a safer place to go down.

"Where should I cross?" I ask and wait for his answer. "Juan?" I turn and no one is there. He's gone back into the bushes and trees. I'm sorry we didn't give each other proper goodbyes. But I know that for Guachis there are no farewells until someone dies.

I study the chasm and the distant, darkened hills. Suddenly, I feel alone and abandoned. What would Father tell me? What would he would tell a client whose house had burned down?

Bear and forebear.

I'm forgetting his refrains. I'm sitting on the edge of the canyon rim, trying to remember some of his sayings, but they stay hidden in a rush of random English words. The canyon is rich with birds and plants. I wish Izel and the children could see this. The thought of them and my mission to flee, hide and return fills me with a sense of purpose. But, as they say, "*Del dicho al hecho hay mucho trecho.*" Or, as Father would put it, "Easy to say, hard to do."

I get up. I figure the river flows to the sea and probably flattens out once it leaves the canyon. So I start off along the rim in that direction. It takes me two days of finding my way through brush and tangles of vines and branches. By the time I leave the cliff and descend to the water, leaving the canyon behind, the river widens and I swim across.

Out of the mountains, I travel south through warmer land. The farther south I travel, the more I see trails and paths marked by the passing of mules and horses. In time I know I'll encounter someone who will raise an alarm at seeing a "white" savage. And if I run, I might be hunted and shot. As it is, I'm getting weaker and can barely keep a walking pace. I'm so hungry that my deerskin hangs over my bony shoulders in tatters. I must look like a skeleton with skin and hair.

I meet a mule train coming from the east on a trail that leads to the western mountains. I count more than thirty pack animals, tied together and loaded with bulging bags, baskets and piles of hides. Six mule drivers—one of them with a musket and the others with poles—walk beside the line of moving cargo.

I decide to reveal myself as a kneeling beggar, hands out, palms up, pleading for something to eat. The passing native muleteers ignore me—until the man at the end of the mule train hands me some dried meat with a few corn tortillas. I thank him in

Náhuatl and start eating. At the same time, I keep up with my Good Samaritan. When I finish, I ask in Spanish where they are going, and the man points ahead with his staff. "Metztitlán."

I ask if I can walk with them. The Nahua looks me over, his gaze going from my bushy, tangled hair to my blackened bare feet. And then he asks in Spanish, "Who are you?"

"I escaped from the Guachichiles," I answer, repeating a truth from years before.

"I was their slave."

The Nahua whistles ahead to the others and soon the mule train stops. "Wait here," he says and walks ahead to meet the lead mule driver midway up the line. The two men speak and then the trailing Nahua returns and tells me I can ride on one of the mules after they shift some of the animal's load to other mules.

Days later, the mule train reaches Metztitlán. It's a town built on a rise near the cultivated bottom of a barranca. Abundio, the Nahua muleteer who fed me, insists we go together to the church and convent overlooking the valley. "Escaping the savages is a miracle," Abundio says. "You must give thanks to the Virgin."

We enter a massive structure that reminds me of a fortress, not a temple of worship. Abundio, a short, thick-bodied man with intense eyes, quickly finds his way to a wall painting of Mary floating in the clouds, the hem of her robe only inches above the

RON ARIAS

open mouth of a fearsome-looking dragon. Rather than kneel and pray, as Abundio does, I remain standing, searching the painting's many images surrounding Mary for a hint of England's patron saint. At Greyfriars my classmates and I imagined we were Saint George looking for a dragon to slay. Lost in memories, I'm roused by a tug on my shirt, the one Abundio gave me. "Kneel," the muleteer says.

After years of going to church services with Izel, I know all the Catholic rituals and prayers—genuflections, candle lighting, making confessions and taking the Communion host on the tongue, if it comes to that. I'm not a good-faith believer but I pretend well and look sincere. Without looking at Abundio, I kneel, make the sign of the cross, and we recite our prayers and wishes in whispers.

Back on the trail, this time going to Pachuca, I feel strong enough to walk alongside the line of mules. Twice I impress the mule drivers by dropping a deer and a rabbit with unerring bow shots. Each time, I announce that the meat will be shared by all.

Several days into the journey, I recognize a cut between two hills. It's the way to Emilio's place. Thanking the mule drivers for helping me, I tell them I'm going to a friend who lives a day's walk away. Abundio gives me a bulging leather water bag and offers me meat for my journey. I take the bag and tell him he should keep the meat. My friend will feed me. As I leave them, I'm glad I didn't give my true name or tell them about myself—and Abundio never asked.

304

A day later, I pass by a small herd of grazing cattle and then approach Emilio's house. I see a man carrying a bucket into the corral, followed by three dogs. By the time I walk up to the corral gate, the dogs have caught my scent and are barking. As soon as the door to the house opens, I see over the gate that Luisito has grown to manhood. He approaches me with a quick step and a machete in one hand. He's followed out the door by two other young men, both with machetes.

"Luisito!" I shout, looking over the corral fence. "It's me."

"José?"

"As a savage!"

Luisito orders the dogs back and opens the gate. We hug, then step back and look at each other. "Welcome," Luisito says. "And Izel—where is she?"

"In the north."

"And the children? Antonio told me you have two."

"Yes, two. They're fine."

"What happened to you?"

"A long story."

"Come," he says, turning and moving toward the door. "I want to hear it."

I stay with Luisito and his cattle drivers for six days. More than ten years have passed since Izel and I left Emilio, and now I learn that the Portuguese farmer died a year ago. But he lived to see his son, Antonio, marry and to hold his first and only grandson. "That pleased him as much as anything in his life," Luisito says. "I owe everything to Don Emilio. He gave me this house, his livestock, this land."

During my visit, I often pass through the doorway to the corral, each time pressing two fingers on the spot where Emilio buried his family's mezuzah. After days of doing this, I tap the depression between the adobe bricks as I step into the corral. Except for the chickens, I'm alone. I realize the habit is more for the memory of my old friend than for any religious feeling. Mountain spirits make more sense to me than do amulets or the Virgin Mary's image floating above a dragon. But I told my children that I buried my penknife to leave them something of myself so they wouldn't forget me. I see their faces and begin to cry, not for long but long enough to feel I'm embracing them, one in each arm.

***

I'll travel south to Puebla. It's where Hassan went to make pottery. Luisito has no news of the freed African, so I don't know if my old friend is still there. What he does know is that *cocoliztli* took the lives of Oreja and his sisters. I was so sorry to hear this news. Such kind people, and oh, how much the sisters loved Izel and the children.

I start my journey to Puebla wearing clothes that Luisito gave me—along with food, water and a small but sturdy bay mare to ride. Over the next two days, I cross flat brushland, avoid native villages and guide myself by keeping Orizaba, the great volcano Nahuas call Citlaltépetl, on my left and the white mantles of Popocatépetl and Iztaccíhuatl on my right. The three volcanoes, seen like sentinels so clearly against the sharp blue sky, lead me to the main road running between the port of Veracruz and the city of Mexico. They are my guides, my spirits.

Following the traffic of people and products, I turn onto a road leading to the streets of Puebla. It's midday when I ride into a town that's busy with pack animals, porters, carts, wagons, children and dogs. At the central plaza, I get down from the rickety wooden saddle and lead the mare through a crowd of natives to the edge of a small *tianguis*. I stop before a display of clay bowls stacked in front of a young woman sitting back on her heels. I point at the bowls and ask her in Spanish where they are made. She waves an arm in one direction, gesturing with her hand. "Not far," she says. I nod and then I feel a tap on my shoulder. "Is it José?" a man's voice says. "Are you José Campos?"

I turn around and stare at a face that's slightly familiar. I know the eyes but not the gray hair and goatee. And then it comes to me. "Captain González!"

"Yes, but captain no more."

We hug each other, me using one arm, the other holding the reins to my horse.

"Where are your bow and arrows?" González asks. He's looking at the rolled blanket and bags tied to the saddle. "I thought you were a savage."

"Savage no more," I answer. We laugh at the memory of my Guachichil disguise. "Well, we all change," González says. "Look at me. I'm a trader of means now. Much better than a soldier's life."

"Gentlemen, please," the woman behind the bowls says. "Can you talk somewhere else?" I pull the mare away through the crowd. We move to an open space across the cobblestones and I start to answer his questions about my life after we last saw each other in Zacatecas.

"But you must come to my house," he says. "We can celebrate your arrival there. Yes?"

Before I can answer, he steps away. "Follow me."

In the courtyard of his home, crowded with mules, my horse is taken away to be watered and fed. Then I follow González inside to drink cups of sweetened chocolate. He tells me how he went from a poorly paid officer doing dangerous duty on the frontier to making big profits transporting and selling cacao and other goods from the south, from the part of New Spain they call the Kingdom of Guatemala. He says that after we left each other in Zacatecas, he continued escorting caravans during the war with the Chichimeca tribes. In one attack an arrow hit him just above his breastplate, bringing him down off his horse. When he got to Zacatecas he was taken to a hospital to have the arrowhead removed.

He tells me that in the cot next to him was a wealthy trader, a childless, married man who also had deep arrow wounds in his thigh and back. The two already had become friends during the journey north from Mexico to Zacatecas, and now in the hospital they became closer still. But while González healed, the trader grew sicker and his infections worsened. Before the merchant died, he had his physician write and witness his last will and testament. In the event of his death, he whispered to the doctor, he wanted his entire transport and trading enterprise to be given to the captain.

"That gift was the first of two blessings," González says. "The second was the man's wife. You see, when I got out of the army, I got busy learning about his business. I also fell in love with his widow. She was a beautiful, clever woman and— would you believe—a princess from a royal family in Texcoco. She lives in Mexico with our two sons. I want you to meet them."

"I'd like to," I say, "but I can't because I'm a fugitive. I'm hunted by the Holy Office for heresy. And by now I'm also wanted for murder."

"I heard about that," González says. "The word is that you, José Campos de Medina, are the killer of an Irish Catholic."

"I didn't kill him."

"I believe you, José. But even if you were guilty, I'm sure you would have good reason to kill."

I describe what happened to Red Beard and about Juan, the Guachichil slave who saved me from the man's whip.

González stands and paces. He seems to be thinking about my problem. His erect figure reminds me of the soldier he once was. "Well," he says, "Puebla is the worst place for you to be. The clerics and viceroyal officers are watching everywhere. You have to leave. I'm surprised they haven't arrested you yet. You stick out like a Spaniard in a sea of Indians, blacks, mestizos and other *castas*. An easy catch."

"I'll leave Puebla," I say, "but first I want to see two old friends."

"No, sir! Not if you want to save your life. Tell me their names and where they are. I'll send someone to find them."

I describe Hassan and Minoru and explain that they might be making pottery.

"African and *chino* potters should be easy to find," González says. "Do they make Talavera? It's becoming very popular. Or do they make what the Indians use?" I remember the colorful glazed pitcher and bowls Hassan gave us at the home of Oreja's sisters, María and Xuchitl. "Talavera, I think."

González quickly finds Hassan and Minoru working at the same pottery. The trader invites them to his home for dinner, and when they arrive, it's as if my friends and I never left one another. We embrace and begin trading stories. When Hassan hears about my plight, he says, "Don Alejandro is right. You'll be caught like a rat in daylight. You have to go." I look at him and Minoru.

"Where can I go?" I ask.

Minoru suggests that I leave the Indies. "Run, leave this land."

"You sound like Izel and my father. She told me to run away from the Holy Office, and my father told me to run away from England."

"Minoru's right, José," González says. He sits at the head of a long table with pitchers of wine and goblets spread out among plates of bread, cheese and sausages.

"You must hide somewhere else."

"And my family?" I say.

"Someday you can return."

"Where will I go?"

"Veracruz or Acapulco," Hassan says. "Ships always need crewmen."

"That's a death sentence," González says. "There are more eyes in those ports in service to the church, the viceroy and the King than even here in Puebla. But I have an idea."

Again he paces about the room, then stops and outlines a plan for me to avoid capture and leave the Indies. He says I will travel to Guatemala in the guise of a mule driver in one of his pack trains. I'll go by way of Oaxaca and then to the cacao farms of Soconusco near the coast. The mules will be loaded with cocoa beans, then travel across Guatemala to Puerto Caballos in the province of Honduras.

"Caballos is a small port," González says, "not nearly as watched as Veracruz. Once you get there, you can clean yourself up, change clothes and turn yourself into a merchant who's taking cacao beans to Seville. My agent will see to it that you board a galleon sailing in the treasure fleet to Havana and Seville."

"But I have no money," I say.

"I'll give you enough to board as a passenger and to pay for the shipment. Just go with the cacao to Seville and your job is done—you can disappear. The city's a stew of every kind of person."

Hassan agrees, having lived there himself when he was a slave. "You'll have no trouble hiding," he says. "It's a refuge for everyone."

"Unless you're Jewish," I add. "Or Muslim."

"Well, yes, there's that."

"To board the galleon I'll have to change my name again—and change the story of my life."

Minoru lifts his glass vessel. "A toast, then. To the new José."

"To the new José!" González and Hassan repeat. My three friends lift their goblets and drink more of the Rioja red.

They make more toasts to my new identity, inventing details as they drink more wine, wishing me good health and Godspeed on my journey to the Kingdom of Guatemala and on my voyage to Seville.

"From now on my name is Abundio," I say, recalling the face and name of the mule driver whose last name I never knew.

"Abundio what?" Minoru asks.

"I don't know," I say. "Hernández, Gómez, García."

"Fine," Minoru says and again raises his goblet. "To Abundio García." "To García," I say and finish pouring from the pitcher.

Chapter 22 – Disguises

The train of twenty-six mules plods into the port of Caballos during a heavy afternoon rain. Everything is soaked except the cacao beans. They're sealed in clay jars to protect against rain, rats and rot. In five weeks we've traveled more than 250 leagues along mountain trails and rutted roads. We've forded swollen streams in the jungle forests and once crossed a river on log rafts. I'm exhausted. Short steps for a long journey, as Oreja would say.

We stop the pack train by a storage shed close to the main wharf, where a galleon is tied fast. Two other ships are anchored in the harbor, and the town's meager waterfront of streets and wooden structures appears deserted. The only movement besides the downpour and the mule train's arrival comes from a lone figure on the foredeck of the galleon that's moored at the wharf. I see the man through the sweeping curtains of rain. He paces from one side of the deck to the other, now and then stopping to watch us unload the big jars and set them next to the shed.

After this is done, the two Tlascalteca mule drivers stay under the roof's overhang, while I follow the third muleteer, a mestizo, and the mules across a muddy clearing to a corral on higher ground. After the animals file in, we unburden them of tethers, blankets, chests and bags of barley feed.

At the home of the agent working for González, I give the man a pouch of silver ducats and a letter about arranging payment and passage for myself and the cacao. My host, a stooped, gray-haired Spaniard, takes the money and begins reading the letter. Several times he looks up and nods. When he finishes, he says the cacao has arrived in good time because the ships that are in the port will be leaving for Havana within the week. "Until then you will stay with me. But remember, from now on you must look like a merchant of some wealth. When the rain stops, the cacao will be loaded on the ship now at the wharf."

The agent doesn't ask why I have to change my appearance from that of a mule driver to one of a merchant. He asks no questions. Maybe he thinks the less he knows about what González and I are up to, the safer it is for him. In any case, all that matters is that González wants the agent to help me. In the mule train he has even sent a wooden chest filled with a gentleman's clothes and boots.

"And you need your hair cut and beard trimmed," the agent says. "I'll have a barber come to the house."

Hours later, I lie in the dark on a bag of straw and sheep's wool, listening to the thrum of rain on the roof tiles. I'm tired and normally I have no trouble falling asleep, usually with visions of Izel and the children easing the way. But anxiety has seized my mind. I worry about my family constantly, especially after seeing so many empty villages in the mountain valleys of Oaxaca. I fear the scourge by now might have swept through frontier settlements. Have they been spared? How can I know? Returning is impossible because very soon I'll have to meet the ship's captain and pretend to be Abundio García, a merchant sailing for Spain.

The old agent assures me I'll be expected and welcomed aboard. He tells me the jars of cacao beans will be stored below, and I—along with my caged hens, hard biscuits and dried foods—will probably be given sleeping space in the aft quarters with the officers. I'll never be asked to pull a line or lift a cask. Compared to my time on the *Mynion*, this voyage promises to be one of ease and comfort.

That's the plan. Then what? What will happen after hiding and waiting in Seville? How and when can I return to New Spain and home? Thoughts of the possible dangers ahead keep me awake until I finally imagine joining a crew on a galleon bound for Veracruz. From there I see myself traveling north to my family and home.

I enter the garden of my dreams, the one Izel and I created with seeds we brought with us. We got to where we could grow all that we needed. We even had a surplus to trade and sell to the miners and others in Santa Bárbara—everything from wheat and corn to squash, beans, peppers and tuna cactus. After five years, we harvested our first olives and oranges from our young trees.

We celebrate our good fortune. I see other settlers, whole families coming for the occasion. They bring food and wine. They sing, a young man plays a guitar, and couples dance while others clap their hands to a beat. Children and dogs run about, then everything dims.

Morning? If only I can quiet my mind—stop seeing, stop thinking. I hear rain. Am I awake? Am I dreaming? I try to see my garden, see me tending rows of corn and squash, harvesting olives with my children and watching David shoot an arrow through an orange hanging in a tree. Izel brushes her hair while singing something soft until all I hear is the fading sound of rain on the roof.

***

After more than two months of sailing—with a stop in Havana to join the fleet of thirty-two vessels—I see the coast of Spain. No pirates have attacked this Indies run, storms have been weak and now the flotilla is passing over the sandbar at the mouth of the Guadalquivir, catching the tide to move upriver to Seville. For me, the voyage has been pleasant and free of problems. And I get on well with the captain and officers.

Their stories during the crossing kept me entertained. But there was one tale that brought me great joy and it was told by the ship's surgeon, a veteran of many voyages to the Indies. He said that not long ago he was on a galleon that anchored for a few days in a cove on the west side of the island of Dominica. Water casks needed filling and repairs had to be made. It was then that he heard from an island trader about an Englishman who had adopted Carib ways. He lived with a native wife and their children on the island's east side, where most of the Carib villages were, and was known for his swimming and diving feats. "They said he was the best lobster diver on Dominica. And no native could swim faster than this man."

Hearing this, I smile, thinking the English swimmer had to be Nicky. He must have recovered from his illness after he was left on the island. My friend Fish Boy had found his own slice of Eden.

***

All hands are now on the main deck cheering as we leave the sea with a fair wind filling our sails. From the aftcastle deck, I've been watching us pass over the bar. I feel relief, as if the burden of my disguise and escape to Spain is becoming lighter. But what's this? The young captain, normally a good-natured fellow, is coming my way, looking grim, glaring at me.

"Sir," he says. "I must arrest you. You will be confined to the cabin until we reach Seville, where the King's authority and the Holy Office will decide your fate."

Since leaving Havana, I thought I might be arrested—all because of a sailor's suspicions that I was not who I said I was—certainly not the cacao merchant Abundio García. Instead I'm being called out as a wanted man, an Englishman, a heretic Lutheran, and a murderer whose criminal name is José Campos de Medina.

I deny the charges. The captain and I are both in our early thirties and formed a bantering friendship during the voyage. Yet the arrest, while not a surprise to me, leaves the captain with a puzzled expression when he delivers the charges. Twice he points to the accusing sailor, who stands below on the main deck among other crewmen. One calls me "heretic scum," shouting that I should be flogged.

The sailor is the same lone figure on the galleon who watched me and the mule drivers unload the jars of cacao beans in Puerto Caballos. He saw the four of us in sheepskin cloaks, me taller than the others. And then when I appeared on the ship as a gentleman passenger, he recognized me as the rustic muleteer he'd seen in the rain. Why else would I now be wearing a shirt with ruffled sleeves and collar, a leather waistcoat, crimson linen breeches and high boots? Why would I change my look so radically if not to avoid detection?

At first, the sailor, a Basque usually found in the rigging, kept quiet about his suspicions. But in Havana he told me he'd heard from other crewmen on ships coming from Veracruz about an Englishman wanted for heresy and murder. From then on during the voyage across the Atlantic, the Basque sailor would come up to me and whisper in my ear that for a generous sum of money he would remain silent about my true identity. He always addressed me as "Your Highness." But I refused to be blackmailed. I fended off the man's offers with lighthearted denials, insisting that I couldn't speak a word of English.

Now, as the captain finishes his words about arrest and confinement, I tell him, "You're the law on the ship. I will do as you order and stay in my berth."

The captain glances at the restless sailors, then looks at me. "Go to your cabin," he says, "and may God be by your side."

***

Hours pass. The galleon moves slowly and darkness comes quickly on a moonless night. For some reason—perhaps disbelief or sympathy—the captain has not given the order to have me bound to a post or to have my ankles shackled. Nor has he ordered the cabin door to be bolted on the outside. This is probably because three officers and one page also sleep in the cabin and might have to be ordered out during the night for some duty or another. I worry that the ship's scrivener, a jittery man who is one of the few aboard sleeping in a kind of sling he bought in Havana, will fall from his swinging fish net—and that would be the end of my escape plan.

I listen for a time to the usual creaks and squeaks of a ship on the move. I hear the bell and the changing of the watch, listen to the snores of my cabinmates, and then I hear the order for the anchor to be dropped. The snoring stops but after a while begins again. The galleon must be close to Seville, so I swing my legs off the bunk and stand.

Leaving everything behind—except the nightshirt and short pants I wear—I slowly slide across the floor planks until I reach the cabin door. I lift the inside latch and push. Suddenly, the soft wetness of fog brushes my face. I step out on the deck and close the door behind me. I pause a moment, hoping I won't be noticed by anyone, maybe by someone curled up on the deck but awake. A hanging lantern above me shines a dim light through the fog. There, near me, I make out a pair of outstretched legs. I step around the sleeping figure and move to the portside rail. I feel the ropes of the shrouds and pull myself up with both hands to clear the rail. Slowly, I climb down alongside the hull. Feeling the water, I let go.

The river is cool and I begin to swim. I want to get as far from the galleon as possible. But the darkness and the fog make it impossible to see anything. All I can do is swim across the slight current. I don't want to collide with another ship or boat that might be anchored or moving. I think ebb tide has begun because I'm moving to the left, downstream and probably heading for the opposite bank of the river.

With each downward pull of my arms, I imagine hearing Nicky shouting, "Kickkick stroke! Kick-kick stroke!" Twice I swim around barely discernible shapes of other unmoving vessels, lights coming from lanterns on the fore- and aftdecks.

By the time my feet touch the muddy bottom, I no longer feel a wetness in the air. I slog ahead, unable to see anything. Reeds. I touch the tops of tall reeds. I move them aside with my hands, step ahead out of the wetness. I stand on dry earth. I look back in the direction of the river and notice a faint glow in the sky. I must have drifted far enough downriver because I see no silhouettes of ships.

The sky still sparkles and in the dark I can only feel around, hoping to find a grassy patch. But I feel only dirt. I stretch out on the hard ground, intending to rest until dawn.

I open my eyes and blink. I must have slept for a while because the sky has brightened. Now, faintly and then louder, I hear a man's voice singing about falling in love with three pretty girls, Moorish girls. For a moment I think I'm dreaming.

"Good God, man!" the voice shouts. "Out of the way!"

I turn over and get to my knees. I've been sleeping in the middle of a narrow road. I look up at the wet snouts of two oxen, inches from my face. Their breath showers me with spittle. Beyond the snouts, I see a large man sitting at the front of a two-wheeled cart, holding the reins in one hand.

"Do you want to be crushed under these wheels?" he asks.

I get to my feet and tell him I didn't know where I was. "Are you drunk? Or are you here so your friends can rob me?"

I step out of the way, telling him I'm alone.

"Good," the man says and glances around. "All I have are the bricks I make."

"I'm not a thief."

"I see that. Or you're very bad at stealing."

"I'm sorry I stopped you," I say, gesturing to my two pieces of clothing. "And sorry for how I look."

"I don't care what you wear. Go naked if you want. Goodbye." The brickmaker mouths a clicking sound and shakes the reins over the backs of the oxen. As the animals start to move, I ask if he's going to Seville.

"Triana."

"I'm going there too. Can I ride with you?"

"Whoa!" the brickmaker yells. He pulls the reins back. "I'm going to the Castle of Saint George. I'll take you there if you help me unload the bricks."

"Yes, sir. I'll help."

"Then, get on."

I step up on the axle, climb over the side board and sit on top of the stack of bricks. Soon the cart is on its way, moving at a steady, ponderous pace amid wavy shades of brown wheat fields. I give my name as Alonso, after the mestizo mule driver in the pack train. No more Abundio. I will now be Alonso, a farmworker who left the countryside to find work in Seville.

The brickmaker, whose name is Celestino Camacho, starts singing again. I'm excited about going to a castle, especially one named for England's patron saint. The only castle I've ever seen—and only from the outside—is the one I saw in Rochester when I crossed the bridge over the Medway.

I can only imagine what might be inside a real castle. Rows of cannon, a wall of pikes and harquebuses, suits of armor lined up and ready to be worn, a bustling of soldiers, knights, stables and horses, sentries on every tower. And what would be the meals of people in Spanish castles? Surely plates of cherries, succulent strawberries, the finest wines, the best cuts of beef, mutton, pork.

My reverie is broken when Celestino stops singing and cries out, "Look at that! The fleet—it's back!" He points across the river to the dozens of vessels in the distance with their sails down. He calls them "fish bones pointed upward."

As we near the riverside outskirts of Triana, we share the road with more carts and wagons, more people on foot and horseback. Across the water, the ships now look bigger and taller, as do the towers, spires and outer walls of Seville. I want to ask if the tower next to the riverbank is the Tower of Gold, the one Captain González mentioned years ago. But I don't want to show my ignorance.

In talking about his work, Celestino says his father taught him brickmaking, and his grandfather taught his father before that. "All the way back, the Camacho men, all good Christians, have made bricks. And you, Alonso? Has your family always worked the land?"

I hesitate in answering.

"Alonso? Alonso what?"

Celestino waits for a family name. We have just passed a woman standing by the side of the road selling rosemary, so I say, "Romero." I sense that Celestino also wants to know about my religious lineage, who my ancestors are. "The Romero family," I tell him, "has always worked a poor piece of land. That's the misfortune of some

Christian families. So I left to find other work."

"Are you married?"

"I'm a widower. The plague took her."

"I'm sorry."

"And children?"

"Four. I left them with their grandmother."

Celestino stops asking questions, and I stay silent, thinking I've told a convincing story in a few words.

When we get to a point where the road veers close to the river, Celestino points ahead to a long, dark structure with square towers looming over the river. "That's where we're going."

"The castle?"

"Yes. We'll go inside, unload the bricks, and then they'll feed us!" He laughs, slapping his belly. "My brother lives there and he makes sure I'm well-fed."

"He lives in a castle?"

Celestino looks back at me with a surprised expression. "Alonso, it's not a real castle. It used to be—hundreds of years ago. Nowadays it belongs to our holy fathers."

I stiffen at the mention of priests. How do I get out of my promise to help unload the bricks? Jump off the cart and bolt? Run barefoot through unfamiliar streets?

Escaping now would be dangerous, foolish. Celestino would shout for me to stop and someone on the street would chase and probably catch me. No, the last thing I want is to draw attention to myself.

As we approach the castle, I see that the bridge over the river to Seville is simply a line of planks laid across what looks like a string of flat boats. On the Seville side the roadway opens on to a wide stretch of land alongside the river where the ships are tied up. From the city wall to the water, people and horses are moving among the shapes of shacks, tents, small boats and wagons.

Before reaching the bridge, Celestino turns the cart onto a cobblestone street that leads beneath an arched entrance to the castle. He calls out that he has arrived with another order of bricks. We wait, then the thick doors draw back and the oxen lumber past two men. They greet Celestino by name.

I promise myself that I will do what he asks of me, then leave and cross the bridge to what I hope will be safety in the crowds of Seville.

Hours later, we finish removing the bricks from the cart and then haul them four at a time to a kitchen. There, I help Celestino stack them near a broken brick oven that needs to be rebuilt. When we finish, we move to a long table where we sit down and wait to eat lunch with Celestino's brother. He's also a large man. He wears a hooded brown robe and enters the kitchen with other clerics in brown robes. Even as they sit, the talking continues.

The beef and vegetable stew that other monks serve us turns out to be the most satisfying food I've eaten since my last dinner in Puebla with González, Hassan and Minoru.

While Celestino and his brother talk about their family and what sounds like hometown gossip, I eat in delicious silence, savoring every spoonful of the stew. At one point, the friar asks his brother if I'm a good worker.

"Yes," Celestino says. "Strong, quick, and listens well. He does everything I ask of him."

"Do you trust him?"

"I know what you're thinking. With the rags he's wearing he looks like a drifter, a thief. But from what I've seen, I believe Alonso Romero is an honest Christian man." They speak of me as if I were not present. I pretend not to listen, slowly sopping up liquid with a chunk of soft bread.

"Alonso," the friar says. "We need your pair of arms and hands, someone to help a bricklayer build a new oven. Will you work for us?"

"Uh, yes, sir."

"He has nowhere to sleep," Celestino says.

The friar waves away flies moving around the rim of his

bowl. "Don't worry, you can sleep here. We'll pay you something. Not much, but you'll be fed and given better clothing."

"So that's it," Celestino says. He stands and claps me on the back. "I have to go now."

The brothers embrace, then Celestino turns to leave. "You're in good hands," he tells me. "You're better working here than crossing the bridge to Arenal and looking for work among thieves and cutthroats. Here, you're in the safest place in all of Christendom. Tell him, brother. He doesn't know. He's been living in the farmlands all his life."

"Yes, you're safe here," the brother says, "where our worst sinners are locked up and in chains. You have nothing to fear."

I'm still puzzled and look at Celestino.

"My dear Alonso," the brickmaker says, "you are in the heart of the Holy Office."

"Sir?"

"The Holy Inquisition."

***

After months of hiding, any kindness of thought I had toward religion withered away in the Castle of Saint George. I've been living among men in brown robes who treat condemned heretics and blasphemers no better than caged chickens on their way to slaughter. Worse even. They are tortured, made to confess their sins and held in chains. Day and night I hear their cries and pleadings. And yet the friars I see go about looking pious and content to be doing the Lord's work.

I'm afraid of being exposed and of someday being caged myself. I never leave the castle, keeping to my labors with an Italian bricklayer whose name is Marcelo. We've removed most of the old oven and have built a new one. I learn to prepare mortar and to lay bricks for the oven and also for walls, doorways, floors and stairway steps.

Marcelo is a pious man who says he believes in the mission of the Holy Office.

At night, the two of us share a small space in a kitchen storage room. I hear him praying in the dark and sometimes we talk about our faith. He thinks it is our duty to follow Christ's example in everything. Marcelo presses me to swear that "everything" also means the elimination of Lutherans and secret Jews in Spain. "Heretics," he says, "like the English vermin who were burned here in Seville and in the Indies."

I must agree with him. But he thinks my response is weak. "Alonso," he says, "why do you change direction when we talk? Are you hiding something?"

"Not at all," I answer, trying to sound calm and unbothered. "I'm just sleepy and not listening too well."

"That's a dangerous attitude, Alonso. But fine. We'll talk tomorrow."

In the morning when I see Celestino's brother I approach and ask for permission to quit work for a week to visit my children.

"Yes, of course," the friar says. "But tend to your duties today."

Later, Marcelo and I finish cementing an iron base for chains on a wall of an empty cell. I've been hearing moans coming from another cell—a steady sound of pain. I pick up my trowel and bucket of mortar and follow Marcelo, who is lighting our way with a lantern. We pass the source of the moaning. I look into the cell and see a naked woman stretched sideways across the floor. She's pulling on the two chains that bind her to the wall.

"We did God's work today," Marcelo says. "Don't you think so, Alonso?"

"Yes," I answer softly.

"What did you say?"

"Yes!" I say loudly. "God's work!"

I inform Marcelo that I'm going to be gone for a week to visit my family. He frowns but says nothing. I wonder if the expression is only annoyance. Or is he suspicious of some kind of trickery? Maybe he senses I'm about to leave and never return, about to flee with my thin disguise of faith.

In the morning I tell him goodbye and I will return soon. He's still silent, watching me cross the castle entryway and walk out beneath the arch of the main gate. I have good woolen trousers, a clean tunic and sturdy sandals. I feel free and content for the first time in months. But before stepping out into the streets of Triana, I look back. Should I wave? But Celestino is gone. Good. I never want to see him again.

At the boat bridge over the Guadalquivir, I cross to the Arenal. Marcelo often spoke against the evils tempting sailors and others in this strip of sin outside the city walls. I wander over the muddy expanse. I watch the porters toting sacks, inspectors counting what comes off or goes on the ships. I stop by men and women busy at different chores—from fishmongers to carpenters. They are people of dark skin and light, farmers, peasants, slaves and servants. I see monkeys, parrots and a giant, lizardlike animal with many teeth, its body hanging on a pole carried by two men at each end.

I'm free to do as I wish, free of commands, free of the Inquisition's prison and the sounds of torture. I stop and pay for grilled sardines on a stick. I watch a carpenter smooth a rough plank of wood. I meander more, then squat down and just gaze at the passing faces and figures, playing my old game of make-believe good and bad stones, the same as I taught my children.

What are they doing now? What's Izel doing? Probably cooking or reading to the children, maybe washing clothes at the river's edge. I close my eyes for a moment and am struck by a jolt of sadness.

The voices and noise around me soften, and tears drop from my face.

"Eh?" a thick voice says. I look up to see a stooped-over young man in tattered clothes. He's leaning on a crudely made crutch. "Are you a sailor?" he asks.

"Yes," I answer.

"Why the tears? Don't tell me—the fleet left without you."

"No, it's not that."

"You need help?"

"It's nothing. I got something in my eye."

"You sailors have stories, no?"

"Yes."

"I have stories too."

"I'm not interested," I say and wave him away.

Celestino and Marcelo warned me about a group of imposters called the Liars, men and women who tell tales of their miserable lives. The stories are so good that even the most suspicious listener can be deceived and end up placing money in an outstretched hand.

The crippled stranger lingers, trying to make me speak to him. I keep shaking my head and gesturing with my hand for him to leave. Finally, he curses me and walks away. After a while, I stand and walk over near the city wall. Then I move alongside the workhouses where the galleys are being built. Looking into one of the entryways, I watch the carpenters setting planks on the skeleton of a hull. Such long and low boats are nothing like the wide and tall galleons.

Beyond the galleys being built, I walk on until I reach several two and three story buildings—brothels. Women are out on balconies calling down. Same as the women of the London stews.

Down an alley alongside one of the brothels, I spot a crooked hanging sign offering "wine and more." I'm thirsty and start for the tavern. Ahead of me are two men by the door, talking and gesturing with their hands. As I step by them, suddenly my arms are grabbed from behind and held. The two men pull me away from the doorway and begin to hit me with their fists in the face, stomach and ribs. Then something hard strikes my left shoulder and upper arm. As I bend over in awful pain, I turn my head enough to see the crippled young man who spoke to me earlier. This time he's holding his crutch in the air, standing tall and looking as if he's about to strike me again. But the other men are now searching my clothes. My pouch of money is ripped from the leather cord around my waist.

"A few coins," one of the men says and punches me in the chest, and I fall down. He's about to hit me again when I hear a voice shout, "Leave him!"

I lift my head to see the three men run off past the tavern and disappear around a corner. Then I look back toward the open area of Arenal and see a figure running toward me, waving a stick with one hand as he would a sword. When he reaches me, he drops his stick and with his right hand grips me by my left arm to help me up.

"Thugs," he says, "cowards."

I'm dazed and can barely stand, hurting everywhere.

"Broken bones?" the stranger asks.

I shake my head. I touch my throbbing left shoulder and move my arm. "No, I don't think so."

I thank my rescuer. He's a tall figure with a trimmed beard and a concerned expression. He's probably about ten years my senior.

"What did they take?"

"My money, all I had."

"How about something to drink? It will help with the pain."

"But I—"

"Come, you look as if you need a drink."

With the man's help I step slowly to the tavern door. I figure his left arm may be lame because he's using only his right arm and hand to steady me and open the door.

We make our way to the middle of a nearly empty room and sit at a table. He calls for red wine, which a young man serves to us in pewter mugs. My savior asks why some men enjoy inflicting pain on others. "Why would scoundrels like that strike again and again, when one well-placed blow would do?"

I nod, guessing that such men must like dominating others with punishments, like the extra burdens given to me by Red Beard at the Purísima mine. Or maybe it's a matter of revenge, like what the Guachis do to the Spaniards, laughing and dancing as they kill them. "Or," I say, "is it like a code or command, like what the church orders done to heretics?"

"That's it," he says. "Or the man with the whip on a galley, which is the reverse of the code of chivalry. And they both follow rules of conduct. They both know how to hurt and kill. "

"What about the slaves?" I say. "Beaten and made to suffer because they're sick or because they're Africans."

The lame-arm stranger pours more wine into the mugs. My shoulder and ribs are sore, but the sharp pains have eased up.

"How do you know about such suffering?" he asks. "What kind of work do you do? "

I answer that I've worked as a sailor on a galleon taking men and women from Africa to sell in the Indies. "But I really want to live a farmer's life."

He tilts his head and winces. "I would like to go to the Indies someday, but first I have to finish my work for the Crown. I travel around to collect wheat as tribute for the king."

"Seems like hard work."

"No one likes to see me coming. I'm sure they would prefer other forms of torture. But I tell them the king needs their wheat so we can make biscuit for the armada."

"Armada?"

"Yes."

Just then, more men enter, many of them sailors. I look around the tavern, then lower my head.

"What's wrong?"

I think I can trust the man. He saved me from a worse beating. I owe him some honesty. I tell him that I'm a wanted man, accused of a murder I did not commit. To my surprise, he smiles and says that he, too, knows about life as a fugitive. He once had problems with authorities and had to escape.

"I need to hide," I say. "If I'm caught I'll be executed."

"Lisbon," he said. "Go to Lisbon."

"Lisbon?"

"The armada leaves from there. They need sailors. You can hide on a ship until the invasion's over."

"Invasion?"

"Of England."

Now it's my turn to smile.

"So this is a solution to your problem, yes?"

I want to agree but wonder about the authorities. "Won't I be walking into their arms?"

"Don't worry. They're so desperate for men that unless you're dead, they'll recruit you. No one will care or notice who you really are."

He reaches for the pitcher. "More?"

"Yes!"

He pours what's left into the mugs. "I'm surprised you haven't heard of the armada."

"I've been living in the Castle of Saint George for months. I was laying bricks and patching things and I never went out."

"The armada's a mighty force—thousands of sailors, soldiers, more than a hundred galleons. I'm certain someone will take you on."

"How far is Lisbon?"

"Far enough. They leave in a month or so. I'll give you some ducats for the journey."

"Thank you."

"Whatever you do, don't let them stick you in a galley. A rower's life might as well be a rower's death."

For a moment I'm lost in thought, my mind filled with a possible return to England, my thoughts brimming with images of my childhood in Greenwich and London.

My savior raises his eyebrows. "Did you hear what I said?"

"No, not really. I'm thinking about the invasion."

"Of course, but first comes Lisbon."

I nod.

"And stay away from galleys."

"Yes, sir, no galleys."

Chapter 23 – Armada

I join a ragtag group of other men seeking work in the armada. They've been drawn by the same mix of news and rumor sweeping all of Spain—that King Philip needs more hands to build a sea force big enough to invade England. Ships are still being repaired and cargo vessels have to be loaded with everything from munitions and gunpowder to horses and barrels of biscuits, dried fish, olive oil, rice, water and wine.

The nearly week-long trek to Lisbon is tiring, but we're determined to find work and few of the men lag behind. I hardly speak with the others, and when darkness comes, I follow the group off the road to what looks like a spot where all of us can stretch out. Even in sleep we stay together in case we have to face robbers. But none ever appear. When we finally near the city by the Tagus, we stop on a hill to marvel at the many anchored galleons, caravels, hulks and other craft that stretch up and down the river. None of us has ever seen such a gathering of maritime might. We start down the hill and soon enter a jumble of crooked cobblestone streets that take us by Lisbon's cathedral and then down to the riverside plaza. Most of the men go to the uniformed figures or to the officials sitting at their dockside tables. I decide to feed my empty stomach first.

I make my way to an open market where a woman stands behind a large pot, serving porridge into whatever the men hold out—bowls, gourds, mugs, leather pouches. I hope she can offer me something to hold the porridge, because two nights ago my clay bowl slipped from my hands and broke.

I get in line and wait my turn behind a man who tells me that the woman's fare is so much better than the awful gruel he has to eat aboard the galleass *San Lorenzo*.

"Galleass," I say, "like a galley?"

"Much bigger. It's a warship—three masts, fifty guns, soldiers, and a load of poor devils behind the oars."

"What do you do?"

"I'm up in the rigging most of the time."

I ask if the *San Lorenzo* needs more seamen.

"Maybe. Have you sailed?"

"Yes."

"Well, if my ship doesn't take you, I'm sure another will."

We move closer to the woman serving the porridge and the sailor points with his chin. "I see you have no bowl."

"No."

He reaches into his shoulder bag and pulls out a clay mug. "Here, use this," he says, giving it to me.

When he reaches the black pot, he gives the serving woman a coin with one hand and extends his bowl with the other. She scoops up the thick brown liquid with a wooden ladle and pours it into his bowl. Then she takes my coin and fills my mug. Looking up at me and the sailor with a concerned expression, she tilts her head back and tells us we are very brave and that God will guide and protect us.

***

I speak with the boatswain of the *San Lorenzo*, a man everyone calls "Bear" because of his overly hairy arms, neck and back. After I ask about work available for a common sailor, Bear studies me for a moment, then tells me that for now I can join a work crew that's cutting down pine and oak trees in a forest not far away.

Before long, I'm trimming and moving logs on wagons pulled by oxen to the port, where carpenters are still shaping hull planks, rudders and oars.

It's nearly summer and work in the heat is exhausting, but I expect to find work aboard the galleass *San Lorenzo, doing anything but rowing*. Storms and contrary winds at sea have delayed the armada's departure for weeks. But we all believe the order to launch will soon be given. And if the invasion goes as well as many are describing it, I believe I can somehow give the Spaniards the slip and take refuge in London.

340

Everywhere but especially in the taverns I hear how easy the victory will be, that England's persecuted Catholics will embrace the invaders and that King Philip will rescue the people of England from their heretic queen. Only he can bring them back to the true church.

By the time we hear the order to sail, I can only get hired as a rower among mostly criminals and slaves. Maybe I should have paid more attention to what the tribute collector of Sevilla told me about avoiding galleys, but I must get to England and now I don't care what kind of vessel I board. So I join some three hundred shavenheaded oarsmen belowdecks aboard the *San Lorenzo*. We're a motley collection of Italians, Turks, Berbers, other Moors and some Spaniards, Portuguese, Germans and black Africans. Except for me and a score of other hired men, the rowers are chained at the ankles to their benches. We sit together, six to a bench behind one of fifty heavy oars, each the length of four men stretched out head to toe.

I'm put in the ship's midsection on my feet behind the narrow end of an oar. This standing position is considered the least strenuous place to be, unlike the seated men closer to the hull. But the unfortunate part of my spot, I soon discover, is that it's also closest to the catwalk that runs above and between the rowers on each side of the vessel. And Bear is in charge of keeping the oarsmen working at the same pace by using his whip on those closest to him as he moves up and down the catwalk.

My first day at sea includes three cuts of the whip, painfully testing my resolve to get to England. The first stripe comes when we're towing another vessel over the bar at the mouth of the Tagus and into the ocean swells. "Pull!" Bear screams. "Pull hard, you stinking, worthless bastards! Pull!" And that's when I'm momentarily blinded by the stinging lash on my bare back.

"Don't stop, keep rowing," says my neighbor, a scrawny thief from Málaga, who's also standing. "The Bear loves it when his whip stops a man. It makes him want to strike again."

I settle into a kind of monotonous trance in the gloom below the gun deck, keeping to a steady, rhythmic motion. The last thing I need is another lash.

Most of us pull the oars silently, unless we're moaning and cursing about some injury or sickness. We often praise God with a shout when Bear orders us to stop rowing because the wind is good for sailing and the oars can be raised and set down.

Rest is always blissful, allowing me to sit still or curl up beneath the bench. I can gnaw at a hard biscuit or pass the time telling a story or listening to one by another rower. Some of the men use the time to turn splinters into small bundles of toothpicks, which are used as barter with the crew and soldiers. To relieve ourselves we use waste buckets, and if the bucket spills, then whatever mess doesn't reach the bilges is pushed aside and left for the rats to pick over.

During lulls, we like hearing the bark of Mata, the ship's rat-hunting dog. The first time the black-and-white terrier barks, the rowers cheer. Mata allows anyone to pet him as he moves about, sniffing around legs and under benches, hunting his prey in the shadows of the hull timbers, alert to whistles and sweet words.

"Why is he called Mata?" I ask my bench mate.

"He's a matador, a real killer. If we see a rat, there's nothing we can do because we got on these chains. But give Mata a whistle and he's all business. When he catches one, he shakes it, sometimes chews and swallows it, or he'll give it to someone, give it to him like a gift!"

Listening to the scrawny *malagueño* talk of killing or eating rats reminds me of my time with the slaves on the *Mynion*, when hunger drove me to eat anything, even newborn rats.

Living below, we seldom know where the ship is unless we hear the navigation orders from the top decks. After leaving Lisbon, this is how we know we're about to sail north on a course toward the enemy. We're listening to the captain deliver a kind of sermon above us. He's shouting about the sins and the crimes of England and its heretic queen and about how we must protect the Indies and the treasure fleets. And we will plunder, the captain is now saying, "for the endless riches we shall gather in England."

Everyone is cheering and I join in, shouting as loudly as the men around me. I think I'm pretending. Or am I? I've become such a chameleon, changing colors, inventing, lying with no convictions. I can still hear Father's and Izel's words warning me that sooner or later the chickens come home to roost.

***

After long delays caused by storms and a detour to La Coruña to repair a broken rudder, we finally cross the Bay of Biscay and enter the great channel between England and France. It's near the end of July, off the Dorset coast, when we hear orders to engage the enemy. The Bear is yelling to pull harder. We need speed. "Harder! Pull, you mealy worms!" I tighten my grip. I push and pull, push and pull. I call my calluses my gloves, protecting my fingers, my palms, my very bones.

I hear voices from above, then the Bear shouts, "Stop!" and he snaps the whip. We raise oars, wait, listen. I hear coughing, chains moving, then suddenly there's a blast of a distant cannon, then another and another, then a crash and cracking of wood above us. Cries and shouts. Again something hits us and the ship shudders and heels to the side.

"Pull!" the Bear orders with another snap of his whip. After hard pulling, we're halted. Then louder cannon blasts begin on the deck above us, deafening and shaking us with each explosion. Over the shouting I can hear the rolling of cannon carriages, the clank and thud of reloading, the cracks of faraway shots. All I can see in the gloom ahead of me are the glints of backs and arms and heads, all of us bending and moving hard to the task. We stop, wait, then pull again, stopping and starting. "English dogs, devils!" my skinny neighbor mutters. "All of you and your mothers should rot in hell."

The day darkens; the deafening mayhem dies down. There are fewer booming bursts until there are none, not even the popping jolts from smaller arms. We can now sleep. Bear has left us.

***

Days later, off the French coast near Calais, our galleass is again in battle. This time, after we give and take fire, I hear metal clanking and wood shearing coming from the stern. Above us, a voice shouts that the mainmast and rudder are entangled, fouled by another ship coming too close. More breaking noise, then a commotion of voices about what to do.

We drift, pushed by tide and wind. We rowers sit, grumbling, complaining, all of us afraid for our lives. I hear it all around me, men in chains pleading for the Virgin Mary to intercede for us, to save us from death by English swords. The *San Lorenzo* is a floating target, a coffin that will sink. "Help!" a voice cries. "Take off our chains!"

I say nothing because I know I can free myself if we begin to sink. It's been a while that we've been drifting, even as the commotion above deck goes on about the damaged rudder. It seems a miracle that none of us has been hit or hurt in the attacks on our ship. But now with no more shots fired, are these chained men going to drown?

A thump and the ship shudders and begins to tilt sideways. Voices up top cry out and the word runs back to us that we've run aground beneath the ramparts of Calais Castle. Under the bashing of heavy surf, the great vessel slowly turns on its side.

Our filthy world of oars, waste buckets and the whip also topples over. Water floods in through the hatches. I get down on my knees and try to free my bench mate from the chain around his ankle. I can't, unless somehow I can break the thick bench leg. My skinny neighbor has passed out and is slumped over. Save myself? In the early morning light, men are screaming to be free, and just as I lift my head, I'm thrown forward and up onto the catwalk with other unchained rowers. From outside I hear words in English. "Cut them down!" the voice yells. "Give no quarter!"

Do I surrender? No, no time for that. I'd never make sense quick enough. They'd run me through before I could say, "I'm English!"

There, over there, above me, is a gunport. I crawl up to the opening, scramble through and fall into the water. Other men are flailing or drowning. The eyes and screams of panic are all around me. Our soldiers are being pulled down by the weight of their armor. My feet haven't touched bottom. I look for something to hold on to. In the distance, not floundering at all, sits Mata on a floating timber. I try to swim in his direction but can't get around the burning sails and clusters of hysterical men.

I swim away from the chaos next to the ship and move with the current, swimming and floating far from the rooftops of Calais. It seems like an eternity passing but I manage to put distance between me and the keeled-over *San Lorenzo* and all the other ships and longboats. My bony rower's body is barely stroking and kicking. I'm drifting toward a deserted beach with a line of dunes beyond the flat sand. A breaking wave pushes me forward and my toes touch bottom. I stumble out of the surf onto dry sand. I lie back and look across the water. Far away I see the red and yellow bursts of cannon shots and through the smoke watch ships on fire close in on the Spanish galleons.

I think I'm alone on the beach. But why take a chance of being found? I must hide—maybe in the cover of grass and brush beyond the dunes. I want to rest but I can't stay where I am. I must drag myself into the maze of smooth mounds of sand. I have to cross them. I climb one, then roll down to the bottom. I can't move. Will rest a bit, then move on.

***

Something touches my face. I open my eyes and see Mata's black snout, pink tongue, black eyes and pointed ears. His smooth coat is wet and his tail is wagging.

"Well, aren't you a sight," I say in English and give him a hug. I'm hungry and thirsty but feel rested and warmed under the sun. I get to my feet and tell Mata that we both need to eat and drink. I speak to Mata slowly and in English. "Come," I say, gesturing with my hand. I climb a dune to have a look around. I know Mata obeys commands in Spanish, but now he'll have to pick up the gist of the English words. I say them with gestures that must look familiar to him. Come, stay, down, quiet, drop it, fetch. I think he'll get used to the new sounds.

I walk out of the dunes and enter a plain of high grass, brush and windblown pine trees leaning away from the beach. "Fetch food," I tell Mata, repeatedly moving the fingers of one hand to my mouth. "Go on, fetch a mouse, a snake, anything." I fall to the ground and pretend I'm catching something on the ground with my mouth, shaking my head as he would a rat. Then I point inland. He's watching me with motionless attention. I tell him to fetch again and he runs off into the waves of grass.

I go back to the beach, looking for shells that I can use as knives and scrapers, tools for skinning and cutting small game. I'm assuming my new companion will come back with a meal in his mouth.

After finding what I need, I sit and study the horizon, especially the line of distant white cliffs, which must be England. I figure it's about seven or eight leagues across to the cliffs.

Mata returns with a dead rabbit dangling from his mouth. I accept the gift and scratch my hunter behind his ears. "Good boy. This will do fine."

348

In the following days, the forays of my terrier produce more rabbits, squirrels, wood rats and birds. Along with water taken from streams and ponds inland, the wild game sustains us very well. We avoid fires and hide from the likes of fishermen passing near the shore.

I tell Mata to find us a boat to get across the channel. I even say the word "boat" in Spanish, *bote*, and repeat it in English. Then with two hands I mimic a rower's motion. Mata's ears perk up when I point to a fishing boat in the distance. Suddenly, he races off on the beach away from me. I chase after him but he's far ahead of me.

He disappears into a jumble of seaweed and driftwood. As I run up to the mound of debris, Mata comes out from behind what appears to be a fat log washed up on the shore. As I approach the thick shape I realize it's a battered skiff. Head erect, tail wagging, Mata stands triumphantly next to the flat-bottomed little boat.

"Now find the oars," I say, pointing to the fishermen and making a rowing motion. "*¡Anda!* Go!"

Mata tilts his head, looking at me as I continue rowing in the air. I wait and then he runs farther down the beach, darting among a jumble of rocks and more debris. It's not long before I see him return dragging what looks like an oar. He has the narrow end in his mouth and is dragging it across the sand. When I reach him, he drops it and begins barking.

I'm overjoyed but I still make it clear that we need one more oar. He runs off again but he never does find one. So I end up making one with a plank of driftwood tied to a straight tree branch that fits into one of the skiff's oarlocks.

The skiff has no mast but appears to be sound and free of leaks. If the weather and sea are good, I'm sure I can row the distance to the cliffs. After two days, we wake to a morning of almost no wind and a calm sea. I shove the skiff down the beach into the shallows. I lift Mata and place him in the stern, along with a leather water bag I found among the flotsam. Then I push off through the light surf and clamber over the side. I'm wearing only a loincloth and hope I won't be too cold on the water.

I sit on a cross plank with my back to the bow and begin to row. There are no clouds that I can see. As the French coast recedes, with Mata as my only audience, I start to speak my thoughts in English, as if to a mute friend. "You know, Mata, I think the invincible armada lost the battle. No invasion, galleys gone. What do you think? You saw the battles, I didn't. You got the best seat up top. Did the Spaniards run off, tails between legs? Ah, we'll be in England soon. Halfway across and our little lifeboat is holding course. The only sails I see, my friend, are far away."

Mata stares back at me, his tongue hanging from the side of his mouth.

"You thirsty? One bark for yes, two for no."

Mata tilts his head and I laugh.

I offer him water in cupped hands, which he laps up, then I drink some and continue rowing. The only sound comes from the wind and steady splash of the oars dipping into the sea. For a long while I practice random words, happy that my English is starting to feel normal, that words are coming back to me. I'm thinking in English again. I begin to hum, trying to remember a melody. I start singing the old Rose Red song, just as I did years ago with the boatman Wayne and the two yeomen on the Thames. "Rose! Rose! Rose! Rose! Will I ever see thee wed?" I repeat the words, which seems to puzzle my silent shipmate.

My voice grows louder, and the words become "Izel! Izel! Izel! Will I ever see thee again?" Mata joins in with a long yowl. If only Izel and the children could see us know. How long has it been? Maybe a year and a half since I left them. I stop singing.

Mata looks up at a pair of gulls passing overhead.

I shield my eyes to get a better look at the birds, then turn around to see the white cliffs so close that I can make out figures moving along the top. The current's now pushing the skiff to the left and toward a beach.

"What say ye, Mata? Shall we put in there? Is that a yes? How about one bark?"

I try making sounds of barking and then he joins in.

We slide to a stop on the pebbly beach. Mata hops out into the meager surf, cavorting in the water. As soon as I step out of the boat and stumble up to the dry, smooth stones, I hear shouts coming from above on the cliff. I look up at a group of some twenty men, many of them carrying weapons. They're coming down a steep trail leading to the beach. "Mata, my friend, we're about to be welcomed to England. Let's hope they're friendly. You leave the talking to me."

I squat, one arm around Mata, and wait. "Quiet, boy, *quieto*," I say as the strangers reach the bottom of the trail. The men carry swords, poles, halberds, bows and long-barreled guns. They begin shouting and rush toward me, looking as if they're going to cut me down on the spot. I don't move, my arm still around Mata. Good dog, good dog.

The men surround us. "Who are you?" a helmeted figure in full armor demands in English. "We've been watching you!"

I clear my throat and look at the glaring eyes under the visor. "Joseph Fields, sir, an Englishman."

"English?"

"Yes, captured by the Spaniards and made a galley slave in their fleet."

"You don't say."

"Yes, sir."

"And how did that happen?"

"I'll tell you, sir, but first I must do one thing."

I let go of Mata, get to my knees and bend down to kiss the small stones. Then I rise and begin to speak. The gesture, I say, is in gratitude to God for returning me to the land of my queen. After a moment of silence, I look up and say, "I've reached

England, have I not?"

"Indeed you have."

"What year is this?"

"The year of our Lord, fifteen eighty-eight."

"As I said," I begin in a stronger voice, "I was a slave of the Spaniard."

It's not long before the men relax their threatening postures. Eyes widen and there are ahs and murmurs as they listen to my tale of an orphan boy from Greenwich who shipped out with Hawkyns in 1567, lived a perilous twenty years in the New World, then was arrested by the Inquisition's priests, sent to Spain and condemned to a galley. I was a fugitive among the Spaniards.

I'm stretching the truth because if they know that I signed up to row for money, then I might be seen as a traitor. So I emphasize the harsher side of my life among the Spanish, omitting the kindness of benefactors like Captain González.

353

By the time I describe my escape from the grounded *San Lorenzo*, the men are shouting for death to the invaders. By the end of my account, I think I've become a hero to the gathering, an innocent who defied the odds and the hated papists. I've returned to my homeland through luck and lots of English grit.

The men around me and Mata are generous in their offers of a place to stay, feast and rest. They tell me they're part of a militia from Dover and the surrounding farms and towns, assembled to protect England from the invader. Two men offer to carry me to the top of the cliffs, and one fellow promises to guard my skiff.

"No need to carry me," I tell him. "And keep the boat. I won't need it."

***

I tell my tale many times in churches, homes, inns, taverns and village squares. The darker I can paint the Spaniard, the better. The explosion of emotion after I describe the burning of Cornelius always brings out the angriest oaths and jeers against King Philip and the Inquisition.

My hosts in Dover and in the countryside of Kent treat me with awe and kindness, taking me and Mata in their wagons and carts or on horseback from one place to another. Some convince me to stay with them awhile. They give me clothes, feed me well, and we celebrate our victory over the armada ships.

I speak of my time with the savage Guachichiles, of my life in the floating city, Venice of the New World, of *cocoliztli* and my days as a scout in a caravan going to the northern frontier. I even demonstrate my skill with a bow. Mine is shorter than the longbow, but I can still wow local folks with my accuracy at short range. I tell them how I single-handedly fought off a band of savages.

I sometimes invent details for effect, to add force to the story, despite Izel's warning about stepping on "snakes and spines," about how bending the truth can be a trap, sure to bring me pain and great trouble. So far, no one has caught me in a deception, but I sense it might happen.

"Long live the Queen!" someone shouts in a crowd I've just spoken to.

"And God bless Joseph Fields!" a woman yells, and the cry continues until another voice tells me I should join the ranks of the Queen's advisers. After all, I speak the enemy's tongue and know his ways. "What do you say, Mr. Fields?"

For a moment, I'm stuck and cannot speak. Such a move would surely cook my goose. Near me, a barefoot boy shrieks, "You must talk to the Queen!"

"Yes, yes, we'll see," I say, determined not to do any such thing.

Chapter 24 – London

Early one morning, I leave the warm hospitality of Sittingbourne. Mata and I walk to Chatham and climb onto a wagon loaded with a harvest of wheat and oats bound for London. We pass by the Rochester castle and over the Medway on the very bridge where I discovered I had been robbed. And not long after we cross the river, I tell the wagon driver we have to leave him and walk away from the main road. "I want to find the woman who fed me," I explain. "I believe she lives not far from here."

"But you tell such a yarn," he says. "Sorry I won't hear the end of it."

"But, sir, you have the end. I am here, safe and sound."

"Thank God for that." He reaches back and pats Mata on the head, then stops the wagon and we jump down. I wave goodbye and Mata and I start off along a path that I expect will lead us to Millie's place.

As we roam along paths between harvested fields, I begin another one-sided chat with my companion, ordering him to stay by my side and not go after every squirrel, snake, rat and rabbit that moves. "They spoiled you, Mata," I say. "All those people fed you like a royal pet. I know, you want to show me how you can still catch small game. You were born to hunt. But let's do that later, not now.

We have another, more urgent mission. We must find Millie. Have I told you about her hound, Scout? He was larger than you and probably died years ago."

We can't find Millie's cottage. It's hopeless. I stop and ask passing farmers and yeomen about the widow in the stone cottage who raised pigs and had a big floppyeared dog. No one seems to know. I give up and hike along the Thames.

At Gravesend I pay a waterman for a seat in a wherry going upstream with the tide to London. I have more than enough money from the coins given to me after my talks to pay the fare to Greenwich. I want to see where we used to live, where I spent the first nine years of my life. But when Mata and I leave the Greenwich wharf and walk the streets, I see that my old home has been replaced by a building three stories high. There's a shop on the first selling fabrics. "It's gone," I tell Mata.

I'm standing in front of a window display of colored linens. I look around, thinking I might have the wrong place. But no, the blacksmith forge across the street is the same. Different blacksmith but the same place. So I walk away to wander the streets, looking for something else familiar besides the Queen's palace. At last, along the riverside I recognize the wall where I sat with Mother, where I watched a passing slave with a noose around his neck. Again I sit where we were that day, watching the man led about as if he were no more than a donkey. I close my eyes and clearly make out Mother's face. After years of being unable to remember her, I now see her hazel eyes, her smile and rosy cheeks.

Mother, unless you've been with me all along, I wager you'd be more than concerned about the life your Joey has led these many years. I've lost count the number of times I almost joined you, Father and Mary in the hereafter. But I do cherish my adventures, all the kind or the few malevolent folk I've met along the way, the places I've seen, the mountains I've crossed, the New World's Venice where I lived.

Most of all, I cherish Izel and my children. If only you could meet them, meet a bit of your flesh and blood. I know they would take to you, Father and Mary, and you with them.

After a while, I stand and walk toward the wharf. "Come, Mata, let's go to London."

***

Reaching the city, the wherry lets us off near the customhouse between the tower and the bridge. I'm excited to be back. After paying the waterman, we walk away from the traffic thick with carts and porters. I lecture Mata about not tangling with the street curs roving the waterfront. "They're everywhere, all skinny and with no masters," I tell him. "They're desperate and hungry. Ignore them." I scoop him up in my arms and hurry into a candlemaker's shop, closing the door behind me.

"May I help you?" asks a bald man behind a counter.

"Sorry, sir," I say, "but I had to escape the scruffy dogs."

"Ah, yes. Such is London these days. More of everything, including them. But you're welcome to stay a bit and let the danger pass."

When I guess the dogs have gone, I say goodbye to the candlemaker and walk out with Mata beside me. On the way to Greyfriars, I keep dodging the coaches, carts and wagons. I keep calling Mata to my side, afraid he might be run over. There seem to be more streets paved with cobblestones, so that the horses' hooves striking the stones make a loud clopping noise. Along Fish and Lombard Streets the noise grows louder and the air feels thicker, warmer. There are more people, more shoppers, more merchants.

I reach the markets on Cheapside, then walk on to Newgate Street, where Mata and I go as far as the city wall and the prison. At the turn I find my way to Stinking Lane and the wall close to the dormitory I left so long ago. Walking alongside the wall to the gate where I escaped, I stop to listen.

"This is it, Mata. Hear the voices? There are children in the classroom, but I don't hear Deacon Brown's voice. He must be gone, dear man. Someone else there."

With Mata trotting beside me, I hurry toward Saint Paul's Cathedral, whose spire looms in the distance. After twice losing my way, I ask a well-dressed woman for directions to Bucklesbury, the street of apothecaries and grocers. "That way," she says, pointing with her parasol. "Just follow your nose."

Sure enough, I soon enter the realm of sweet scents and earthy, delicious odors. As I join the crowd on the narrow street, I inhale the mix of spices, elixirs, herbal confections, syrups and tobacco leaves. I'm hoping to see some name or coat of arms above the stores that might pull me in. I pick up Mata and enter one of the many shops of medicinals. Inside, a stooped man is weighing a tiny mound of powder on a balance scale. "Excuse me, sir," I say. "I'm looking for the apothecary Jacob. Where might he be?"

"Dead," the man answers, unsmiling, his steady hand removing powder from the little mound with the flat tip of a stick. "But he left a widow and son. Three doors down on the right beneath the green turtle. The son's the apothecary now."

I thank him and leave with Mata still in my arms.

Beneath the hanging green turtle sign, I open the shop door, step in and wait until a man wearing a smock has finished attending to a large woman complaining of gout. They're standing by a tall counter or worktable, behind which are shelves filled with ceramic jars, bowls, glass vials and hanging instruments.

When the customer leaves, I ask if I can speak to Jacob's widow, explaining that my father many years ago used to travel here from Greenwich to buy ink from Jacob the apothecary.

"Jacob was my father," says the man by the counter, who appears to be about my age.

"Would your mother see me?"

"I'll ask if she's up for a visitor. She's frail and stays upstairs."

The young man disappears behind a hanging curtain at the back of the shop. While the he's gone, Mata explores the floor with his nose, poking into cracks and corners and under the work table. Finding a broken piece of a ceramic bowl, he drops it at my feet. His next gift is a dried bone about the length of a small finger. I pick it up just as the apothecary appears from the back doorway, saying his mother will be down shortly.

"My dog found this on the floor," I say.

The apothecary takes the bone. "Thank you, Rover. I've been looking for this. Sorry there's no meat on it." He sets the bone on a shelf, then turns to welcome a customer entering the shop, a young woman with a baby in her arms.

"I need something for the rash on his chest," she says.

"Well, let's have a look."

While the woman and the apothecary are talking and looking at the infant's chest, Jacob's widow emerges, steadied by a cane. A small, wrinkled figure in a plain frock, she waves a welcoming hand at me and slowly lowers herself onto a chair that's near the entrance.

I step around the counter and tell Mata to sit and stay. Then I turn to greet the widow and ask if she knew my father, David Fields.

"I did," she says. "And the same plague that took him took my Jacob."

"I've been gone across the sea for many years," I say, "but before I left, I remember my dying father telling me to leave England, that I was not wanted here. I didn't understand why he said that. All he told me was to find the apothecary Jacob."

The widow nods. "I knew your father," she says softly. "But tell me your name, son. Mine is Elena."

"Joseph, ma'am."

"Once a month, your father would come to have Jacob mix his ink. But the real reason for his visits was something else. And here I must ask you, do you know who you are or what you are?"

"I don't understand."

"David was a Jew, as I am, as my son is, as Jacob was."

"So *I* am?"

"You are because your parents were. Years ago, our families had to flee our homes in Spain, then again leave Portugal for the same reason. We could stay if we converted to the Catholic faith. But some of us, like your father's family and mine, escaped to Amsterdam, then to London, Bristol and other places."

"Why didn't he tell me and my sister we were Jews?"

"To protect you from those who hate us, who think we killed Christ. They believe we're evil people who poison wells with their babies. They believe we brought the Black Death to England."

Elena looks down and is quiet. I think of Father's gift to me and tell her he gave me his penknife with the Hebrew symbol of life on the handle.

Elena looks up and smiles. "A precious gift, son."

"It's the only thing I have of his."

"David Fields came here for Sabbath services. He and others came through a back door, one by one and never together. They made the minyan of men who met upstairs."

"Minyan?"

"The ten or more men needed to worship."

"Why did they come here?"

"My Jacob led the prayers. He was their leader, their rabbi. You have no idea how careful we had to be to keep these meetings secret, keep our faith secret. You too, Joseph, even if you were raised a Protestant, you don't want anyone to know you are the son of Jews."

"My family name is Fields. Is that a name from Spain? It sounds so English."

"Your grandparents on your father's side, I knew them after they arrived from Portugal. I was just a girl but I remember their name was Curiel. Then they changed it. We all did. When Jacob was a boy, he was called Jacobo. Jacobo Mendes, not Martin. I was Elena Cardoso de Souza. And you would be Joseph Curiel, or José

Curiel if our families were still in Spain."

"I'll stay with Fields. I've had to change my name so many times already."

"Why?"

"A very long story."

"Well," Elena says, sighing, "next time you come by, you can tell me all about it. I need to rest now." She leans forward, gripping her cane, and stands. "I don't know you, son, but I have a feeling your parents would be proud of you. May you be well and live in righteous ways."

***

Later that afternoon, I rent a room in Bankside, then find a tavern. I enter with Mata by my side and look around for an empty stool. At a corner table to my right a young man is gesturing for me to join him. I make my way over and sit down. "Have some ale," he says, lifting a pitcher and pouring into a tankard. "This for you, and I'll drink from this vessel. You look as if you've just left a ship, which I venture to say is now free of rats thanks to the hunting instincts of your canine companion." I thank the young man, who says he's an actor, and boast that Mata is indeed a seagoing rat killer. Before long, I'm spinning tales of my life aboard ships and of my adventures in the Spanish Indies. He's especially delighted to hear the description of me dressed in leaves, cavorting by a waterfall and pool amid a sprinkling of butterflies. I say it was a garden of freedom after my nightmare crossing in the *Mynion*.

"Magical," the actor says. "A forest sprite dancing with the butterflies."

"Until I was hit on the head."

"Well, it was heavenly for a time. Another pitcher?"

"No. Actually, I'm tired and pickled. I should go."

"Where are you staying?"

"The inn down by the water."

"Ah, then you and your furry friend must not keep the fleas waiting."

I laugh and rise on wobbly legs.

"Thank you for the stories." The young man raises his mug in salute. "You must write them down. Or someone must."

"What's that?" I ask and put a hand to my ear.

The man stands and steps around the table to be heard over the din in the tavern.

"Write it all down, sir."

"I suppose so."

He taps me on the back, smiling. "If you write such stories, in the end your world of words is all you leave behind."

"I'll remember that," I say. I wave a hand and weave my way toward the tavern door.

***

I peddle myself as a scrivener on the streets of Southwark, but the work pays little and I'm hounded by decrees, new rules and guilds. My time sneaking about writing for others is nothing like my unfettered early days in Bankside. So I move to Greenwich, find lodging above a butcher's shop and start my scrivener business with Mata at my side, often with a bone from the butcher. I also begin writing an account of my twenty years in a world new to the English nation.

I buy a sheaf of vellum, make holes through one side of the sheets, then stitch the lot together between two leather end pieces. I begin.

I Joseph Fields lived twenty yeeres as prisoner, slave, servaynt, scrivener and miner in the Viceroyalty of Newe Spaine lately in the northern hamlet of Olivos. I was but nine yeeres thereabouts when the Black Death came to Greenwich and tooke my parents and sister Mary. In time the Queens men took me to Christ Hospital a school for orphans and urchins formerly Graiefryers where I continyud readynge and wrytynge as my scrivener father taught me. In the yeare 1567 when I was but thirteen I fled and found work in the Fleete of Generall Master John Hawkyns.

Early every morning I write, and in little more than three months' time I finish my story up to the present day. The butcher has heard bits, and though he can't read a word, he urges me to keep "marking it all down."

But try as I might, my scrivener duties have fallen and I have almost nothing to pay the rent for a room I share with two countinghouse clerks. I hear that ships are being built in southern ports for use in the ongoing war with Spain. So in January of 1589, as cold as it is, Mata and I leave Greenwich and find our way to the port of Plymouth.

Chapter 25 – Home

I'm hired as a caulker and carpenter's helper on the *Black Dog*, a privateer bound for the Spanish Indies. Once we're aboard, officers and crew warmly welcome Mata because the ship has no hunter of rats.

We hoist sail, but I wish I were not leaving Greenwich without my manuscript, which I entrusted to the butcher for safekeeping. If I'm ever to see my wife and children again, I want to read them my story, for it's also their story. But I shake my regret and tend to my shipboard duties.

Weeks of fair winds and following seas take us south toward the Canaries and then push us westward across the ocean. A few gales sweep over us but they're not so strong that they keep us swinging and sick in our fishnet slings. I like my airy bed. It's much better than sleeping on wooden deck planks at eye level to a rat, as I did on my first English voyage.

On the morning we make out the Spanish frigate and the cry goes up to give chase, I leave my sling and scramble up to the main deck with some of the crew. My duty that day is to replace a broken section of a railing on the top deck, working with the carpenter in his cabin. But not today. I want to be up top on deck to see the enemy ship as we close in—and I'm as eager to see it as are the forty sailors and soldiers around me.

They're a regular, rough mix of young men and some fellows like me—all with stories of hard work on land and perilous times at sea. Now, as privateers or licensed pirates, they're allowed to take whatever they can from the enemy. The call suddenly seems to transform them into a brutish, bloodthirsty lot—full of bluster and hateful oaths against all things Spanish.

The frigate stays along the southern coast of Hispaniola. Captain Michelson orders the attack and we run the frigate ashore. Our longboat is full of soldiers who storm aboard the grounded vessel, overwhelming the crew. Many of the Spaniards are jumping off into the surf and running away. Our men injure many with their swords and halberds and they soon take what they can find of silver, weapons, food and casks of wine. It's a long, laborious task to transfer the loot from the grounded frigate to our vessel. I join in, carrying goods on my back across the main deck, down the ladders to the storage deck. At this moment, I don't care who has been hurt or killed or what treasure is taken, because all my will is pointed to finding my family. Before I began this voyage, I vowed that I would do whatever it takes to reach them. And if this means looking away from such plundering, then so be it.

Not long after the pillaging, we attack and loot more of the enemy's ships off the southern coast of Cuba. Finally, the captain takes ten of our crew aboard one of the captured vessels and sails west to see about joining other English ships to blockade Havana's harbor.

Our pilot, Roger Hingson, and Master William Mace now command the *Black Dog*. We weigh anchor near Cape San Antonio and are soon chasing a Spanish galleon riding low in the water and probably carrying heavy cargo. But awful winds and currents force the galleon and our ship toward the Yucatán coast and into the harbor of San Francisco de Campeche. While we're at anchor and preparing to attack yet another galleon—this one tied to a dock—I tell the boatswain that I need to drop into the water to check on a worrisome wormhole in the aft hull. "Won't take long, sir," I say, holding a caulking iron and a wad of oakum in one hand.

"Hurry!" the boatswain says.

"Aye, aye, bosun!" I answer and turn to climb down to the busy gun deck. Since I'm not a soldier or one of the fighting crew, I don't think he'll miss me for long.

I signal to Mata to follow me over the side, and before I finish the gesture, my rat hunter leaps high in the air and easily clears the midship rail. I follow over the rail and we sink down in the water together. I let go of the iron and oakum and swim underwater without surfacing for some distance, away from the ship. After surfacing for air, I go down again and keep on going toward a wide, empty beach. Mata takes longer to reach the sand, but when he does, he runs up the slope to the bushes and vines where I'm hiding. "That's a good fellow," I say in English, gathering him in my arms for a hug. "Welcome to New Spain, Mata. But here I'll speak to you only in Spanish. *¿Entiendes, Mendes?*"

I begin moving away from the harbor alongside a gentle surf, headed south, judging from the sun's position. Mata keeps ahead of me, occasionally stopping to sniff at shells, seaweed and bird droppings. I no longer care what the men of the *Black Dog* are doing, so long as they aren't pursuing me. All that matters is reaching Izel and the children. Almost three years have passed since I left Olivos, and I hope the authorities believe I'm dead.

Now and then I leave the moist sand and cross the softer white beach to look for trails or tracks into the thick vegetation. I know nothing of this coast but believe Mata and I might move in greater safety on trails in the forest rather than by traveling on an exposed open shore. But I can't find such breaks leading inland through mangrove roots and other growth. We keep to the sand just above the onshore waves, twice having to swim around rocky points.

In the late afternoon, we stop at the mouth of a stream beneath a palm tree to drink and rest. Mata immediately splays himself out on the sand, his head resting on one paw, eyes closed. I stare at the darkening sea, no longer blue and translucent. Though I'm not thirsty, I crave food. "We need to eat," I say in Spanish. Mata rises, alert, ears up. I also stand and begin moving my hand repeatedly to my mouth while loudly pronouncing the words "go,

371

RON ARIAS

find" in Spanish—*anda, busca*—and pointing across the stream.

Mata bolts and springs into the air, clearing the entire stream. Then he scampers away and disappears into the brush. I lie back on the sand, close my eyes and imagine Millie's stew, then remember Mother's meat pie, and finally, I see a warm piece of bread baked in Plymouth and served with a slab of grilled mackerel.

Just after sunset, Mata returns, barks once and licks my face. I sit up and see a dead snake next to me. It's about the length of my arm and twice as thick as my thumb. "Thank you. Now we have to figure out a way to eat this creature."

Soon, the two of us are chewing on lengths of raw snake—a messy, bloody dinner but at least it quiets the hunger.

***

In the morning, I emerge from a cocoon of palm fronds and leafy branches I gathered and settled down in a hollow I dug in the sand. I stretch my arms, yawning and feeling the moist, chilly air on my face and bare arms. I scan the flat sea, then look around for Mata. I whistle. He appears from the brush far down the beach and races back to me.

I decide to follow the shallow stream to see where it might lead. Maybe we should get something bigger to eat than a small snake. For that, I need a bow and several arrows. It takes a while but I collect enough reeds and strips of bark to twist the fibers into a

372

cord that will be strong enough for use with a bow. Then I comb the shore and vegetation for suitable driftwood and branches. In the end, the pieces I find aren't neatly straight, but they'll do. When I finish tying on the stone arrowheads and feathers from a dead seagull for fletching, I test my crude weapon along the beach. I hit random targets of washed-up objects. "Not so bad, Mata. Let's go hunting."

Helped by Mata's knack for rousting animals from the underbrush, I soon shoot and kill a bluish-green lizard the length of my arm scrambling across the sand. Then I gather enough fallen branches and twigs to build a fire. I start by rolling a stick between my hands, working the pointed end on a piece of driftwood layered with dry leaves. A tiny smoldering glow grows into flames as I add twigs and branches. Once the fire is crackling, I skewer the lizard with a branch and turn it over the fire until it is good and roasted.

When Mata and I begin to eat, two natives approach us from along the beach, both wielding hand axes. Undaunted by Mata's growling, they come to the fire and nod to me. In Spanish I offer them some of the skewered lizard's meat. Without hesitation, they squat by the fire and wait. Bare-chested, barefoot and wearing only short trousers, they smile and thank me as they accept strips of meat that I hand to them.

Mata has stopped growling and returns to gnawing a piece of the big lizard. As we eat, I tell them in Spanish that I've escaped from a pirate ship and want to reach Puebla and then travel on to the north to find my family. My listeners are both much shorter than I am. The one with a red headband is Manuel and the other, with a white cloth over his forehead, is Aapo. They make sympathetic expressions and nod when I explain I'm English and not Spanish. When I ask them what work they do, Aapo says they take wood by boat to traders near Veracruz.

I offer to help them in exchange for taking us to Veracruz. The men are silent for a moment, and then Manuel asks me if I can fight.

"Yes," I say, holding up my bow. "I lived with Chichimecas and learned to use

this."

"Then come with us."

"Who are you fighting?"

"Men who will kill for the wood."

"Kill for wood?"

"Not just any wood," Manuel says. "It's Campeche, for making dyes."

"Contraband?"

"They tax Campeche, so we stay away from Veracruz."

He's waiting for my answer. I look at Mata. "What do you say? Want to sail again?"

Mata lifts his head, tail twitching. I smile and nod.

***

After three days of chopping wood at their inland camp, the Mayans and I make repeated trips to the beach carrying bundles of wood on our backs. On the final trek each of us carries either food or water. I'm bearing a sack of cooked sweet potatoes.

At the beach, we pull an open one-masted boat out from the tangle of brush and trees. Then we load the bundles of wood in the center of a craft that's about twenty feet long, rigged with one sail, and equipped with two sets of oars and four bench planks.

When everything is aboard, Mata and I settle ourselves in the bow. Manuel begins rowing the boat into the small surf. Once we're past the break, he raises the sail and Aapo takes the tiller. "We go out far enough from anyone wanting to steal what we have," Manuel says, "but not so far that we can't run to land if a storm comes up."

Over the next three days, the boat keeps its steady course with only one day when the wind dies and we all take turns rowing. When we reach the cove that's their destination, the Mayans meet with a trader whose bearers immediately begin unloading the wood. I ask Manuel why the trader doesn't use burros or mules to carry the wood. "Where these men go," he says, "not even burros go. They follow no trails. They're more like jaguar tracks in the wet forests and over the mountains."

"And roads?"

"Oh, no. Those are all watched. That's why you're safer with these men."

Manuel turns to join Aapo in the emptied boat.

"When do they leave?" I ask.

"Now! They already know you're going with them."

"Then goodbye," I say. Manuel waves a hand. I watch the stocky figure with the red headband wade into the water and pull himself into the boat to join Aapo. Suddenly, he calls out, "Here!" and tosses me a pair of huaraches. "Where you're going, you'll need them more than I will."

Mata rushes across the sand to retrieve the leather sandals and bring them to me. They're stiff and the fit is tight, but they'll have to do until I have the time to make my own huaraches.

The porters with their bundles of wood are already moving off the beach and disappearing into a wall of tropical trees and bushes. I sling my bow and arrows over my shoulder and back, pick up the bag with my portion of sweet potatoes, and run with Mata to catch up to the line of porters.

***

The first days I follow the bearers as they push through hot, dense, muddy forests. Mario, the mestizo smuggler, and a few native

376

men stay at the head of the line, hacking a way through the underbrush. When we reach the foothills we have to ford streams and cross gullies, all the while avoiding villages, plantations and other people. Finally, we climb up along a narrow valley to cooler air and then over a mountain pass and down along the lower slope of the Orizaba volcano. In the distance across a plain that spreads below me, I can see the cluster of structures that is Puebla. And beyond the town rise the peaks of Popocatépetl and Ixtáxcihuatl.

Morning, noon and at sundown, I've shared meager meals with Mario and his bearers. We all complain about our cuts, bruises, blisters and sores. I don't talk much about myself, saving banter for Mata. He feeds himself well enough on his own. We sometimes amuse the men, me shooting arrows at targets and Mata retrieving the arrows after tugging them out of tree trunks or cactus plants. When I hit a pinecone, he runs off and returns with it held in his mouth. The feat always gets him the loudest cheers.

On the afternoon we approach Puebla, I see the first proper road I've seen since leaving England. Mario tells me I should avoid it because trails coming from eastern farmlands are safer and less watched. But impatience gets the better of me and I decide to leave and continue on my own. I signal farewell to Mario and the porters, then Mata and I leave on the main road to Puebla. My old friend González warned me that the town was full of clerics and others on the hunt for fugitives like me. So after entering the town on cobblestone streets, I think I should lose myself in the big *tianguis* by the central plaza where years ago González surprised me with a tap on the shoulder. I can then retrace my way to my friend's house.

I wear the same shabby clothes I've been wearing since I jumped ship, looking more like a grimy beggar than a person of respect. With Mata following closely, I reach the *tianguis* vendors without having to ask directions. But when I try to find the González place, I lose my way and decide I might have more luck on the streets where they make pottery. When I find the workshop neighborhood, I stop a black porter bearing a large clay urn and ask if he knows the potter Hassan.

"Who doesn't?" the porter says, smiling, and indicates with his chin an open doorway. "Hassan works there."

I cross over to a long adobe structure and walk in. It's not long before I see Minoru at the back of the workshop, where he's hunched over a spinning potter's wheel, both hands giving shape to a bowl. He's one of about ten potters working at wheels.

Walking across the workshop, I keep Mata close to me. Then I step close to my Japanese friend and whisper in his ear, "No more baskets?"

Minoru turns his head slightly, his hands never leaving the clay. He holds his breath for a moment, then exhales with a wide grin. "You're back!"

"Only for a short time."

"Does Hassan know?"

"No, where is he?"

"Outside loading pots."

Minoru stops kicking the foot wheel and withdraws his hands from the bowl, wiping them on a wet rag. "What happened to you—after you left?" he asks.

"I got to a ship, reached Spain, even England. But I missed Izel and the children so much that I had to come back. I was lucky to be taken aboard a ship sailing to the

Spanish Indies. And here I am."

"You look awful," Minoru says.

"But alive."

Minoru rises from his stool, turns, nods, then bows in an almost prayerful greeting.

"And you?" I ask. "How've you been?"

"Married and a father. But come, let's go surprise Hassan."

Noticing Mata sitting back on his haunches, Minoru bends down and extends a hand. "And who is this?"

"His name is Mata."

Minoru again bows his head. I raise my right hand, palm up. Mata stands, tail wagging, and Minoru pats his head. "Let's go find the boss."

We head across to the back door and step into sunlight. Near us five women squat on the ground, painting colorful designs on unglazed pots. At the far side of the yard near the kiln, Hassan sees me and hurries over, smiling all the way. He wraps his arms around me, hugging and lifting me off the ground, an excited Mata barking and yipping next to us. Still as trim and muscular as when I last saw him, my slave mate from the *Mynion* has become the workshop's foreman. "I run the place," he says with a laugh. "The owner just collects the money."

Minoru and Hassan leave the workshop earlier than usual in order to take me to meet González. The cacao trader is delighted to see me but insists I bathe and change into clothes and boots he'll provide. "There's still some danger of you being caught," he says, "but the situation is different from what it was when I last saw you. No more

English heretics. Now the Inquisition's going after secret Jews."

"How do I get to the north?"

"On one of my wagons."

"Wagons now?"

"I've expanded."

"And cacao?"

"I still have that in the south, but there's good money to be made taking goods to

Zacatecas and the other mining towns. And the wagons return with silver."

"What about Chichimeca attacks?"

"The war has almost ended. You'll be safe. No need for your bow and arrows."

"I'll take them just the same."

"Stay awhile?"

"I can't wait another day."

"You'll have to," González says. "My next wagons don't leave for another four days."

"Don't worry," Minoru says. "We'll take good care of you."

In the days before leaving, my trio of friends treat me as they would a prince, although one kept in hiding. Fine food, fine company, and the softest beds and pillows. I also meet the three lively but courteous wives and their children. Minoru's two young ones strike me as entirely native, born of parents with similar eyes. Actually, since all three men have married Nahua women, all the children have a native look to them, although Hassan's four are mulatto dark.

During a final gathering of the three families in the González home, I have a moment of clarity, the kind that I haven't felt since Izel and I decided to flee the city of Mexico to escape the great pestilence. Here in Puebla, at a table set with lavish care and covered

381

with sumptuous food and drink, around me sit the many faces of a new people—native, Spaniard, African, Asian. As my glass is filled for another toast, I watch the children play with Mata in the courtyard, thinking this land and its people are changing and I just got a peek at the road ahead.

***

As González predicted, there are no attacks on the caravan wagons. We make our way north on the silver roads without incident. But before reaching Zacatecas I lose all patience with the plodding pace of the oxen teams and buy a runty bay stallion from a fellow traveler, using nearly all the coins my Puebla friends gave me. The seller is an Asturian with a small herd of common cows, one bull and three horses. In buying the least of his mounts, I figure the animal can take me and Mata to Olivos in weeks instead of months.

So I ride on with Mata draped between me and the bay's withers. I avoid Zacatecas altogether, and Mata helps me hunt game and forage for anything we can eat. I come near other travelers going north and south but I don't speak with anyone.

I wave and keep on. I also stay away from Fresnillo and Sombrerete, and I go around Durango. From there on, I make better time, for a few days finding good pasture for the horse and plenty of small game in a cultivated river valley. Farther north I come near Santa Bárbara but go around the mining town where I once lived.

Three days later, on a windy afternoon, I put Mata in a sack that hangs from the saddle. His head is out, ears up and eyes darting back and forth. I'm on foot, pulling my runt of a stallion by a rope tied to the reins. We're heading up a rocky canyon to a mountain pass, and for this part of the journey I figure Mata doesn't need to be on the ground exhausting himself. As it is, I'm thinking exhaustion and worn-down hooves might kill my horse. When we reach the pass, at last I see the river that gives water to the people and fields of Los Olivos. For a long while I stare at my dream that's about to come alive. I'm in tears, overjoyed.

How are Izel, Yetzi and David? Will they recognize me? What do they look like now? And the crops. The corn. The olive trees. Our livestock.

We start down the mountain slope and enter the valley. In the midday sunlight I see no cattle on the higher pastures. Closer to Los Olivos, I see structures but no movement, no smoke trails, no animals, no people, no voices, no sound but the wind.

Nothing moves but the dust. The sickening, hopeless feeling of a great fear grips me. *Cocoliztli?* Did it finally reach this valley? I look up and scan the sky. No birds are circling above, but then the pestilence may have swept in and disappeared long ago. I don't want to know. The closer I get to the houses, the more I dread the truth. I let Mata out of his sack and he runs ahead.

All that he and I find are empty houses. The ground and blackened stains of old fires have been taken over by weeds, grasses, dust piles and dunes. There are hardly any wood frames around doors and windows. Pieces of posts and broken roof tiles lie in the dirt by the houses and among dead or dying trees.

At my house I let go of the horse and step over a mound of dirt to look around. Dust blows through the place we built. It blows through open doorways and frameless windows, through the courtyard and out into the corral, pushing tumbleweeds against the wall of stones David and I piled up. The same wind and dust rushes on through the leafless, dead olive trees and across weedy, brush-covered fields.

I see no signs of a fight. "They're gone, Mata." I squat by the front doorway. What happened? I run my fingers over Mata's back. Nothing left. No cattle, no neighbors, no clues. Nothing, not even flies.

What had I expected? My family to be safe? Good harvests? No attacks by Conchos or Tepehuanes? And where were my friends, the Rarámuri?

I feel an aching sadness I haven't felt since losing my family in Greenwich.

I wander through empty rooms with dirt and weeds piling up in the corners. I step out through the courtyard and into the corral. What can I do?

Only a dozen or so homes. I walk among them, in them, around them, and there are no clues about what might have happened. Dwellings for ghosts.

I circle my home and again move through the courtyard. Then I step up to the frameless doorway at the rear of the house. With my dagger I begin poking at the spot next to the doorjamb where I buried my penknife. After jabbing away the hard dirt, I see something lodged in the crevice. I scrape again, enough so that I can pinch the leather pouch. I tug it out, expecting to feel the shape and stiffness of a knife blade and handle, but I feel nothing. I pull back the crusty leather flap and find a folded scrap of paper. I open it and read the English words "Going north David."

***

As I am leaving the shell of what was Los Olivos, other men arrive, natives of a tribe I can't identify. I shush Mata, then pull the nag by the reins and we hide in the hills to the east.

When I see them go, we return. They took nothing—since there was nothing to take but dirt bricks and stone walls.

For many days the old stallion, Mata and I move north along the river and on the bluff above the valley. My dear family must have gone northward, downriver, to better lands. Maybe they joined the Rarámuri and built a shelter and planted crops and more trees. Something like that must have happened. Why else would my hamlet be empty of tools, pots and the other things we need to live?

I just want to find my family. How far did they go? Maybe a long journey, maybe as far as the gleaming houses of Cíbola.

***

Days later, I'm on foot, pulling the horse while slogging through a patch of weeds by the river that comes out of the mountains to the west, out from the deep and fertile canyons my old friends showed me once when we hunted. Some Spaniards call them Tarahumara, but to me they are the people who run, the Rarámuri. I will go north and west and hope the mountain spirits will let me pass.

I feel a sting on my right leg just beneath the knee. Whatever it is—spider, scorpion, snake or something else—I'm soon feeling weak and dizzy and then my right leg goes numb, my head hurts and I'm shaking all over. I let go of the horse and fall down. I'm on my back, hidden in deep grass.

Now the leg hurts. I can't move. I shout for Mata but he doesn't appear and I hear nothing. I try moving my head but that's impossible. Am I passing out? I'm shaking. I hear my last words. What are the words? Do I babble? Am I moaning? Is this how I die? Pain in the leg on fire. I want to crawl but I can't move even a finger. Will I die here in the weeds with no one, not even Mata? I want to feel him licking my face. Where is my friend? Come, friend, come back to me.

The lower part of my leg is throbbing. It's a stabbing, pulsing throb. I close my eyes and I wait and wait. Minutes, maybe hours. The pain is going away. I'm no longer shaking. But I still can't move my legs, my arms. And my eyes won't open. All the running and hiding I've done in my years, all the many times I've been bumped and brushed by death, and now some little creature's poisonous bite might finish me off. What did the fellow in the pub say? Life's like a dream, like a play. When it ends, our time is over. Is that what's happening?

I feel the grass on my face, I hear the steady sound of water flowing, splashing on rocks, rippling against the riverbank. My hands are wet. I want to squeeze the mud between my fingers but I can't. I can smell the grass but I can't see what's around me. I wait. And wait. Am I leaving the stage? Is it time to vanish?

What's that? Barking, Mata's barking. Coming closer. I feel hands lifting up my head. I try to open my eyes. I can't. I can't move.

I hear a soft voice, Izel's voice. She's calling me. And is that David and Yetzi calling me, "Papá, Papá." Is this heaven?

I hear Izel's voice again: "English! You don't fool me!"

Hands hold my head, soft, gentle.

"Wake up."

I feel her breath, her lips. I try to speak. "Shh," she says. "We're here."

I clear my throat. "Izel."

"Yes, my love."

"Am I alive?"

"Yes."

I open my eyes. She's smiling and Mata is barking.

"Alive, José. We're all alive."

About The Author

A former English teacher and journalist, most recently for 22 years at *People*, Ron Arias has published the following books: *The Road to Tamazunchale*, a novel nominated for a National Book Award; *Five Against the Sea*, a true survival saga; *Healing from the Heart*, with Dr. Mehmet Oz; *Moving Target, A Memoir of Pursuit*; *White's Rules, Saving Our Youth One Kid at a Time,* with Paul D. White; *My Life As A Pencil*, a chapbook of stories about his life as a journalist, and *The Wetback and Other Stories*.

08e20ef7-be29-4ef7-9fb6-9cc873cb0ef5R02